"Mr. Koch, you're a lawyer. You know that the way Arthur Wien was murdered wasn't a spur-of-the-moment whim. You don't walk around with an ice pick in your pocket if you're not planning to use it."

"That's what I would argue if I were the D.A."

"Someone hated him. Assuming it was someone in your group—or a wife—it's hard for me to believe no one outside the victim and his killer knew what was going on."

"I can tell you I didn't know."

"Then who would?"

"You've got me. What my wife said to you yesterday? That Art was having an affair with a wife of one of the group? That was the first I ever heard of it."

"Then I guess it's the wives I should be talking to."

He looked at me and smiled. . . .

Please turn to the back of the book for an interview with Lee Harris.

By Lee Harris
Published by Fawcett Books:

THE GOOD FRIDAY MURDER
THE YOM KIPPUR MURDER
THE CHRISTENING DAY MURDER
THE ST. PATRICK'S DAY MURDER
THE CHRISTMAS NIGHT MURDER
THE THANKSGIVING DAY MURDER
THE PASSOVER MURDER
THE VALENTINE'S DAY MURDER
THE NEW YEAR'S EVE MURDER
THE LABOR DAY MURDER
THE FATHER'S DAY MURDER

THE FATHER'S DAY MURDER

Lee Harris

FAWCETT GOLD MEDAL • NEW YORK

A Fawcett Gold Medal Book
Published by The Ballantine Publishing Group
Copyright © 1999 by Lee Harris

All rights reserved under International and Pan-American Copyright Conventions. Published in the United States by The Ballantine Publishing Group, a division of Random House, Inc., New York, and simultaneously in Canada by Random House of Canada Limited, Toronto.

Fawcett Gold Medal and colophon are trademarks of Random House, Inc.

www.randomhouse.com/BB/

Library of Congress Catalog Card Number: 98-96977

ISBN 0-449-00441-4

Manufactured in the United States of America

First Edition: June 1999

10 9 8 7 6 5 4 3 2

In memory of my aunt and uncle,
Sally and Max Shulman

With many thanks to Ana M. Soler and James L. V. Wegman and to my cousins, Martin Shulman, M.D., Cecille Shulman, and Irwin Shulman, for their time, their tales, and their wonderful memories.

At the beginning of the cask and at the end take thy fill, but be saving in the middle; for at the bottom saving comes too late. Let the price fixed with a friend be sufficient, and even dealing with a brother call in witnesses, but laughingly.

HESIOD
Eighth Century B.C.

Prologue

In the four years I had known my husband, he had been a daytime detective sergeant with the New York Police Department (NYPD) and an evening law student. Although I had never liked his four late nights a week during the academic year, I had gotten rather used to it, using the time alone to read, prepare the poetry course I teach, or correct papers. In a way that I have come to believe is typically me, I had more or less expected life to continue that way forever, although rationally I knew it would not.

So it came as something of a jolt when Jack announced that his last series of finals was coming up and, with luck, a graduation not long after that. His law school days were coming to an end, and our lives and routine would begin to change.

He worked as hard as ever to prepare for the finals, even taking a few of what the job calls "chart days," a concept so complicated that I simply accept they're time coming to him, to do his studying. The rest of his accumulated days would be used, God willing, to study for the bar exams.

And then one bright spring day I found myself standing on the campus in the sun with our year-and-a-half-old son, Eddie, and my in-laws, all of us dressed for the happy occasion of Jack's graduation. It had really happened. All those hours and nights, weeks and months, semesters and years had paid off. The day of recognition had come.

It was a wonderful occasion. There were as many smiles as people, and mine was surely the biggest and proudest. Jack was ten years older than most of the graduates, and all I could think of was how hard he had worked to achieve this, putting in full-time days at the Sixty-fifth Precinct in Brooklyn and dashing off to hours of evening classes, not eating dinner till he got home to Oakwood, our suburban town on the north shore of the Long Island Sound.

When the celebrating was over, Jack settled into his summer schedule, working five days a week with evenings free now, for studying for the bar. But a big change was in the works for him. The legal department of NYPD offered him a temporary position at One Police Plaza, New York's police headquarters in Manhattan, where he would be on call to answer legal questions, a service provided around the clock for police officers. To start, he would work days, but this might change in the fall. What was so great was that he would have a law library at his fingertips and time to study. Later in the year, as the date for the bar exams drew near, he planned to take every second of chart time, lost time, and vacation time that he had earned and bury himself in his books. Like a monk, he said. His joke. I am an ex-nun.

He delayed the start of the job at One Police Plaza until early in July, feeling sentimental about the precinct where he had spent many of his years on the job, where he had developed firm friends and a good working relationship. Also, he had cases he wanted to clear, if possible, and a sense that he did not want to walk out on a lot of good people who would have to pick up what he left behind.

This was all fine with me. I never find change very easy, and easing slowly into something new seemed a good way to accomplish it.

This left me to finish teaching my own course at a local college in Westchester County, give my exam, mark my papers, say good-bye to my students, and adjust to a few months of leisure, time to spend with my nineteen-month-old son, get my garden planted, and swim in the nearby cove from the beach that a bunch of homeowners own jointly. I love spring and summer because they allow me to do all those things.

June was almost a lazy month when I finished my teaching. Jack was not yet hyper about his coming exams, although he spent an awful lot of time studying, and Eddie and I enjoyed his company and his fairly relaxed manner.

Jack and I could hardly have come from more different backgrounds. At the age of fifteen, having lived with my aunt and uncle since the death of my mother a year before, family problems produced a second upheaval in my life. I went to live at St. Stephen's Convent, not as a novice but as someone who needed a stable home, someone who wanted eventually to become a nun. In my twenties I took my vows, and I remained a committed nun until, at age thirty, after much thought and consideration, I was released from them. It was a few weeks after that that I met Jack at the station house in Brooklyn where he was working. My life has changed a lot more than his since that moment.

On Father's Day we drove into the city to spend the afternoon with Jack's family. Since I was orphaned as a teenager, the Brookses are all the family I have, and I love them all. It was a great day. Jack's sister, Eileen, was there, and she had arranged for a catered dinner, courtesy of the small catering company she and her mother run. Eileen just gets better at what she does and the food was superb. And my father-in-law was absolutely ecstatic.

I had picked up my cousin Gene, who lives in a home for retarded adults not too far from where our house is, and after mass we took him along to celebrate the day with us. He and Eddie have a great relationship, and they kept up a giggly banter in the backseat as we drove to Brooklyn. It was as though they shared secrets and jokes in a language only they could understand. I don't remember doing anything like that with Gene when we were children, but something about Eddie appeals to Gene, who is a sweet person in any circumstance and has loved Eddie since he came into the world.

After Father's Day, Jack had only a couple of weeks left at the Six-Five. Each evening he came home with a few things from his desk—a pen that belonged to him; snapshots of him and several buddies, one of them now dead; a box of stale crackers; a small solar calculator that I immediately took possession of when he said he had no use for it; and a number of other small treasures he had not remembered were there. His notebooks were the property of NYPD and would be returned to his lieutenant on his last day, but he had some file folders with notes on cases he had worked on which he still had questions about or which hadn't been solved or which had something interesting about them he wanted to remember.

I watched him move slowly toward his first change in years, the first since we had met. I sensed his eagerness to move on and his reluctance to give up what he knew and loved. I tried to help him in any way I could, to be around when he wanted to talk or to make myself scarce when he wanted to study or whatever else he did in that room upstairs that we kept as an office. I was free till September and available anytime, and I made sure he knew it.

All that ended just before the end of June with a phone call.

1

The call came at nine in the morning as though the caller had been sitting by the phone waiting for a polite time to call. After I answered, a girlish voice asked tentatively, "Ms. Bennett?"

"Yes."

"This is Janet Stern?" She said it like a question I might be able to give her an answer to.

"Janet, yes. How are you?" She had been a student in my poetry class and I wondered how she had gotten my phone number. Jack is very particular about not giving it out and I use my maiden name to teach.

"Uh fine. It's just—I have a problem."

"Grades are in, Janet. And I think you did very well in the course."

"It's not that. It has nothing to do with school. I'm sorry. I'm a little nervous. Uh, I'm calling about something else. The student paper did a write-up on you last fall?" Again she said it like a question.

"Yes, it did." It had been a nice article, well written, complete with a picture. It was a profile of me and included a description of a murder I had had a hand in solving last summer on Fire Island.

"We have a terrible problem in my family. It's my

6

grandfather. Somebody he knows was murdered and he's—well, the police used the word *suspect*. Could we talk about it?"

More things rushed through my mind than I could count or consider. I should say no because Jack would be coming home to dinner every night and I wanted his life as comfortable as possible. I should say no because I had gardening to do and books to read, because I had put in two semesters' worth of work and I wanted a little time to indulge my whims. But murder is serious, and this girl was nervous and scared and it wouldn't hurt to talk to her and find out what was going on. "I'd be glad to talk about it with you," I said.

I could hear her exhale. "Thank you. Thanks a lot. Could we meet for lunch?"

"Today?"

"Today would be great."

"I have to make arrangements for my son, Janet. Can I call you back?"

"Sure." She gave me a number, and I called my mother's friend Elsie Rivers, my number one sitter, and asked if she was free. Elsie always makes me feel as though I'm doing her a big favor by leaving Eddie with her. I hadn't left him for some time so I didn't feel too guilty about asking, and she was thrilled. She had some small errand that could easily wait and she knew Eddie would love to play in her garden. All in all, I was very grateful.

I called Janet back, and she gave me the name of a restaurant I had heard of but had never visited in one of the towns along the Sound, the kind of restaurant that would require my putting on a dress and looking like a lady. I didn't mind. My usual life was so casual, it was a treat to dress up once in a while.

Eddie was happy enough to be going to Elsie's. Her lunches were far more appealing than anything I put together. My lunches emphasized tuna fish, but Elsie is inventive and always manages to have cookies for good little boys. He took along some toys, and I managed to get him in and out of the car without ripping my stockings. Elsie was impressed with the restaurant I was being taken to and assured me I was dressed appropriately.

I kissed them both and left.

The restaurant was on a busy street with elegant shops up and down the block, a movie theater featuring four current films, and people window-shopping as well as carrying the kind of small, pretty shopping bags that indicated expensive purchases. I parked around the corner at a meter I was lucky to find and put in enough coins for two hours. Then, since I was a few minutes early, I did my own window-shopping, looking at handbags too expensive even to consider and handmade jewelry that spoke of a designer with real talent.

The restaurant, Maurice's, had a heavy oak door with a small, cloudy window at about eye level. I pulled it open and went inside, a cool darkness greeting me. Tables were set with white linen and candles burned on the occupied ones.

"Yes, madam."

I am not often addressed with such formality and I attempted to take it in stride. Where I live, I'm Chris unless I see an old friend and then I'm more likely to be Kix, a childhood name that has stuck. "I'm meeting Miss Stern," I said.

"Oh yes. They're here. Come this way, please."

The *they* surprised me. Janet hadn't said anything about anyone else joining us, but as we approached the table, I could see it was her mother who was with her. The two faces were as alike as such a relationship could produce, but the mother's face was clouded with worry.

She looked up as she saw me and stood to greet me. "Ms. Bennett, thank you so much for coming. I'm Lila Stern. Please sit down and make yourself comfortable."

"Thank you." The place reserved for me was to her left with Janet sitting directly opposite me which I liked. I would be able to look at both of them easily. "Please call me Chris. I've just been called madam and I'm a little startled by it."

Lila Stern gave me a quick smile that faded immediately. "I'm Lila. I somehow thought you would be older."

"I'm thirty-four," I said.

"Well, I'm past forty so that sounds pretty young to me. Why don't you have a look at the menu before we start to talk? They do a wonderful cioppino here."

My taste in food is rather simple, and I looked through the menu a couple of times before deciding on a pasta dish with all sorts of good things added. Janet chose the same thing but Lila ordered a plain fish dish and a green salad. No wonder she was pencil slim.

She then asked for the wine list, and I told her I would not be drinking. I like wine although I'm not much of a connoisseur, but I don't hold it well and I wanted to fall asleep neither while we were discussing something very important to these two people nor while I was at the wheel of my car driving home. She ordered a glass of wine for herself and then turned to me.

"Janet told you what happened?"

"Not really. Why don't you start from the beginning?"

"Well." She smiled, more to herself than to me. "The beginning goes way back, long before I was born. My grandparents were immigrants. They came to this country separately and met and married in New York. They started with nothing, as you can imagine, but they did well enough by working hard. After my uncle was born, they moved into an apartment in the Bronx. It was a residential neighborhood near Morris Avenue." She paused as though she expected me to acknowledge the name.

"I don't know much about the Bronx," I said.

"Well, it was a place where people grew up in the thirties and forties. There were parks and schools and stores and lots of apartment houses. It was a safe place to live, with children playing in the street and women schmoozing. It was a few blocks from the Grand Concourse—"

"I know the Concourse," I said, finally recognizing a name.

"Yes, a magnificent street, a boulevard, almost like Paris if you think about it; the subway runs just underneath it. It was a wonderful place to bring up children."

She paused, as though to consider when to begin the substance of her story. "That's where my father, Morton Horowitz, grew up. He went to school there, and he became friends with a group of other little boys who were just like him in many ways, children of immigrants or even immigrants themselves, with families that placed tremendous importance on education and hard work. Some of them became friends when they were in kindergarten, others when they were a little older. But altogether there were nine of them by the time they were eleven years old and thinking about high school. They called themselves the Morris Avenue Boys." She smiled wistfully, as though she were talking about her own friends and their child-hood. I could imagine that her father had regaled her with tales of his youth, his friends, their practical jokes.

"Are they still friends?" I asked.

"Most of them, yes. Not all. And those that are are as close as brothers. They've scattered, of course. Nobody lives in the Bronx any more, and a couple of them don't even live in the East. But they have reunions every so many years, the ones who keep in touch. The last reunion was last Sunday, Father's Day."

"Did they pick that day for any special reason?"

"It was spring and it was a good time to travel. I think they felt it was a good day to be in the New York area. Many of their children and grandchildren live around here, and they could spend the day with their families and then have their celebration at night."

"I gather from what Janet told me that something ter-rible happened that night."

"It did."

Our first courses were just arriving, and we said nothing while the waiter placed them artfully in front of us. Before beginning to eat her salad, Lila opened her bag and pulled out a small black-and-white snapshot. She put it on the table between us, and I picked it up and looked at it.

Two rows of young boys grinned impishly at me, boys with pudgy cheeks and unruly hair, sparkling eyes and smudged shirts. There were five in the back row, four in the front, and the background appeared to be brick with a window frame at the left end, probably an apartment house they lived in or near. It was hard not to smile back at them.

Above the heads of the ones in the back row and on the

shirts of the ones in the front, someone had lettered in black ink the first name of each boy.

"This one's Dad," Lila said, pointing to Morty, who stood between Ernie and Bruce in the back row.

Morty was taller than either of the boys around him, and although he was smiling, he wasn't mugging for the camera the way some of the others were.

"George Fried died several years ago," she said, pointing to the boy in the front row second from the right. "He lived out west somewhere. Here, let me go through them in order. In the back row is Dave Koch. He's a lawyer now. Bernie Reskin was a schoolteacher till he retired but he still works part-time. Ernie Greene—they always used to laugh about Bernie and Ernie—Ernie went into medicine but never practiced. He's been in research his whole life. There are rumors he's been considered for a Nobel Prize."

"That's amazing."

"They're an amazing group of men. Then there's Dad; he's also a doctor but he's been cutting back for a few years. Bruce had a hard life. He went into his father-in-law's business and got mixed up in an embezzling scandal. He wasn't the embezzler, but I think he covered up for someone to save the other man's skin. In the front row, Fred Beller hasn't shown up at the reunions for years, and I don't know if anyone knows what's become of him. Art Wien is a writer and has a lovely sense of humor. George is the one who died. And the last one on the right is Joe Meyer. Joe has had a long career as a concert violinist but I hear he's thinking of retiring." She had been careful not to let on which of them had been murdered.

"I can hardly believe that a group of children connected only by the place they lived could have turned out to be such astounding people."

"They were motivated and they were smart."

"I gather one of them was murdered last Sunday."

"Yes." She looked at the picture as though she had the power of life and death over them, as though they were all alive until her finger came down on one little smiling face. "It was Art who was murdered, Arthur Wien, the writer. I have something to show you." She took an envelope out of her bag and pulled a color photo out of it. This one was about four by six and showed gray and graying men, several with paunches, all wearing suits and ties, all smiling. They were also standing in two rows with gaps in the front row.

"They arranged themselves the way they were in the old snap. The space on the left here in the front is for Fred, the one who never comes to reunions, and the space between Art and Joe is for George, the one who died. It was taken before the murder, and we just got the pictures back yesterday."

"Mom," Janet said, speaking for the first time, "will you let her eat?"

"Oh I'm so sorry, Chris. Please. Your soup is getting cold."

I lined the pictures up with the new one above the old one and looked at them as I ate. I kept trying to describe for myself what I was feeling. It was startling, astounding, confounding, and amazing. A motley group of boys had become men of stature and importance in a variety of respected fields. I found myself wondering whether there was something in the water they drank or the air they breathed. Had they all had parents who drove them relentlessly or had they simply been instilled with such desire to achieve that they made wonderful things happen?

When we finished, our plates were whisked away by

waiters obviously anxious to deliver our main course. Lila apologized again, and I assured her I was interested in hearing everything.

"I wasn't at the reunion," she said. "It was just the men and their wives. Dad said they had an oval table so they could all sit together. He said everyone was in a good mood; they all gave speeches, short ones, and had a good time."

"Who took the pictures?" I asked.

"A waiter. There are other pictures besides this one. They took a bunch, some of them with their wives. I have all of them."

"Tell me about the murder."

"As near as they can determine, it took place about nine-thirty. They had all gathered at the restaurant at seven. They were in a private room, but they had to use the men's and women's rooms for the regular restaurant. Dad said he didn't take particular notice of who got up and left the room, but he was aware that people did as the evening went on. By nine they had finished eating and were making toasts and doing their usual telling of tales, which always got them laughing and sometimes a little teary eyed. There was music piped in and some of the couples were dancing. Dad went to the men's room about nine-thirty and he found Art's body on the floor. He had been stabbed with an ice pick. Dad thought it had just happened. His body was still warm. No one else was in the men's room."

"Was it a room for one or were there several stalls?"

"I never asked."

"I assume your father called the police immediately."

"He did. And they came very fast; he told me that."

"And everyone was questioned."

"And questioned and questioned. They're all suspects,

and unfortunately, my father is suspect number one because he found the body only minutes after the murder. It puts him on the spot. I can't tell you what this has done to my family."

I could imagine. "When you say that your father is the main suspect, have the police let you know that?"

"Not in so many words, but they've been back to ask him questions several times, and my mother too. My folks have hired a lawyer."

"Does your father have a feeling about who may have done it?"

"Not at all. Quite the contrary, he's ready to vouch for the character of any one of the boys. Men." She smiled. "He's never called them anything but boys when he's talked about them, and I've never known them as anything but men."

"Lila, this is not only an ongoing police investigation but a very new one. I'm not sure how I can help you without getting in the way of the police, and I won't do that."

"I know. I knew you would say that." She had been picking at her fish. Now she laid her fork down.

"Mom," Janet said, "you promised."

That's when I realized Lila was holding back tears. "I'm so worried about him," she said unsteadily. "I don't really expect you to figure out who did this terrible thing. I hoped you might be able to clear my father, to find something that would prove he couldn't have done it. He's not a young man any more and this is taking its toll. Janet was so impressed with you, both as a teacher and as a person."

I let it all rush through my head. Her family was surely in turmoil. If her father were innocent, this burden would affect his life every day until the police decided he was not their man. If he had committed the murder, and he might have, I would hate to be the one to dig up the evidence that pointed to him. I wasn't sure how much I could accomplish toward either end. From what Lila had said, some of the men at the dinner lived far from the New York area, and I had a young child whom I couldn't just drop off for days with a sitter while I went flying around the country, not to mention Jack's precarious situation with a new job and the bar exams not far down the road.

"It's all right," Lila said, sounding recovered. "I was asking too much. Why don't we just have a nice lunch and not talk about it any more?"

"Let me talk to your father," I said. I could see Janet's eyes widen across the table. She broke into a smile, and I remembered what a pretty girl she was, how much more forthcoming she was in class.

"He'll probably regale you with stories of the old neighborhood."

"That's OK. I kind of like that sort of thing. And maybe I'll begin to understand how this group of little boys turned into such fine old men."

"Don't call Dad an old man if you value your life. He's only in his late sixties, and he's as powerful a human being as he was in his forties."

"Sounds good."

Lila pressed a tissue to her eyes. "Thank you." She smiled. "I think I'll have dessert today."

"You, Mom?" her daughter asked in apparent disbelief.

"Yes, me."

"Then I will too," Janet said.

I wasn't about to be the odd man out.

2

I came home with a large envelope from Lila. After I had told her I would look into the murder, she had held out her hand to Janet who had given her the envelope on cue. It had been on the floor next to Janet during our conversation. What was inside would be the beginning of my investigation if I took it on.

The envelope contained not only the photographs but also jottings that Dr. Horowitz, Lila's father, had made, not for me but for himself. She had xeroxed them that morning and given me the copies. It was a place to start my thinking. Tonight, she would call her father and arrange for me to meet him as soon as he could make time for me. Eddie had been pretty rambunctious when I picked him up at Elsie's, and I didn't get a chance to look at the pictures and writings till a few minutes before Jack walked in the door.

I put Eddie to bed before Jack came home. His tour was ten to six, but he was lucky to leave on time and it was a long drive from Brooklyn to Oakwood, especially at that hour of the day. I had roasted a chicken according to my friend Melanie Gross's fail-safe recipe, the only kind of recipe I ever use, and the kitchen smelled wonderful, full of garlic and rosemary and lemon.

When I heard the car, I put the stuff back in the envelope and opened the family room door, the closest door to the garage.

He came inside, gave me a kiss, and looked at me strangely. "What's up?"

"What do you mean?"

"What's happened? Is Eddie OK?"

"Eddie's fine. We're both fine. Dinner's ready."

"You look a little—I don't know. What did you do today?"

"I had an interesting day. Sit down and eat your melon."

We sat down at the kitchen table, which was already set, and started to eat.

"Nice and sweet," Jack said. "You gonna tell me?" He took another bite and looked at me. "You're on a case."

I started to laugh. "You saw that in my face?"

"I saw something. You had that look like you were really fixed on something. Is that it? You walk into a murder this afternoon?"

"One of my students called," I said. I told him about it as he carved the chicken and I got the potatoes and string beans on the table.

"Maurice's, huh? You're gonna need a whole new wardrobe for this one."

"I doubt whether I'll be eating many more lunches there. Lila's going to arrange for me to meet her father, and I'll see if there's anything I can do. She was in tears, Jack. I tried to say no because I want to be around while you study."

"Honey, I can study alone. I just won't make a very good baby-sitter. I'll really have to concentrate."

"I know."

"But it sounds interesting, a bunch of guys who love

each other except that two of them don't. At least the things you stumble into don't involve drugs and gangs."

"These men could hardly be called a gang. I'd love to drive over to where they lived when they were children and get a look at it."

"Where's that?"

"The Bronx. A Hundred Seventy-fourth Street and Morris Avenue. They called themselves the Morris Avenue Boys."

"You're kidding. You want to *go* there?"

"Why not?"

"Because that's just above Claremont Park. It's drugs and gangs and you don't want to know what all else in the street."

"That bad?"

"It can be."

"I guess Lila was right. She said nobody lived there anymore."

"It's gone way downhill since the forties and fifties. The young people left; the older people left or died. Look at this guy's pictures. They're a lot better than reality."

I mulled it over after dinner. Jack sat down in the family room, which he likes better than the office upstairs, and I sat down away from him with my envelope of goodies after we'd had coffee and some extraordinary Jersey strawberries I had picked up on my way home from lunch. Eddie had eaten several with relish and his father did the same hours later.

I emptied the envelope and took out the smaller envelope of pictures. It was thick enough that they must have used a whole roll of film to record the evening's activities. Lila had said they were in chronological order, and I was anxious to keep them that way. With a pencil, I numbered the backs before I sat back to look at them.

They told the story of a happy reunion, a festive dinner, a group of men who, as far as I could see, cared about each other. There were no solemn faces, no hints of anger, no tense, nervous wives. I was particularly interested in Arthur Wien, the victim. Using the first picture Lila had shown me as a key, I identified him in picture after picture, a man of average height, hair still mostly dark, thickening at the midsection, standing close to a wife who was many years younger than he and very attractive. He had a good-looking face that had probably been quite handsome when he was young, and he was dressed, like the others, in a well-cut suit. Instead of the dress shirt that most of the others wore, he had on a white turtleneck. His wife, whose name was Cindy, was wearing a dazzling low-cut dress that showed off an enviable figure. Even in these amateur snapshots, the sequins on her dress caught the light. Like everyone else there, they seemed to be very happy and enjoying the evening.

As a boy he had been shorter than most of the others, his hair dark, although hair color in black-and-white pictures is hard to determine, and a bit on the pudgy side. There was nothing about his looks that would indicate he would grow up successful and famous in a competitive field.

A sudden thought sent me to the bag of recyclable paper, which we keep in the family room where we read newspapers, magazines, and mail. I pulled out *The New York Times* from Monday and turned to the obituary page. There was no mention of Wien, but if he had died during the night, that was understandable. But Tuesday's edition had a paid notice that read: "Wien, Arthur A., suddenly on Father's Day, beloved husband of Cynthia (Cindy)

Porter, devoted father of Michael and Katherine, Robert and Sondra, and Melissa and John Beck." It went on to name numerous grandchildren and then said, "Author of *The Lost Boulevard* and many other respected novels, Art was a good father, a good husband, and a good friend. In lieu of flowers, contributions to the Authors Guild will be welcome."

I thought that last was very generous. I was about to tear out the small square of paper when I noticed that just below it was a second, smaller notice for Arthur Wien: "A good man and a great friend. We will miss him forever. The Morris Avenue Boys."

I tore the tiny notices out of the paper and slipped the clipping into my envelope. Then I checked yesterday's paper and found the same family notice again but no *Times* obit. Today's paper was an arm's length away, and I reached over and pulled it toward me. This time there was a long obituary with a photograph taken about ten years ago.

Arthur Wien, novelist and author of *The Lost Boulevard*, died Sunday night, the victim of an apparent homicide. Police said there were no immediate suspects.

Born in the Bronx to immigrant parents who owned a grocery store in which he often worked after school, Mr. Wien attended City College where he majored in English and graduated after World War II. He held a number of teaching jobs until, days before his thirtieth birthday, his first novel, *The Lost Boulevard*, was published to great critical acclaim. The *Times* called it "a searing, incisive study of the generation that came of age during and after the war."

It went on to note the titles of his other books, not all of them critical successes although apparently they did well enough commercially. The obituary mentioned places he had lived—he had apparently become an expatriate for a while and taken up residence in Paris—and some of the people he had known.

> He is survived by his second wife, Cynthia Porter, and three children of his first marriage, which ended in divorce, his sons Michael of New York, Robert of Short Hills, and one daughter, Melissa Beck of San Francisco.

When I tore the section out of the paper, Jack looked up to see what I was doing and then went quickly back to his books. As I put the obituary in the envelope, the phone rang.

It was Lila Stern with an appointment for me to see her father. He would talk to me after his last morning patient; it was the best she could do. His office was in New York, and if I didn't mind, he would order a take-out lunch so he could eat while we talked. I didn't mind at all. That was one tuna fish sandwich less I had to make for myself.

I went back to my comfortable seat in the family room and took out the several sheets of xeroxed handwritten notes. They had been written in pencil, and there were places where words were so faint they were not legible. To make matters worse, the handwriting was that of a doctor who was used to scribbling so that no one but a pharmacist could read it. But as I looked the first page over, I realized he had tried to put down on paper a chronology of the events of the Father's Day dinner, starting with the arrival of the men and their wives at the restaurant.

Arrived before seven. Dave, Bernie, and Joe already there with wives. Room set up. Nice. Joe very thin but said no recurrence. Ernie and Bruce came next, I think. Art was last but not late. All stood up for our regular picture.

Then picture of the women. Cindy (Wien) very gorgeous. Ellen (Koch) looking good too. Bernie still overweight; Art looking better than last time. Can't remember when that was. Bruce in good spirits and drinking a lot, but Arlene covers her glass when waiter comes around. Art eats fish; so does Joe. Didn't notice the wives.

Everyone talks. Everyone in good spirits. Art tells funny story about Hollywood. Dave tells lawyer joke. Ernie tells doctor joke. Joe tells jokes so old we all laugh before he finishes.

Several couples dance after appetizer; not sure who. Robin (my wife) insists we dance and we do, but the food comes right away and we sit down. Waiter takes pictures throughout meal. Joe eats little. I worry.

I found myself feeling confused about who was who and who was married to whom. I looked through the remaining pages and found that the last one, the one that should have been on top of the pile, was a key.

Here Dr. Horowitz had sketched out the group complete with last names, professions, and wives. He had taken the men in the order of the famous half-century-old snapshot, which made it easy for me to put names onto faces.

The first man in the back row was Dave Koch, an attorney, whom Dr. Horowitz identified as "my best friend in the world." His wife was Ellen, and I found her in the wives' pictures, contemporary with her husband, a pretty face, and an excellent figure. To the right of Dave Koch was Bernie Reskin, the schoolteacher, married to Marilyn. Third in line was Dr. Ernie Greene, who might or might not be in line for a Nobel Prize. He was married to Kathy. To the right of him in the picture was Dr. Horowitz himself. His wife's name was Robin. And last was Bruce Kaplan, dubbed a businessman, the one Lila said had been caught in some sort of embezzling scheme. He was married to Arlene.

The front row had only two men. Fred Beller was absent as usual and not further described. Next to his empty space was Arthur Wien, the writer who had been murdered. To the right was the empty space for poor George Fried next to whose name Dr. Horowitz had written "dec." And finally, at the right end of the first row stood Joe Meyer, the violinist, whose wife's name was Judy.

Now, at least, the names began to mean something to me. When I went back to the narrative and saw that Judy had ordered a vegetable plate instead of the filet mignon or fish alternative, I knew he was talking about the violinist's wife.

Most of what followed struck me as mundane; this didn't mean it wasn't important or wouldn't yield something crucial. From time to time he would note that this man danced with that man's wife, but there was no comment about how close they danced or whether they seemed enamored of each other. There was just the fact: they danced.

He noted the wines that were served but was unable to say who drank red and who drank white. Champagne had been ordered for the traditional toast with dessert—a sheet cake with a schematic of Morris Avenue and 174th Street drawn on it—and "even Joe took a sip of bubbly."

It was while the cake was being cut that Dr. Horowitz

left the table to find the men's room. Arthur Wien had gotten there first, and someone had found him and killed him before Dr. Horowitz entered the room.

The chronology ended there but he continued to write his musings.

> Why Artie? If he offended one of us, I know nothing of it. If he had his eye on someone's wife, no one has told me. And why would he? His is the youngest and prettiest wife in the group. Who among us could have been offended? Artie lives in Cal. We only see him at reunions.

As I read these rambling comments, I could feel the doctor crying out in despair. He was convinced one of the group had committed the murder, but he could find no reason for it and could not believe one of his boyhood friends could have done such a thing.

I put the photos and notes back in the envelope and groped around for the small rectangle of newsprint that was the family's notice of Arthur Wien's death. I took it out and read it again. "Suddenly on Father's Day." The phrase did something to me. I had never written an obituary notice. When Aunt Meg died, while I was still a nun at St. Stephen's, I had not thought about a notice until the funeral director asked me. I gave him the facts of her life and death, and he composed it for me and sent it to the paper.

But each day as I read the *Times*, I looked at them, letting my eye move over the names to see if one sounded familiar, so I knew what form they took. I had seen similar phrases, "Suddenly on the twenty-seventh of November," and understood the shock that a family felt at the unexpected passing of someone loved. But this one was somehow more poignant: "Suddenly on Father's Day," as though there were some significance to the fact that the death happened on that day.

I would have to ask the good doctor when I saw him tomorrow after his last morning patient.

3

Dr. Morton Horowitz's office was on Lexington Avenue in the Seventies, not far from Hunter College. I had forgotten to ask Lila what kind of doctor he was, but I found out when I reached his address and read the brass sign next to his door: gastroenterologist. That stretch of Lexington had doctors' offices at just about every ground level door of apartment houses, often two or three together. You could walk up the street and pick an obstetrician, a cardiologist, an internist, whatever your body needed.

I rang the bell next to the barred door, and the receptionist buzzed me in. When I gave her my name, she said the doctor was expecting me and should be available quite soon. I took a copy of *The New Yorker* off a table and sat down to wait.

It was the kind of old-fashioned office that made me feel comfortable and secure. The furniture was both leather and upholstered, with mahogany showing here and there. The carpet was worn, the pictures on the wall dark prints of old masters. The obstetrician I had used when I was pregnant was young, and her office was new and high tech. Here I felt as if I were visiting someone's parents.

Except for me the waiting room was empty so I assumed the doctor was treating his final patient of the morning. As I sat, I heard a buzz and then a man's voice asking for something. The young woman at the desk got up and disappeared.

About ten minutes later, a middle-aged couple came into the waiting room with a man I recognized as Dr. Horowitz. They had a brief, pleasant conversation and then the couple left.

"I bet you're my lunch date," the doctor said with a smile, holding out his hand.

I stood and shook it. "I'm Chris Bennett. Glad to meet you."

"So am I. Come with me and I'll give you a menu. The restaurant isn't the Grill Room but it's second best. It serves very good food."

We went into a large room filled with bookcases, a mahogany desk, family pictures almost everywhere, and a barred window looking out onto Lexington Avenue.

"First things first. Here's your menu. Pick anything, eat hearty, and we'll have it delivered in fifteen minutes or so."

I thanked him and looked at the card. There were several selections, all appearing more like dinner than lunch. I must have taken a long time because he said, "It's all good. Close your eyes and point to something. You won't be sorry."

At his insistence, I started with a seafood salad and then took a veal dish that sounded wonderful. He gave our order to his receptionist and then sat down on his side of the desk and smiled.

"Explain to me how I come to be having lunch with someone like you."

"Your granddaughter took a poetry course from me. She called yesterday and asked if I could help with the investigation of Arthur Wien's murder. Your daughter took us both to lunch and told me all about it." I showed him the envelope. "And I've read a xerox of your notes and looked at all the pictures."

"Gotcha. Well, I don't really know what you—or anybody else—can do about this. Somebody murdered poor Artie last Sunday night while we were all celebrating, and I'd vouch for every man in the group."

"What about the women?"

"The women, yes. Well, he was found in the men's room so I'd think that would exclude the women. Wouldn't you?"

"It's rather early to exclude anyone. I can imagine a woman getting inside a men's room. How big a room was it?"

"Not big. You're right. At this point, anything's possible. The police seem to think one of us did it—that's not an unreasonable assumption from their point of view—but nothing's turned up pointing to anyone. I found the body; Lila probably told you that. So I seem to be suspect number one. And since my lawyer is my best friend since boyhood and a member of the group, I can't even use him. He's also a suspect. It's a mess, Ms. Bennett."

"Chris," I said. "I read the *Times* obituary and the paid notice that Mr. Wien's family put in. Tell me about his first wife and what happened."

"His first wife was a lovely person, someone he met after school and before his first book was published. She loved him, she struggled with him, she bore his children, enjoyed their rise into affluence as his books began to sell, and watched as he became disenchanted with her and enchanted with other women."

"Did he go directly from wife number one to wife number two?"

"No, they lived apart for some time. I'm sure she hoped he would return to her, but those of us looking in from the outside knew it would never happen."

"Where is she now?"

"I think she still has an apartment here in New York."

"How did his children feel about their relationship?"

"As you might expect, not very happy. From what I know, they maintained separate relationships with their parents. And if you wonder whether he paid her alimony, my understanding is that he did. If there had been any court battles, I would have heard."

Since his best friend was an attorney, I could see why that was so. "The other men," I said. "Are any of them divorced or widowed?"

"There was one other, George Fried. But he died several years ago while married to his second wife."

"Who is now his widow."

"Right."

"Did he die a natural death?"

The doctor smiled. "You are certainly a suspicious young woman. But it turns out that that's an interesting question or at least a question that has an interesting answer. His wife wrote a letter to each of us after he died, after the funeral, after it was too late for us to go to see him for the last time."

"How strange. Was there a problem? Was he angry at the group?"

"Not at all or, at least, not that I know of."

"Where did he live?"

There was a knock on the door and the receptionist brought our lunch inside, set the bags on the desk, and said she would bring fresh coffee. She returned with a silvered flask that she set down beside two mugs. It occurred to me that the doctor must visit with people from time to time over this lunch.

We got our lunches out and began to eat, my pen and notebook near my right hand. After a few minutes, Dr. Horowitz said, "You were asking me something about George Fried."

I glanced at my notes. "I think I was asking where George Fried lived."

"Yes. George was one of two in our group who hated living in New York. George's father died when he was pretty young; I remember when it happened. His mother couldn't quite accept that she had been widowed, that she had a son she had to bring up alone. They had a hard life, the two of them. Add to that that George never liked the winter weather, never liked living in an apartment. Finally, when he was in his twenties, he and his mother picked up and moved out to southern California, somewhere around San Diego."

"That's certainly a place with warmer winters," I said. "It's too bad he didn't live longer to enjoy it. And he had two wives, you said?"

"He married a few years after he moved west. Most of us flew out there—or took the train; that was a long time ago—for the wedding. The marriage didn't last all that long, maybe ten or fifteen years. When he married his second wife, we heard about it afterward."

"Did you ever meet her?"

"Oh yes. They came east for a reunion or two. I'm afraid I can't tell you the dates."

"Perhaps before I leave you'll give me the addresses and phone numbers of these people, dead or alive."

"I will certainly do that." He opened a Rolodex on his desk and began to look through it.

"And the other man who was missing, Fred Beller, what can you tell me about him?"

"Fred just doesn't come. He's alive and well as far as I know, but he doesn't want to see us. At least, he doesn't want to see us in a group."

"Is there someone he doesn't get along with?"

"Chris, we are a very agreeable group of aging boys. We're probably split down the middle politically, and we have spent many hours raising our voices in a very ungentlemanly manner when we argued politics. But we were friends. We care about each other more than we care about who is running the government or how. We all get along."

"Can we go through the group that came to the Father's Day reunion?"

"That's easy. I don't even have to look at the picture to see where we're all standing. It's the same place we were standing when we were kids. Dave Koch, who I already told you was my best friend, is a lawyer. He's a liberal lawyer but he's managed to make a lot of money anyway. He went to the Bronx High School of Science even though he wasn't much of a scientist." The doctor smiled. "Good marriage, good wife, nice kids. And he's in good health. Next in line is Bernie. He's a teacher, a very good one. He's given his heart and soul to his students. He should lose a little weight but shouldn't we all? He went to Taft—"

"Taft?"

"High School."

"Oh."

"Yes. And then City. Met his wife there, I think. She

taught too. Sometimes in the summer they'd lead a group to some exotic place somewhere in the world. I believe he's had a rewarding life. Ernie's a doctor, a researcher as it happens, went to Bronx Science with me. Then we both went to Cornell and on to Cornell Med. So now you know about me. I'm married to the same wonderful woman I was married to when I graduated from medical school. And then next to me in the picture is Bruce Kaplan." He stopped as though it were my turn to ask a question.

"Your daughter said something about him."

"There was a troublesome incident. It happened a good many years ago, and you can be sure I don't know the whole story. Bruce worked for his father-in-law. Some money disappeared, and the long and short of it is that Bruce stood trial and was convicted of embezzling. He served about a year in prison."

"How terrible."

"More terrible than anything I can imagine ever happening to me. Not only did he have to spend that time incarcerated, but his parents, his wife, his children all suffered with him. When he got out, we had a reunion to welcome him back."

"You're a very kind group of people."

"He was one of us. I don't think any of us believed he had done what he was charged with."

"Do you think he was protecting someone, like his father-in-law?"

"I suppose that's the obvious answer, but personally I don't know."

"Was Arthur Wien involved with that incident in any way?" I asked.

He looked at me across the desk, a look of confusion on his face. "It never occurred to me. . . . I thought—when

Lila told me about you, I thought asking you to investigate was rather foolhardy, but I see the relevance of your question. Sometimes resentments do take a long time to boil over. But I'm afraid this is a dead end. If Artie had anything to do with that incident, I know nothing of it, and I don't think that Artie and Bruce were particularly close, that they had anything to do with each other between reunions."

"Sometimes people need money," I said. "Sometimes they give the appearance of having it when they really don't. If a man suddenly needed a great deal of money, which of the members of your group would he go to?"

"No one's ever come to me, I can tell you that. I don't know the answer, but it's a good question. Bruce did well. And from the time Artie's first book was published, he always seemed to have plenty of money. Some of us—Dave and myself—were starting out in professions that required expensive equipment, insurance, nice offices, and we sure didn't make a lot in those early years."

"Why don't you think about it, Dr. Horowitz? I'll leave my name and phone number with you. Something may come to you over the next few days."

"Yes." He looked troubled. He took a sheet of paper and copied something from a Rolodex card, then flipped to another and wrote some more.

"Tell me about the boys in the front row," I said.

He put his pen down. "Fred Beller married a girl from the Midwest and moved to Minneapolis or just outside Minneapolis. I visited him there once. He seemed very happy, had a huge house, nice kids. He said he'd never really liked New York and that was one reason he didn't come for reunions. It can happen. I don't think he had any beef with Artie. In fact, he had Artie's books on a shelf in his bookcase."

"The next one is Mr. Wien, then George Fried. You've told me about him. And the last is Joe Meyer."

"Joe is the gentle soul in our group. How he managed to play ball with us when we were kids is still a mystery. His great love was playing the violin. He started young and spent more hours at it than I spent studying. His mother was always afraid he'd break a finger, and he nearly did once," the doctor said with a smile. "But his parents wanted him to have a normal childhood and they sent him out to play with us. He wasn't much of a hitter, but he could catch pretty well. I mean in the field, not behind the plate. And we played other games besides baseball—stoopball, handball, stickball. We managed to break a few windows while we were at it. And paid for them, God help me. Joe went to Music and Art."

"Is that a high school?"

"Yes, in New York. He took the subway every day, carrying his violin back and forth. He went to Juilliard when he graduated and got himself auditioned for professional playing. He picked up jobs here and there and then landed the big one with the New York Philharmonic, and he's been there for his entire career. I've gone to some of his recitals. He's very good. He's taught students in the past but he hasn't been well lately."

"I gathered that from your notes."

"It's cancer. He's in remission now. I hope it lasts another twenty years." He spoke with great sadness.

"What was his relationship with Arthur Wien?"

"As a matter of fact, I think Joe admired Artie for not being a scientist or a lawyer or a businessman. Artie may not have been to literature what Joe was to music, but he was a creative person and Joe loved that. I believe they had a friendly relationship, the way Dave Koch and I do. When Artie came to town, they saw each other."

"And that's it."

"I would say that's it. They were friends."

"What about Mr. Meyer's wife?"

"Oh they've been married forever. Judy was a young singer when they met. She's had parts in operas at the Met and she's done work in Broadway musicals. They're a wonderful combination. Their daughter is a fine cellist and their son plays the viola, I believe."

We had gone through every boy in the original picture. I had a question that I didn't look forward to asking, but I knew I had to. I had to let Dr. Horowitz know where I was heading if I continued to look into Arthur Wien's murder. "Dr. Horowitz, did the group or some of the group get involved when you were younger in something that was illegal or unethical or could cause you problems today if it were discovered?"

He looked at me as though he didn't understand or believe the question. Then he laughed. "I think you watch too many dramas on television, Chris. You think the group killed some poor girl that we met on a night on the town? We didn't even know what a night on the town was till we had scattered. Our idea of fun was a malted at Shulman's Drugstore on 174th Street. You think we got together and stole a national treasure? I don't know if we had the imagination to do something like that. No, there are no great secrets that some or all of us share, nothing in our background that would embarrass us or our families, that might put us in prison or cost us our jobs or lose us our wives. That one of us could have murdered Artie Wien is so impossible for me to believe I have all but eliminated it as a possibility."

But I hadn't because I couldn't. What he felt with his heart, I would have to learn with my head if the facts were there. "When was your last reunion, Dr. Horowitz?"

"Let's see, it's been a few years. I'd say three, maybe three and a half. I seem to remember it was earlier in the year than June."

"I'm sure I'll have more questions as I sit and think about all this," I said.

"I'm sure you will. The police have been bothering me since Sunday night. It's my impression that they have nothing or at least very little."

"Do you have any objections to my calling these men and their wives?"

"None whatever. If you can find out who did this, we'll all be grateful."

Except, I thought, the man who did it. "I'll keep you informed."

"And I almost have your address list ready. How was lunch?"

"So much better than the tuna sandwich I would have brought along, that I'm doubly satisfied."

"Good." He looked at his watch. "I have a patient to see in a few minutes. If there's anything else—"

"Not for now. Thank you for your time."

"I hope it pays off."

So did I.

4

I spent a little time walking around the East Side of New York. I enjoy looking in shop windows, even if what they offer costs more than I will ever be able to afford. And it was nice to walk in the early summer air.

I had a lot to think about. Dr. Horowitz had given me the addresses for everyone in his group, including Fred Beller who never came and George Fried's widow. Just to make sure that I covered everyone, I would call their numbers as well, although I could not imagine what help the people at the other end would be.

As I was about to finish my little stroll, it occurred to me that the restaurant where Arthur Wien had been murdered was only a few blocks away. I checked the time and, having plenty of it, went off to get a firsthand look at the crime scene.

It was a beautiful place in the East Sixties, a doorman in the street and a maitre d' inside whom I would have to convince to show me the men's room where the homicide occurred. He smiled and asked if I wanted a table for one.

"Thank you, I'm not here for lunch. I'm a friend of Dr. Morton Horowitz of the group that met here last Sunday."

He frowned. "Yes, I recall."

"I'm doing a little research into the murder for Dr. Horowitz," I said, watching his face become more unhappy. "I wonder if someone could show me the room in which the party was held and the men's room where the murder took place."

"This is a police matter. I don't think we can cooperate with—are you a journalist?"

"Not at all. I'm a friend of Dr. Horowitz. He asked me to look into some aspects of the murder."

I wasn't surprised to see him confused. I hadn't said very much of substance.

"Just a minute." He went over to a waiter and said something, then returned. "It'll be a few minutes. What did you say your name was?"

"Christine Bennett."

He looked over my shoulder and smiled broadly as someone came into the restaurant. "Mr. Browning, how nice to see you. I have your table waiting."

I looked out over the linen cloths and well-dressed diners. A waiter came from the kitchen and set his tray down. He carried two dishes to a table where a man and a woman were sitting with glasses of wine at their places.

"Ms. Bennett?"

A busboy was standing next to me. "Yes."

"Come with me, please."

I followed him to the back of the restaurant and into a windowless room with several empty unset tables. "This is where the party was last Sunday evening?"

"Yes, ma'am. There was a different table in here that night, a single table for the whole group. But this is the room."

"Thank you. Is that the only door?"

"Yes, ma'am."

"May I see the men's room now?"

"I'll check to make sure it's empty."

We went out, made a turn, and went down a short hall with two doors. The first was the men's room. The busboy went inside and came out almost immediately. He held the door open for me.

There were two stalls on the right in the back, two urinals on the left, two sinks on the right, one paper towel holder on the wall to the right of the sinks, and a window on the wall where the farther stall was. I walked over to it and tried to open it.

"That's kept locked," the busboy said. "The restaurant is air-conditioned."

"I see." I flipped open my notebook and made a quick sketch of the room. "Thank you. That's fine."

He opened the door for me and we went out. He went back to the kitchen, and I walked through the restaurant to the maitre d' and thanked him. I was sure he was glad to see the last of me.

It's a long drive from New York to the small suburban community where Jack and I live. Oakwood is on the north shore of the Long Island Sound, on the way to Connecticut and New England. I inherited the house from my aunt Meg, who died while I was still at St. Stephen's. I lived there alone for over a year while Jack lived in a tiny, charming apartment in Brooklyn Heights. It broke my heart when he gave it up, but he moved in with me when we married, taking on a long drive twice a day to and from Brooklyn and work.

Before Eddie was born, we added a wing on the back of the house, which gave us a huge family room with a fireplace on the first floor and an equally huge master bedroom and bath on the second. In the course of only a few years, I have gone from living a single life in a small but adequate house to being a wife and mother in a house that seems quite luxurious by my standards. Eddie has his own room with a crib and furniture that bespeak a grandmother's love. While Jack's mother and father are careful spenders for themselves, they seem to have no upper limit where their first grandchild is concerned.

Before going home, I drove to Elsie Rivers's house in a neighboring town. When I got there, I turned up the driveway and saw her in her large backyard holding the hand of my little Eddie. It was a beautiful picture, the grandmotherly woman slightly stooped to be able to hang onto the toddler's little hand. Neither of them heard me drive up, and I got out of the car quietly, watching as Elsie walked Eddie to various plants and flowers and showed them to him. I could barely hear their voices. I stepped onto the grass, waited a minute, then called hello.

Eddie dropped Elsie's hand and turned toward me. As he saw me, his face lit up. "Mommy!" He took off toward me in that bumbling way little ones have of running, and I ran to him, lifted him up, and hugged and kissed him.

"We were just having a nice little walk in the garden," Elsie said. "Eddie had a good nap and a good lunch."

"And kept you busy, I bet." I gave Elsie a hug with my free arm.

"We keep each other busy. We have an understanding." She touched his forehead with hers. "Don't we, my wonderful boy?"

Eddie giggled. We talked for a little while, and then I got Eddie into his car seat and we drove home.

As I went slowly down Pine Brook Road toward our house, I saw my friend Melanie Gross turn into her driveway. As she pulled into her garage, I made the same turn and followed her up the drive.

She got her kids out of the car and came out, smiling, to greet us. "Hi, Eddie," she said through the car window. "Where've you been?"

"I've been to New York. Eddie's been with Elsie."

"New York, huh? That sounds promising. Come on in and let's see what we've got to snack on."

Mel's two children still love to play with Eddie. I suppose that will end one day when they get older and playing with a little kid loses its allure, but now they all grabbed cookies and went upstairs, leaving Mel and me to sit together in quiet. Mel returned to teaching just before Eddie was born so we don't see as much of each other as we did when I first moved to Oakwood.

"You just lazing around New York having a good time?" she asked as the water boiled for tea.

"Nope."

"You're being mysterious. Don't tell me. There's been a murder."

"Oh Mel. They just seem to find me. A student of mine called and took me to lunch with her mother yesterday." I told her the details as she hotted the pot and poured the water. When it was all done, we carried cups and cookies and napkins to the family room.

"Morris Avenue in the Bronx," she said as we sat down. "I wouldn't be surprised if half the people in Westchester came from that part of the Bronx. It was where people started out. It's changed, you know."

"So Jack tells me. I made the mistake of saying I'd like to go over there and look around. I suspect he thought I'd lost my mind."

"I've read some of Arthur Wien's books. Mom's read

them all. I used to see them in the house when I was growing up. I read the obit the other day. I had no idea you were connected."

"You know what they say about degrees of separation. My student's grandfather is a boyhood friend of Arthur Wien."

"Amazing. So I guess the police haven't charged anyone yet."

"Doesn't look like it. If they have any suspects besides my student's grandfather, they aren't saying. I can tell you I don't have any. But I'll talk to the remaining boys—men—and see if anything turns up. I've already had a look at the crime scene, not that I could tell anything from that."

"You went into the men's room?"

"It occurred to me as I was driving home that that was a first in my life."

"Well, you've never been a schoolteacher for little boys. Not a spectacular first, Chris."

There was a screech from upstairs, and we put our cups down and started running.

Eddie was already asleep when Jack came home. He had been called out on a case that had dragged on so he was late and very hungry. He made a quick stop in Eddie's room, changed his clothes, and came down to the kitchen.

"So tell me. You've seen the doctor who you can't believe is a suspect. What else?"

"I can't believe any of them are suspects. Who could imagine that a lawyer, a research doctor who's been thought of for a Nobel Prize, or a concert violinist would murder a lifelong friend?"

"An NYPD detective."

"I know. It's called keeping an open mind. Why does mine close when I sit face to face with a suspect?"

"Because they're real people and, at the time you meet them, you don't know what motivates them."

"True. And it seems very unlikely that someone walked in off the street and did this."

"I agree."

"I visited the restaurant and the maitre d' stands guard near the door. The window in the men's room is kept locked because the restaurant is air-conditioned, so no one got in that way—or out. And I can't believe that a stranger in the restaurant walked into the men's room while Arthur Wien was there, happened to have an ice pick with him, and got mad enough at him that he killed him."

"So you've got six men and seven wives."

"And the wives are less likely to have gone into a men's room."

"But less likely doesn't mean it didn't happen."

I agreed. I told Jack about my conversation with Dr. Horowitz as we ate. When I'd gone through my notes, I said, "I think I'll start making phone calls tonight. I don't know how many of these men will agree to talk to me but I'll try to set something up with all of them. If there's a motive, maybe one of them will know it. It seems to me the two men who might have the best motives are the one who died some time ago and the one who never comes to the reunions."

"Why the one who died?"

"Because he also kind of separated himself from the group a long time ago. And he obviously didn't tell his wife to let his friends know that he was ill. By the time she told them he had died, it was a week or so after the funeral."

"So maybe she's a suspect."

"Jack, I can't go flying all over the country. Let the police look into that."

"Not likely they will. They'll concentrate on the men who are still alive and their wives. Something dramatic would have to happen for them to go looking into the past the way you do. If they don't make an arrest in the next few days, you'll have a better shot at closing the case than they will."

"Except the victim is someone well known."

"Right. That'll keep them going a little longer."

We finished our dinner talking about other things. I told him how Mel and I had dashed up the stairs that afternoon to see who was dismembering whom in her daughter's room, only to find that Eddie had fallen off a little chair and wounded his ego. There had been lots of tears until I picked him up, at which point they dried up pretty quickly. And Mel had sent some cookies home with us so that Jack wouldn't feel left out. He appreciated that.

When we had finished our coffee and all the cookies but one, I sat down in the kitchen near the phone and looked at my list. I decided to start with Dave Koch, the lawyer and Dr. Horowitz's best friend. I was fairly certain he would be expecting my call and would cooperate. The address was Manhattan. His wife answered and called him to the phone.

"Mr. Koch, this is Christine Bennett. I talked to Dr. Horowitz this afternoon about the murder of your friend Arthur Wien."

"Yes, he called me about that. I understand his granddaughter called you."

"That's right. She was a student of mine this year."

"Well, the police don't seem to have a clue what happened. I'll be glad to talk to you if we can set up a time."

"Tomorrow morning?"

There was a sound of a page turning. "That's pretty good for me. Can you meet me at my apartment?"

"Sure."

He gave me the address and said there was parking in the building. I suggested ten o'clock and he said that would be fine. I hung up feeling good. I had a first appointment.

I didn't do so well on my next couple of calls. There was no answer at the home of Bernie Reskin, the teacher, and the woman who answered at Dr. Greene's number said rather curtly that he wasn't there. I decided not to leave a message.

I was a little hesitant about calling Bruce Kaplan, the convicted embezzler, who was my personal choice as suspect number one, although I would not have admitted it out loud. But finally I dialed the number. A woman answered and I asked for Mr. Kaplan.

"He just went out," she said. "Can I take a message?"

"Mrs. Kaplan?"

"Yes."

I told her who I was and what I was calling about.

"Yes, there was a message on the machine this afternoon from Mort. Are you serious about trying to find out who killed Artie Wien?"

"Very serious. I want to interview all the men in the group and their wives as well. I'm hoping to turn up a motive."

"The police have about drained us."

"I have no access to their files. I'd like to talk about the relationships of the men to each other over the years."

"Well, Bruce will love talking about the old days. Can I have him call you?"

I said that would be fine and hung up. I dialed the number of Joseph Meyer, the violinist, and left a message on his machine. That left me with one appointment and nothing else in the offing. I looked at my list. The only two names left were Fred Beller, who never came to reunions, and George Fried, who was dead.

As I looked at the list Dr. Horowitz had given me, I realized there was an address, but no phone number, for both of those men. I am a penny-pincher by nature, going back to the years I spent at St. Stephen's Convent when I usually left the premises with fifty cents in my pocket and came home with change. What this heritage does to me is make me reluctant to spend money in ways I consider frivolous. I knew it would add seventy-five cents to our phone bill to call information for either number, and I thought about it for a minute before I took a deep breath and got the area code for Minneapolis and then called for the number. A minute later, I was listening to a ring at Fred Beller's home.

The phone was answered by a youngish-sounding woman. I asked for Fred Beller.

"He's out of town," she said. "He and Mom went to New York."

It occurred to me that although he might not want to attend reunions, he might feel different about a funeral. "Did he go to New York for the funeral of Arthur Wien?"

"Uh, no, not really. They flew to New York last week. They've been there a week already."

A chill passed through me. "It's really important that I talk to him. Could you tell me where I can reach him?"

"Sure. He's at the Waldorf-Astoria. If you hold on a minute, I can get you the room number."

I held. I had the feeling that all of a sudden I had learned something significant.

5

I sat there with the number of the Waldorf-Astoria and the room the Bellers were staying in staring me in the face. There was no question in my mind that Fred Beller had known well in advance of his trip to New York that the Morris Avenue Boys were having a reunion on Father's Day. Just because he never showed up didn't mean he didn't receive an invitation. He had received one and timed his visit to coincide with the reunion. For all I knew, he might have had dinner in the same restaurant at the same time. I wondered if the detectives investigating the Wien homicide knew about this, and I thought it was very likely that they did not.

I picked up the phone again and dialed the Waldorf. The phone in the Bellers' room rang several times and I was about to give up when a woman answered.

"I'd like to speak to Fred Beller, please."

"Just a minute." Off the phone she called, "Come on back, Fred. It's for you."

He answered a moment later.

"Mr. Beller, my name is Christine Bennett. I'm looking into the murder of your friend Arthur Wien for Dr. Morton Horowitz, and I'd like to talk to you while you're still in New York."

There was a moment of silence. "Mort told you I was here?"

Another bombshell. Morton Horowitz had known all the time we were talking this afternoon that Fred Beller was in town and he had never mentioned it. "He didn't. But I'd like to talk to you."

"My wife and I are on our way out. Can this wait until tomorrow?"

"Tomorrow would be fine. What time is good for you?"

"Uh, let's see." He covered the phone and I heard murmurings. "How's lunchtime tomorrow? We'll be back at the hotel around noon."

"I'll be there."

He told me quickly where to find him—or where he would look for me—and we hung up. I was tempted to call Dr. Horowitz and confront him with what I had learned, but I decided I would gain nothing and I didn't want to alienate him.

Instead, I went into the family room and sat down. I had scarcely read the paper today, and I picked it up and started turning pages while Jack kept his nose in his book.

Finally, he looked up. "For God's sake, Chris, tell me!"

I laughed and put the paper aside. "You were eavesdropping."

"Eavesdropping schmeavesdropping. What the hell is going on?"

"The elusive Mr. Fred Beller, who has not attended a Morris Avenue Boys reunion in lo these many years, was in New York during the reunion and still is."

"That's a big wow. How the hell did you find that out?"

I told him. When I was finished, I asked, "Do I call NYPD and give them this information?"

Jack looked conflicted. He always looks conflicted

when I ask him questions that put the job and me on opposing sides. "Save it," he said. "You're seeing this guy tomorrow?"

"Lunchtime. I better call Elsie."

"I'll watch Eddie. It's OK. We'll talk about it when you come back. If you give this up to the cops now, they'll move in and crowd you out. This is something good, Chris. I want you to run with it before they stop you."

I was glad he'd said it. I have to admit that when I stumble on something as tantalizing as this, I hate to think that it's my duty to tell the police and then politely back off, because it's a personal thing for me. My ego gets involved in the cases I work on even more than it does for the detectives whose jobs are investigating whatever hits their desks. I also know that their case loads pile up while for me a case is the center of my interest. Eventually, if I was successful, everything I knew would be turned over to the proper people, but for the moment, I wanted to track down my lead as far as I was able.

When I finished with the *Times*, I took a few clean sheets of paper and organized what I had learned today about the men who were my best suspects. I listed them and wrote down everything I knew about each one. One of the things I now knew was that Dr. Horowitz had withheld a most important fact from me, that Fred Beller had been in New York for a week, and Dr. Horowitz had probably been in touch with him. Whatever the reason for his silence, I didn't like it.

We were up early on Saturday as we usually were and had breakfast together. I was a little hesitant about leaving Eddie with Jack since Eddie needs constant watching, but Jack assured me he wanted to spend time with his son on weekends, even though there was a lot of studying to do. And there was a long nap in Eddie's afternoon that would give Jack time to hit the books.

I left in plenty of time to get to David Koch's apartment by ten. I arrived a little early, but after leaving my car in the underground garage in the building, I decided to go up right away without wasting any of my precious time. I had to be at the Waldorf by noon, and I had already decided to walk or take a taxi from here to there rather than incur two parking fees, although Janet Stern had promised to pay all my expenses. I'm even a penny-pincher where other people's money is concerned.

The doorman called upstairs and I was directed to an elevator. This was a very luxurious building, fairly new and built like a tower. I was glad I was going to a high floor. I knew the view would be spectacular and I wasn't disappointed.

I stepped out of the elevator into a small hall with two doors, one of which was already ajar. In a second David Koch himself opened it all the way, smiled, and held out his hand.

A tall, powerful-looking man dressed in expensive casual clothes, he said, "Please come inside, Ms. Bennett. It's a pleasure to meet you."

I told him to call me Chris and walked into a magnificent living room with views east and south. "It's breathtaking," I said.

"We enjoy it. We're city people and we enjoy looking at it. That's the East River out there, Roosevelt Island, Queens beyond that, and down the river on the right you can see the Fifty-ninth Street Bridge and then farther down the three bridges to Brooklyn."

I knew he meant the Williamsburg, the Manhattan, and

the Brooklyn Bridges. "And you see the sun come up," I said.

"Well, maybe in the short days of winter. We don't get up early enough to see it at this time of year."

We sat on an arrangement of furniture conducive to conversation, and I pulled out my notebook and pen. "You know why I'm here."

"Somewhat. I gather you know Mort Horowitz's granddaughter."

"She took a poetry course I taught during the spring semester. She thought I might be able to figure out who killed your friend Arthur Wien last Sunday. Her mother seems very worried that because Dr. Horowitz found the body, he's the main suspect."

"That may or may not be true. One way or another, we're probably all suspects, and it does no good to tell the police we were all good friends and wouldn't hurt each other for anything in the world."

"Dr. Horowitz has given me a thumbnail sketch of each of the members of your group. I wonder if you would do the same."

"I'll be glad to."

We were sitting opposite each other. From my chair, I had the better view, both east and south. On this very sunny day, it seemed postcard perfect. A Circle Line boat was making its way up the river and a private yacht was traveling in the opposite direction. It was a remarkable view.

"I suppose," he began, "we all see ourselves in the famous picture of the little boys in the Bronx. I'm the first one in the back row and I'm standing next to Bernie Reskin. Bernie's a fine man, a dedicated teacher, very bright, very thoughtful, would do anything for his students. He probably should have become a college professor, but the money wasn't there for graduate school when he was ready for it, so he got a job teaching high school."

"Do you know how he felt about Arthur Wien?"

"Bernie loves everybody in the world. We were all friends, Chris. We all liked each other. I'm better friends with Mort than with the others, but I'm there for all of them. I'm sure Bernie feels the same way." He paused.

"Ernie Greene is a medical researcher, spends his life with microbes. There are people alive today because of him. They don't know it but I know it. I've always been grateful that there are people like Ernie who give their lives to the kind of work he does. He's the human being behind the word *cure*. He has a good sense of humor, no ego at all, and more energy than I've ever seen in one person. I don't think the word *retire* is part of his vocabulary. And before you ask, he probably didn't care for Arthur Wien that much, but so what? Not every personality gets along with every other one. Ernie isn't into hurting people."

I was taking down phrases as he spoke and starting to wonder if this was such a good idea. Unless I found one man who had a grudge and was willing to be honest, most of what I would hear would be paeans to their friends.

"Do you know what it was that made Dr. Greene feel that way?"

"People are different. Artie's lifestyle didn't appeal to Ernie. Artie was too flamboyant for a man who spends his waking hours in a laboratory and probably dreams about his research when he sleeps."

I nodded although I felt this was all rehearsed.

"You've met Mort. A man couldn't ask for a better friend. He works hard, he has a good family, he has a great sense of humor. I've probably laughed harder in his presence than anywhere else, but I've probably also spent more serious moments with him than with anyone else I know. And I wouldn't take my body to any other doctor in the city of New York."

I smiled.

"Bruce. You've probably heard about his troubles. Bruce is a good man who took the rap for someone else, I'm afraid. He doesn't talk about it and I don't think he ever will."

"Did you represent him in court?"

"No, I didn't."

"Did he ask you?"

He looked at me for the first time as though I were not a recording secretary but someone who might ask an interesting question. "He called me for advice and I recommended a couple of lawyers to him. This happened many years ago and I thought he needed someone with more experience than I had. He didn't ask me to represent him, but that's how I felt."

"You said he took the rap for someone."

"I don't know who that person was."

"Do you think he knows?"

"I think he does."

"But you have suspicions."

"I do, but they're only suspicions, and I don't think it would be right to say anything about them."

Something had changed in him as he spoke. He sounded less rehearsed, less as though he were delivering a practiced monologue. He was talking now, not reciting.

"Thank you for being candid. What about the first row?"

"There isn't much to say about the first row any more, is there? Fred Beller hasn't shown up for years, Art's dead,

George is dead. That leaves Joe Meyer. Joe is a musician, a very fine one. He's a good man. He's not well but he keeps up the good fight. I hope he lives forever and makes music for the rest of his life."

"What was his relationship with Arthur Wien?"

"Probably closer than that of any of the rest of us. I believe Joe and Artie used to get together. I think Joe and Judy went out to California a few times to visit the Wiens."

"Then they were pretty good friends."

"I'd say so."

"What did you think of Arthur Wien?"

He leaned his head back and looked up at the ceiling. "Even when we were in high school," he said, adjusting himself so that he now looked at me, "you knew Artie Wien was going to make it. There was something about him, a sense of direction, of purpose. He loved to write and he was good at it. We would put on skits for one thing or another and he would write them, including the songs, and you knew he was good. I could have thrown a skit together, but it wouldn't have had the wit; it wouldn't have been as clever. He was a talented kid and he worked at it."

"I gather his first book was a success."

"It was phenomenal. Here was a young guy, not yet thirty, and he wrote a best-seller. We were all struggling in our professions, earning in a year what people now earn in a week or even a day, hoping we could pay our rent, and there was Artie Wien a great success. And he deserved it. He earned it."

"Tell me about the old neighborhood."

"Ah." David Koch looked out the window. "You may think that this is a wonderful view, that this apartment is a fantastic location. I can tell you that where I lived as a boy was more beautiful to me then than this is to me now. We had a big, beautiful apartment on Morris Avenue, two bedrooms, a kitchen with a dinette where we ate all our meals, a bathroom in white tile. My brother and I shared a bedroom that was big enough for two beds, the sun came through the window in the afternoon, the kids played in the street outside. Remember the old Robert Louis Stevenson poem about going to bed by day? How you could hear people's feet going by in the street? That's the way it was for us, a safe, happy home. There was nothing to fear. You could walk to school. We had parks nearby. My mother shopped at the stores on 174th Street. When we wanted to go into New York, we walked down to the Grand Concourse and took the D train." He looked at me with a little frown. "Would you like to see where we lived?"

"My husband tells me it's not a safe place to go any more."

"That's an exaggeration, and anyway, I can guarantee your safety. I have a driver who can take us. We could do it tomorrow."

"I'd love to."

"Good. I haven't been back for a couple of years. Do me good to see it again. Give us a chance to talk some more. I'll show you where everyone lived." He turned as someone came into the living room. "Ellen," he said, standing, "this is Chris Bennett."

Ellen Koch came in and shook hands with me. She was a strikingly beautiful woman with a head of beautiful close-cropped gray hair. She was as slim as a girl and had a wonderful smile. "I see Dave has been telling you about his boyhood."

"It's very interesting to me. I didn't grow up in a city."

"Well, he did and he can't ever leave it."

"Did you know Arthur Wien?" I asked.

"I only saw him at reunions. He seemed rather full of himself but he enjoyed being with the old gang. I've read some of his books and I enjoyed them. His wife seemed quite nice."

"Was last Sunday the first you'd met her?"

"Let me think. No, I think she came to the last reunion. They may not have been married then. Do you remember, Dave?"

"She was there last time. She wore kind of a—"

"Yes, that's the one. Then I've met her twice."

"Did you know his first wife?"

"Oh yes. We even ran into her at something a few months ago, some dinner we attended. A very nice woman."

"Your husband has been candid. I'd appreciate it if you were. Who among the men in the group or their wives might have wanted Arthur Wien dead?"

She sat on a chair before answering and I glanced over at her husband to see whether his face might tell me something, but it was quite bland.

"Arthur had women," she said. "I think he felt that it came with being the kind of success he was, a man who was interviewed on talk shows, that sort of thing. There was a rumor—"

When she stopped, I looked at her husband again but he made no move, gave no signal, to stop her.

"A rumor?" I asked.

"That he'd had an affair with the wife of one of the men in the group."

"Do you know which woman it was supposed to be?"

"I don't. I can tell you it wasn't me. Can I get you some coffee?"

I looked at my watch. "No thank you. I have somewhere to go. But it looks as though I'll be back tomorrow for a guided tour."

"A tour through the past. It'll be an eye-opener. When you see where people came from, you begin to understand them."

It was an idea that appealed to me.

6

I felt that the two people I left behind had changed from the people who were there when I first entered the apartment. Ellen Koch seemed troubled and David Koch subdued. There was a lot rushing around in my head that I wished I had time to think about, but I was bordering on being late for my noon appointment with Fred Beller. I dashed over to Third Avenue and hailed a cab. When I got inside and said, "The Waldorf-Astoria," I had the weird feeling that more than the two people I had just left had changed. Something had happened to me too.

The taxi dropped me at the Park Avenue entrance to the huge hotel. It would have been closer if he had left me at the Lexington Avenue side, but I think he hoped to pick up a fare at the front.

I had never been inside before. Beyond the doors was a short flight of stairs that led up to the enormous lobby. Fred Beller had said I should sit in the waiting area to the left. There were a number of people sitting there, reading or just watching the people walking by. I found an empty chair and took it. I had no idea what Beller looked like since he hadn't been photographed, and I didn't relish going up to strangers and asking them who they were.

It was a few minutes after twelve when I got there, and

as I sat, I looked around at the huge chandelier, the people coming and going. No one around me had made a move when I came in and sat down, so I assumed he wasn't there. On the low balcony, a few steps above the foyer, people sat at tables enjoying drinks and lunch. None of them seemed very interested in me.

Finally a middle-aged couple came from the Lexington side, stopped under the chandelier, and looked in my direction. The woman was wearing a colorful summer dress and the man wore a short-sleeved knit shirt with tan pants. I stood so they would see me.

The man smiled, waved, and started over. "Christine Bennett?" he asked.

"Yes, Mr. Beller."

"Sorry we're late. This is my wife Marge."

I shook her hand.

"I've got a table for us in Peacock Alley. Marge'll join us later."

We all walked back toward the restaurant and elevators, and Fred took a light jacket out of one of his wife's shopping bags before she left us. She was carrying several from stores where it was easy to spend money.

"We're leaving tomorrow, so this is our last chance to pick things up. Here we are."

We turned to the restaurant and were seated quickly. Fred Beller was the third tall man I had met in the group. He was slimmer than either Dr. Horowitz or David Koch, wore wire-rimmed glasses, and had an open friendly face. He offered me a drink but I refused. When I left here, I would be driving home. He ordered Scotch on the rocks with a twist for himself, mentioning a single malt brand that I had heard of, Glenfiddich. The waiter brought a small bottle of water and Beller poured a very small amount into the glass.

I looked at the menu next to my place and felt palpitations at the prices. This was only lunch, after all. A dinner at these prices would be expensive.

"I guess my daughter told you I was here," Fred Beller said.

"If that's who answered the phone. I gather Dr. Horowitz knew you were here."

"Yes, I talked to him earlier in the week. He didn't think it was necessary to mention to you that I was in New York."

So they had spoken last night. "Did he mention it to the police?"

He contemplated a moment before saying, "I don't think so."

"Were you at the restaurant last Sunday night where Arthur Wien was murdered?"

"I? No. What would make you think—"

"I'm just asking. It seemed a relevant question."

"I haven't seen any of those people for a long time."

"Except Dr. Horowitz."

"Mort and I are in touch from time to time. What brought you into this very unhappy situation?"

I told him.

"I hope you're successful. The police don't seem to be at this point."

"If I learn anything important, I'll turn it over to them. Could you tell me how you felt about Arthur Wien?"

"Arthur was a very successful man who earned what he achieved. I haven't had a conversation with him for years. Like everyone else in the group, he would have given the shirt off his back for any of us. I didn't like him very much."

"That's an odd sequence of statements."

"It puts into a paragraph what I might otherwise spend an hour explaining."

"Is there anyone else in the group you don't like?"

"I always thought George Fried—who's dead—was a suffocating bore. I never cared for Bruce very much. I guess I don't sound like a good friend."

"You were a large group of men. It would be hard for one of you to find all of them equally attractive."

"That's a nice way of putting it."

The waiter came for our order. I asked for a salad and Fred Beller asked for a sandwich.

"Could you tell me why you felt about Arthur Wien the way you did?"

"We didn't hit it off. I loved basketball and he hated it. When we were in high school I think we had the hots for the same girl."

"Who got her?" I asked.

He smiled. "Does it matter?"

"I don't know yet."

"I think I did for a while, but she lost interest before I did."

"Was he angry?"

"I never cared very much whether Artie was angry."

"Did he ever try to borrow money from you?"

"That's an odd question."

"Did he?"

"No, he didn't. I don't think I've ever lent anyone more than five dollars so it wouldn't make much difference."

"Did he ever ask you for any other kind of favor?"

"Why would he? We weren't close friends." He looked at me. "I know. I'm being evasive. No, he never asked me for money or for any other kind of favor."

"You knew about this reunion, didn't you?"

"They always send me the notice."

"Who's 'they'?"

"I think Bernie Reskin usually arranges these things. There's a nice guy."

"Why did you pick last weekend to come to New York?"

"Very simple. My son gave me the trip as a Father's Day present."

"Does he live here?"

"Yes, he does. And he said he'd rather have me come here than him go to Minnesota. He sent the plane tickets and made the reservation at the Waldorf and got us tickets for a couple of shows."

"That's a wonderful present."

"He's a wonderful son."

I was starting to think that this was one coincidence that was fully explained by what I had been told, that there was nothing mysterious or evil behind Fred Beller's motive for coming east.

"Are you retired?" I asked.

"Semi. I don't go to an office every day any more."

"What do you do?"

"I was a pharmacist for a long time, but I sold my store about fifteen years ago and I do other things now. I work for someone else part-time just because I can't quite stop. And I dabble in the market."

Our lunches came as I was wondering if there was anything else I should bother asking. Both dishes were very elegantly presented, almost too pretty to dig into.

But we did and just at that moment Mrs. Beller showed up. "My, that all looks so good I'm tempted to have something myself." She sat on the other side of her husband. "But I won't."

"Marge isn't a lunch eater," her husband explained. "Want a drink, honey?"

"Maybe something cold like lemonade."

He signaled the waiter and ordered for his wife. She looked very fresh and cool, as though she had just washed in cold water. Her hair was blond, short, and curly and she wore large silver earrings with a pale blue stone.

"Did you know Arthur Wien, Mrs. Beller?" I asked.

"I met him a long time ago. Fred and I were in New York once, it must have been twenty years ago or more, and I met some of the men. They were all very nice. I was impressed with Arthur Wien because I had read his books. Didn't we have him sign one for us, Fred?"

"We did."

"So, you know, I was looking forward to meeting him. To me he was a celebrity."

"Was he married at the time?"

"Mm, maybe not. I don't think he had a wife with him."

"What did you think of him?"

"He was very nice to me. Of course, I told him I had read his books. But he was friendly. I liked him." She smiled. Her lemonade was set in front of her and she sipped it.

"Have you met any of the other men in the group?"

"Some. We were just talking to—" She stopped and looked at her husband.

"Just tell the truth," he said. "Chris knows we've seen Mort."

"Well, we got together with the Horowitzes the other night."

"Did Arthur Wien ever visit you in Minnesota?" I asked.

She didn't answer. I waited.

"Artie never visited us at home," her husband said finally. "We took a trip to California a few years ago and ran into him there. He was very expansive, insisted on showing us around, taking us out, introducing us to his friends. In a weak moment I said, 'Come and see us anytime, Artie.' After that, he actually called and said he was going to be in Minneapolis to do a book signing and he wanted to see us. But it didn't work out."

"He came and you didn't see him?"

"It just didn't work out," Fred Beller said. "He wasn't there very long and he had a TV appearance besides the signing; we just didn't manage to get together." His tone of voice indicated he had said as much as he was going to.

"What made you move to Minnesota?" I asked him.

"I met Marge. She was from Minneapolis, and I went out there and fell in love with the place. I was already in love with her so it wasn't hard."

She was smiling. "My folks had a nice house with a big backyard and this city kid here couldn't believe we didn't live in the middle of a public park."

"Have you ever seen where your husband lived as a boy?"

"We don't come to New York much and I don't think Fred wants to go back, do you, Fred?"

"I left the Bronx because I didn't like it. I don't think it's improved with age."

I decided not to mention that I was taking a guided tour tomorrow. "This is a wonderful lunch," I said to relieve the tension.

"So is mine," my host agreed. "I'm glad you made this

appointment with us or we might not have had a chance to eat here."

I took the envelope of Father's Day photographs out of my bag and put them on the table. "Have you seen these?" I asked.

"The reunion pictures? No, I haven't. May I?"

"Please."

He put his fork down and started through the pictures, looking at each one with interest. As he finished, he passed them along to his wife. "Mort looks good," he said at one point. "This is Artie right here, honey. Is that his wife?" he asked me.

"I believe so."

"Guess he still likes them young."

I waited till both of them had gone through the pack and returned them to me. Then I said, "I would love to have one of you, Mr. Beller, or one of the two of you. Just to complete the set."

Before he could say anything, his wife reached for her bag, which she had stowed under the table. "I have one I can give you." She slipped the photo out of a plastic holder and gave it to me, handing it in front of her husband. I wondered whether he was tempted to grab it and keep it from me, but he didn't. "It's fairly recent," Marge said.

"Thank you very much." I put it in the envelope with the others. "Dr. Horowitz asked me to look into the murder of Arthur Wien. I've had some experience investigating murders, and his daughter and granddaughter were very concerned that the police felt he was the main suspect."

"Is there any evidence?" Beller asked.

"I don't know. It was my impression that because he found the body, he seemed the likeliest suspect. I'm sure they're doing forensic work on the body and whatever they picked up at the crime scene. What I'm doing is talking to the Morris Avenue Boys to see what they think about Arthur Wien, about each other, about what might have happened in the last fifty years that could have made one of the group a killer. What do you think?"

"I think Artie was a womanizer. He married in his twenties and was looking around at other women in his thirties. Is that a motive for murder? Maybe you should ask his first wife."

It was something I intended to do. "He was murdered in a men's room, so it's a little less likely that a woman did it, but I agree, she might have a motive, although if she did it, it took her a long time."

"Maybe hatred ripens with time."

"Maybe it does. Was there anyone else who might have had a grudge?"

"I'm sure there were plenty of people, but murder is very extreme. Most of us work out our displeasures in other ways."

"Besides Dr. Horowitz, did you keep in touch with any other members of the group?"

"Not really. I was always interested to hear how they were doing but not enough interested to pick up a phone or write a letter."

I thought that about covered it. I drank my coffee, declined dessert, and wished them a good trip back home. Then I returned to the Koches' apartment house to retrieve my car. When I went to pay the bill, I was told Mr. Koch had taken care of it.

7

Eddie had not yet woken up when I got home so I had a little time to sit and talk to Jack, who was ready for a break. I told him about my two interviews and the lunch, complete with all my uneasy feelings. Mrs. Beller had never answered my question about whether Arthur Wien had visited them at their home. It was her husband who had picked up for her and said it had never happened, but I wasn't sure he was telling the truth. Nor could I see what difference it made, but it was a question that Mrs. Beller obviously wasn't allowed to answer.

Then there was Mrs. Koch's intriguing statement that there was a rumor that Arthur Wien had had an affair with the wife of one of his friends. How does one know there was an affair without knowing with whom it took place? I wasn't sure. But I now believed I would have to talk to the first Mrs. Wien. I would ask David Koch tomorrow for her name and address.

"So you're going to the Bronx tomorrow," Jack said when I had finished. "What do you expect to get out of that?"

"Maybe nothing, but I'd like to see this magical place that Horowitz and Koch loved so much and that Fred Beller hated."

"Just a lot of brick and concrete," Jack said. "And probably a lot more graffiti than fifty years ago. One neighborhood looks pretty much like another. You get any feelings from these guys?"

"Lots of feelings. Horowitz knew that Fred Beller was in town and he didn't tell me. The two couples got together during the week. Beller didn't answer some questions very forthrightly. Koch was—I don't know—maybe less than candid."

"Sounds to me like you're investigating a homicide. When did everyone tell you the truth before this?"

"I guess never. But Jack, I made a real coup at lunch. I think Fred Beller sensed what I was doing but he couldn't stop his wife. I asked for a picture of him or both of them, and she gave me one."

"What good is that?"

"I want to find out if he was in the restaurant last Sunday night. If he was, he probably didn't make the reservation under his real name. I want to get back there with this picture and see if the maitre d' recognizes them."

"Good thinking."

"He said he wasn't there but what would you expect him to say?"

"By the way, you got some phone calls while you were out." He went to the kitchen and got a couple of message slips. "Someone named Kaplan?"

"Bruce Kaplan, yes, he's the one who served time for embezzling."

"The other one's a Judy Meyer."

"That's the wife of the violinist. Good. Things are moving." I read the messages but they just said I should call back. Before I did, I stood at the foot of the stairs and listened. There were no little cries or other sounds from upstairs so I went to the phone and called Bruce Kaplan first.

"Miss Bennett, yes, I hear you're looking into the murder of our friend. How can I help you?"

For my number one suspect, it was the friendliest overture so far. "I'd like to get together with you and talk to you about Arthur Wien and the rest of your friends who were at the reunion."

"Fine. Name your time."

I thought for a moment. I was meeting David Koch at noon and we were driving up to the Bronx, not a very long drive from what I remembered of the geography of New York. I thought I would be back in mid-Manhattan no later than two. The Kaplans lived in Westchester County, as I did, not a long drive from either Manhattan or Oakwood. I wasn't sure what Mrs. Meyer had in mind so I asked if I could get back to him. Then I called the other number.

"Ms. Bennett," Mrs. Meyer said, "I know you left a message for my husband but he's resting. Can I talk to you instead?"

I told her what I wanted, an interview with him. Tomorrow afternoon was a possibility.

"I think we can manage that. Two to three?"

"I'll be there as close to two as I can make it." Their address was on the West Side of Manhattan, near Riverside Drive.

"We'll be here all afternoon."

I got back to Bruce Kaplan and arranged to see him tomorrow evening. That meant that by Sunday night I would have spoken to all but two members of the group, the teacher and the researcher. The researcher worked in Manhattan and I would try to set something up for Monday. As

I was thinking of that, I heard my little one, and I left my investigative persona in the kitchen and went upstairs.

Having a small child around, I have learned in the last year and a half, is not just time consuming; it's also mind consuming. Eddie gets into things. He also wants attention, specifically mine. I read to him and we play games together. I have also gotten together with other women in the neighborhood who have children about his age so that the little ones can play while the mothers talk and supervise. The women I've met are a very positive addition to my life. They're bright and thoughtful, they're involved in town affairs, and they make good conversation. One of them works part-time, one doesn't work at all, and a third is able to work out of her home on a contract basis, something I do for Arnold Gold, my lawyer friend in New York, when he has the work and I have the time.

So Eddie gets to hang out at this early age with his contemporaries, and my life is richer and pleasanter because of it. But when we are one on one, my attention is at least ninety percent on him.

Not that I mind it. I got Eddie ready for the rest of his day and took him down to see his daddy; then we went out. My phone calls could wait till later.

I suppose Saturday night isn't the best time to call people but it was the only time I had left. Bernie Reskin, the teacher, was still not answering so I tried Dr. Ernest Greene. He answered the phone himself and I explained who I was.

"Yes," he said, "Mort Horowitz said you might call. I'm afraid I don't have much time, Ms. Bennett. And my wife and I are just going out so I can't help you right now."

"I'd be glad to see you at your home or at your office," I said, "whatever is convenient for you."

"I wish you'd just cross my name off your list. I don't know anything. I've known Artie Wien all my life, but he wasn't a special friend of mine and there's not a lot more I can say about him."

"If you could just spare a—"

"I'm very sorry. And I've got to go."

That ended the conversation. I was disappointed, but I knew the doctor had no obligation to talk to me. His only obligation was to the police. At some point I would let Dr. Horowitz know what had happened but I didn't want to bother him right now. Tomorrow, when I was driving through the Bronx with David Koch, I might be able to get some information out of him. And anyway, I had a full day tomorrow.

We ate breakfast early Sunday morning as we always do, and then I picked up my cousin Gene to take him to mass. Gene lives here in town at a residence for retarded adults. We've been buddies since we were Eddie's age, and I try to have him to the house on weekends if I can manage it. Today wasn't a good day for dinner, but I took him to mass, took him home and chatted with him for a while, and then went home myself. I left lunch for Eddie, knowing Jack was better at putting together food for himself than I was, and he said he would make dinner if I promised to be home for it. I promised.

I got to the Koches' apartment house before noon, and David Koch and I went back downstairs to a waiting car. It was just a plain old black car, a Ford, I noticed, and we got in the backseat, assisted by the doorman.

"Chris, this is Sergeant Harry Holt of the NYPD."

We exchanged hellos and I told him my husband was also a sergeant on the job.

"Oh yeah? What precinct?"

"The Six-Five."

"Brooklyn."

"Yes."

"I think I ran into him at a class last year or maybe the year before. Tell him hello for me."

I promised I would.

He drove over to the East River Drive, otherwise known as the FDR Drive, and headed north. The drive runs along the East River and changes its name to the Harlem River Drive when the river changes its name. But we exited just before all the changes, taking the Triboro Bridge to the Bronx. Mr. Koch told Harry to take the Grand Concourse instead of a highway, and we drove north along the beautiful, wide boulevard with apartment houses along both sides.

"This was once one of the finest places to live in New York," Koch said. "It was very beautiful."

"It looks very nice right now," I said.

"Over to the left there is Yankee Stadium. I don't have to tell you we were all Yankee fans. In the summer we lived and breathed baseball, even when we went away. The best thing was to find someone who lived in one of the apartment houses that overlooked the stadium. The stadium was lower in those days. They've added a tier on top. So you could sit on an apartment house roof and watch the game free."

"And feel you were getting something for nothing."

"Oh yes. We always tried. You can turn right at the next block, Harry."

We zigzagged a little and then there we were on 174th Street and Morris Avenue, the corner they all remembered.

"Harry, turn right on Morris Avenue and see if you can park."

Harry made the turn and slid into the only vacant spot on the block.

"That's where Mort and I lived, right in that building across the street on the corner of 174th," David Koch said.

It looked very ordinary, a prewar building of not very clean yellow brick. There were two women standing around and talking, but not the women of David Koch's memory. One way or another they were all gone.

"I've never been up here," Harry said.

"It isn't much to look at any more. Back there," he pointed to 174th Street, "everything's changed. That used to be a bustling street with stores on both sides. In the late fifties, they built the Cross Bronx Expressway, cutting through the rock so that it's way down below the level of the street. To do it, they got rid of half of 174th, so it's just a shadow of what it used to be. At this point, it's one way going east. It used to be a wide, two-way street. Drive up to the corner, Harry."

We passed some single and two family houses, neat and clean, made of brick. At the corner of 173rd, there was Mt. Gilead Baptist Church.

"That was the Mount Eden Jewish Center across the street," Koch said, pointing to an imposing stone building with colorful graffiti along the side. "Take a left, Harry. Go up to your next left turn and take it. This was our school when we were small, P.S. 70," he said as we passed it on our left. "Nice modern school. We even had an indoor pool." He sounded wistful.

"This is like a little village," I said.

"That's just what it was. There's a Yiddish word my mother used to use, *shtetl*. It means 'little village.' We were self-contained here. We had everything we needed. There was a candy store, a dry cleaner, drugstores, grocery stores, bakeries, a locksmith, a barber. If you didn't like the bakery on one side of the street, you could go to the one on the other side. Park here, Harry."

We were on Weeks Avenue, which had become a bridge after it crossed what was left of 174th Street. Koch opened the door and we got out. Railings and fencing enclosed the bridge on both sides; the fencing was to prevent people from dropping objects onto the moving cars below, a frequent New York problem. We stood at the edge and looked down onto the traffic on the Cross Bronx Expressway. Even on Sunday there were trucks; even on Sunday traffic was backed up.

"This is what they did to our community," my host said, indicating the highway far below. "They destroyed our street so that people in cars and trucks could get out of the city faster. What you're standing on used to be the other side of 174th Street."

We got back in the car and Harry drove to the corner, which was marked Cross Bronx Expressway although it was far above it. We went down to Morris Avenue and turned left, then left again at 174th. A Spanish flavor predominated. There were Spanish groceries, a Spanish restaurant, a Spanish travel agency. Harry stopped at a hydrant.

"In the block behind us was Gleitz's Kosher Butcher, where my mother bought her meat. Strasberg's Luncheonette was back there, on the corner of Selwyn Avenue. Across the street on the corner of Morris Avenue," he pointed to the memory of the other side of the street, where now the fumes from the traffic rose in the emptiness that had once been gentle commerce, "was Ernie's Kosher Deli. Once a week my mother would serve deli. We lived for that night. She was a great cook, but what we loved best was the salami and corned beef and hot pastrami on the best bread ever baked."

"Did you go into Manhattan much?"

"Not much, no. My mother would take us downtown for clothes and sometimes a play on Broadway. But the truth is, we were a very provincial group of boys. We lived in the biggest city in the world and all we knew was these few square blocks. If we came from some little town in the Midwest, we couldn't have been more unsophisticated."

"What about Arthur Wien?"

"Yes, I guess Artie was a little different. He always seemed to know there was a world out there, a world that started with the D train and kept going."

Harry had driven the rectangle again, crossing over the expressway, and had pulled to the curb across from David Koch's old home on Morris Avenue.

"Where did he meet his first wife?"

"At City, I think. Maybe after he graduated. They were married at the Concourse Plaza. It was a great place once. It was a beautiful wedding." He sounded depressed. Everything that was good was in the past tense. "Want to get out and walk?"

"Sure."

We all got out, Harry staying slightly behind us. We crossed Morris Avenue to the entrance to the building he and Morton Horowitz had grown up in. He looked in the front door but all you could see was darkness. We walked to the farthest windows on the first floor to the right of the door.

"This was home," he said. "A beautiful home in a small village." He touched the window frame, which was not very far from the street level. "That's my bedroom." He stared at the curtained window for a few silent moments. "My friends used to crawl in through this window in the summer." He smiled. "Claremont Park is up that way. It's a beautiful day, isn't it?"

"Very nice. On a day like this you would all have been out playing in the street."

"You're right. We played stickball and curb ball out here. We used those sewers in the street as our bases."

"What's stickball?" I asked, feeling uninformed.

"You don't have a pitcher. You toss the ball in the air and whack it with your stick. At school we played softball, but not in the street. And every now and then somebody's mother would stick her head out of the window and call for her son who would die of embarrassment. That was a very Bronx thing to do. You don't find mothers on the East Side of Manhattan calling out their windows."

"A cultural change, perhaps."

"Right there across the street in front of that apartment house is where the famous picture was taken. One of the boys lived there, and his father came out with the family camera and arranged us with the tall ones in back and the short ones in the front."

"They didn't all stay that way," I said. "Fred Beller was in the front row but he's a very tall man now."

"Fred Beller? When did you see Fred Beller?"

"Yesterday. I had lunch with him after I talked to you."

He frowned. "Fred was in town? In New York?"

"He spent a week here. His son gave him the trip as a Father's Day present."

"I see."

I was sure he hadn't heard the news before. "He doesn't like New York very much. He said he fell in love with Minneapolis when he visited with his future wife."

"That's what I heard. I haven't seen him in years."

I decided to drop it. "What happened to the parents, Mr. Koch? Did they stay here after their children left?"

"Some did. Some began leaving in the fifties. A couple finally bought a dream house in the suburbs; one or two got an apartment in Mount Vernon, which is just north of the Bronx; some of the older ones retired to Florida or went down to Florida and started new businesses down there. One or two stayed until their children insisted they leave. After my father died, I got my mother into a co-op in Manhattan and later she went to Florida."

Across the street a man carrying a worn leather bag, its contents poking out, walked slowly by. Although it was a warm, breezy day, he wore layers of clothes, baggy pants, a filthy jacket. His face was hairy and dirty, his hair long and unwashed.

Koch sprinted across the street and talked to him. He reached into a pocket, took out bills, and handed them to the man. Peripherally, I saw Harry Holt follow him across the street but remain behind, as good a bodyguard as anyone could want. But Koch was back on my side of Morris Avenue before Harry moved in.

"There were no homeless in those days," he said. "The word was unknown. I hope someday it becomes unknown again, but I'm not optimistic." He watched the man walk toward Claremont Park. "Have you had enough?"

"It's been very interesting. Thank you."

Harry was standing beside the car, ready to open the door for me. "You take a lot of chances, Mr. Koch," he said.

"Not as many as he takes."

"I guess that's the truth."

"Let's drive by the park and then go back the way we came."

When we were back on the Concourse I said, "Did Arthur Wien ever ask you for any favors or borrow money from you?"

He smiled. "I lent someone money once in my life. When I was about eighteen I worked as a waiter in the mountains. *The mountains* means the Catskills for anyone who comes from New York. It was tough work and not a huge amount of money, although there were nice tips. During the summer, the headwaiter asked to borrow fifty dollars from me. If I tell you that five hundred dollars today wouldn't buy fifty dollars then, you'll understand how much money that was. He never paid me back. I found out later that he 'borrowed' from all the waiters. It was how he increased his income. For me it was a rite of passage. After that summer I never lent anyone more money than I could afford to lose. And I never lent money to Artie. I don't remember his ever asking for any."

That seemed to put that question to rest. "Tell me about Arthur Wien's first wife," I said.

"I have her address if you want to see her. She lives on the West Side. Come upstairs when we get home and I'll give it to you."

"Mr. Koch, you're a lawyer. You know that the way Arthur Wien was murdered wasn't a spur-of-the-moment whim. You don't walk around with an ice pick in your pocket if you're not planning to use it."

"That's what I would argue if I were the D.A."

"Someone hated him. Assuming it was someone in your

group—or a wife—it's hard for me to believe no one out-side the victim and his killer knew what was going on."

"I can tell you I didn't know."

"Then who would?"

"You've got me. What my wife said to you yesterday? That Art was having an affair with a wife of one of the group? That was the first I ever heard of it."

"Then I guess it's the wives I should be talking to."

He looked at me and smiled. "Maybe you will do better than the police."

I certainly hoped so.

8

I went down to my car with the address and phone number of Alice Wien in my purse. Once again, my parking bill had been taken care of, and as it turned out, I was able to cross town and get to the Meyers' apartment on West Eighty-sixth Street by two-thirty. I had taken an apple with me in lieu of lunch, and I ate it while sitting in the car in a free parking space on the street.

When I was finished, I wrapped the core in a tissue and walked over to Broadway to find a litter basket. Then I retraced my steps to the Meyers' building and rang the bell.

The Meyers' apartment was one of those huge places they built before the start of the Second World War. In New York, where rent controls from that war are still in effect, an apartment like that, if occupied by the same family since the fifties, might be less expensive than a tiny studio in a new building.

Mrs. Meyer, a small, trim woman in a black suit, the jacket open on a gray blouse, took me into an almost cavernous living room where her husband was sitting near a window, his feet up on a small ottoman. It didn't take any medical expertise to see that this was a sick man, but the smile he gave me was healthy and genuine. He held out a hand and I shook it.

"I'm Joe Meyer. Come and sit down and make yourself comfortable. Mort told us you'd be coming. I'd get up but I'm trying to save my strength."

"Please stay where you are. It's a pleasure to meet both of you. I understand you're both musicians."

"Our whole family is," Mrs. Meyer said.

I had gathered as much walking through the foyer. A dark, windowless area, it displayed photographs of all the Meyers together with more famous people in the music world. There was one photo of Mr. and Mrs. Meyer together with Leonard Bernstein, all three in formal dress, the bottom signed by the great conductor himself.

"That's wonderful," I said. "I'm afraid I missed music as a young person."

"It's never too late," Mrs. Meyer assured me. "I remember my grandfather in the last years of his life. His eyesight was terrible, but he kept a radio tuned to a music station and he was always happy." She smiled, as though the memory gave her pleasure. "I have a little afternoon tea in the kitchen. Why don't you two get started while I bring it in?"

Joseph Meyer watched her go. Then he turned to me. "Mort says you're an amateur detective who does better than the police and you're looking into the death of our friend a week ago."

"I've had some success," I admitted. "And this is a very intriguing case. It would appear that one of your group killed Mr. Wien, and from everything I've heard, it's impossible to believe."

"Absolutely impossible. We were friends. We cared about each other. We've known each other all our lives or practically that long."

"What was your personal relationship with Mr. Wien, Mr. Meyer?"

"Please call us Joe and Judy. We're very informal people as you can see from this room." The room was surely informal. The furniture was old and comfortable and had never seen the hand of a decorator.

"Thank you."

"Artie and I. Well, we go back to about third grade. Artie was always the one the teacher would use as an example of how the rest of us should write. You know, you'd get an assignment: 'How I Spent My Vacation,' and we'd sit and write some dumb, boring paragraph about where we went and what we did when we got there. Artie didn't do anything that was more interesting than what the rest of us did, but it sure sounded good when the teacher read it back to us." He smiled. "He had the touch. The words just did what they were supposed to do; they flowed."

"I'm an English teacher myself," I said. "But I've never taught children."

"Well, I'll have to watch my grammar then." He stopped and took a breath, as though the talk had tired him.

"Were you special friends with him?"

"I'd say we were. He came to my concerts and I read his books."

"I bet they all went to your concerts."

"Yes, I'll say that for the boys. They've been loyal."

"What did you think of his books?"

"Well done. Clever, witty, always page turners, as they say. What he did in his first book, *The Lost Boulevard*, he took the nine of us and sort of melted us down into five young men. He took the two doctors and made them one character. He had a lawyer, a musician, a writer, and a businessman. You can see where he combined two people and made them one. It's very skillful, very artful. He had a tremendous talent."

"Here's something to keep you going," Judy Meyer said, coming in with a huge tray. I jumped up and helped her set it down on a coffee table. "Everyone OK with tea?" she said.

"Fine. It looks lovely." There were small sandwiches and a tray of lovely looking individual cakes. The teapot was old china, the kind of piece I would feel nervous about using. The cups and saucers matched it. I wondered if someone in the generation before theirs had brought it over from Europe or if they had picked it up themselves somewhere. Whatever it was, I admired their taste.

Judy Meyer poured the tea through a strainer and passed the cups to me. I handed Joe his and he propped himself up in his chair so that he was sitting more upright. His wife put an assortment of sandwiches and cakes on a plate and set it on the table beside him. He seemed energized, just looking at the food.

"I heard you talking about Artie's first book," Judy said. "I didn't meet him till he was already working on it. I remember once the gang was getting together and Artie said he couldn't make it; he had to work on the manuscript. But Alice dragged him out, remember, Joe? I think she was just tired of sitting at home doing nothing while he worked."

"Is there anything in that book that anyone in the group would find embarrassing?" I asked.

Joe shrugged. "I haven't looked at that book in twenty, thirty years. I remember at the time that we were all talking about it, identifying who was who, did this really happen, that kind of thing. But remember, even if there were embarrassing things—and I'm not saying there were—the characters were composites. You couldn't take one of his characters and say, 'This is Joe Meyer.' It wasn't like that. There was a musician, but he played a different instrument, he went out with different women, and he had different experiences. Artie wanted to portray people who were typical of the time, not just the boys he grew up with."

"What was Arthur Wien's relationship to Fred Beller?"

"Fred Beller." He seemed surprised to hear the name mentioned. "I haven't seen Fred Beller in so many years, I couldn't swear he was still alive."

"I had lunch with him yesterday," I said.

The surprise on Joe Meyer's face had to be genuine. "Fred's in New York?"

"He was staying at the Waldorf. When I called, he invited me for lunch."

"I can't believe it. Fred hates New York. And as far as I know, he doesn't have the warmest feelings for the guys either."

"Why?"

"Oh I don't know, a clash of personalities maybe. You snub your nose at New York and New Yorkers get their hackles up. They're not the most forgiving people. How did you happen to find Fred?"

"Dr. Horowitz gave me his home address and I telephoned. His daughter said he was in New York. I called his room and he answered."

"Amazing. And he talked to you?"

"He and his wife."

"Wasn't there some to-do between Fred and Artie, Judy? A couple of years ago?"

"There was something but I don't remember what."

"Artie was supposed to see them, I think. Wasn't he out

in Minnesota on a book tour? But something happened and they didn't get together?" He had been talking almost to himself. Now he turned to me. "They just didn't get along."

"Was there anything between Mr. Wien and Mrs. Beller?"

"I don't see how there could have been. Fred was never here. I wonder if—what's Fred's wife's name again?"

"Marge," I said.

"Marge. I wonder if Artie and Marge ever met."

"I'm looking for a motive, some problem that may have erupted a long time ago, something that the killer couldn't forget, couldn't forgive, couldn't live with. Someone walked into that restaurant last Sunday prepared to kill Arthur Wien."

"It wasn't one of us, Chris. There's nothing in the past that could explain one of us killing Artie. And I doubt whether there's anything in the present. We don't see each other that much except for reunions or an occasional get-together."

Judy Meyer got up and carried the teapot over to where I was sitting. "It's a beautiful pot," I said as she poured.

"It was my grandmother's. I've never had an expert look at it because I was afraid I'd be told it was worth a king's ransom and then I couldn't use it any more."

"Do you have any special knowledge of the men or their wives?" I asked her.

"They're all very interesting people. We were close to Art and his first wife, but after they separated, we saw less of Art. His new wife—well, his second wife—Cindy, is a lovely person, but when you've known a couple, it's hard to watch them break up and even harder to accept replacements."

"Did Alice Wien ever remarry?"

"Not that we've heard. She lives around here, you know. I run into her sometimes on Broadway. I saw her at Zabar's about a month ago."

I knew that Zabar's was a place to buy gourmet food, and it didn't surprise me that sophisticated New Yorkers would run into each other there. "She's one of the people on my list to talk to."

"Give her a call," Judy said. "If she's home, she'll probably see you."

"Did she go to the funeral?"

Judy looked at her husband. "I didn't see her there, did you? There was a huge crowd, you know."

"I didn't see her," he said.

"Is she a person who might have wanted to see her ex-husband dead?" I asked.

"I can't see why," Judy said. "I think he was still paying her alimony."

"What about her children? Did they harbor animosity toward their father?"

"They probably did," Joe said. He leaned over and put his cup down on the little table beside him. "But you're talking about a lot more than animosity if it led to murder."

"I keep thinking that it happened on Father's Day," I said.

"I don't think there's any significance to that. It just happens to be the day we picked for our get-together. We once tried to have it on Mother's Day and we couldn't." He laughed. "The wives all objected."

"Any rumors of blackmail?" I tossed out.

"Oh I don't think so," Joe said with a smile. "These are pretty well-behaved people we're talking about."

"But one of them murdered Arthur Wien," I said.

"Maybe there was someone at the restaurant who knew

we'd be there, someone just lying in wait for Artie to detach himself from the group. Did you ever think of that?"

I had and it didn't make my job any easier. "Like Fred Beller?" I said.

They didn't answer. I finished my tea and ate a luscious confection, the last on my plate. Judy offered more but I declined. Jack would have a great dinner waiting for me.

We chatted a little after that; the Meyers told me about their musical careers and those of their children. Judy brought some pictures in for me to look at. Their son, Joshua, was standing next to several other musicians. Their daughter, Marsha, a beautiful young woman in a long gown, was accepting a huge bouquet of roses on stage.

"She looks like you," I said to the proud mother.

"She's much more talented. We're really blessed."

It may have been an exaggeration considering her husband's condition, but she looked and sounded as though she meant it.

Before I left, I called Alice Wien but she wasn't home. I decided to call it a day. I still had an appointment for tonight and a long drive home before dinner.

9

Eddie was very glad to see me. I must say I never tire of walking into a room when I've been away for a while and seeing the smile light up his face as he sees me. I took him out for a little while before his dinner, stopping to talk to neighbors and a couple of dogs. Eddie thinks dogs are the greatest people in the world. My appointment to see Bruce Kaplan was for eight o'clock, giving me just enough time to get Eddie to bed and have dinner with Jack before dashing out again. I would be half dead when I got home, but Jack would have had some useful time alone to study. I hoped we would both have the energy to talk a little tonight. By the time I came home I would have interviewed all the living members of the group except for the famous Bernie and Ernie. I hoped I could still work something out with the doctor, although he had sounded pretty negative on the phone.

Jack had made Hungarian goulash for dinner, which meant we would have lots of leftovers during the week. Those are the meals I appreciate the most, and most of them are winter dishes. We do a lot of grilling in hot weather, and I was glad it was still cool enough to cook something on the stove for a couple of hours. He used the imported paprika that his sister, Eileen, the caterer, had given us. It was hot and left a memory in my mouth and along my throat after I had finished it. I really appreciate my husband.

I looked at a map before I left and wrote down how I would get to the Kaplans' home. I was feeling somewhat deprived, not having so much as glanced at the *Times* today, but it would be there for me when I had some free time during the week. A book review is as good when it's two or three days old as when it's just printed, which isn't generally true of the news. But I much prefer the reviews to the news, so the loss wasn't very great.

We exchanged a quick kiss before I left, and then I was on my way. I reached the Kaplans' house in plenty of time and parked on the street. These were nice older houses with what realtors call mature shrubs and trees. There were none of the scraggly saplings of the newer developments here. These houses and their landscaping had aged like good wine, richly. I walked partway up the driveway and picked up a slate walk curving from the driveway to the front door. Someone must have mowed the grass that day because the scent was heady, and I loved it. I rang the bell and heard half a concert ringing inside.

"Christine Bennett?" the woman who opened the door asked.

"That's right. Mrs. Kaplan?"

"Arlene. Come on in. Bruce is waiting for you, ready to tell you tales out of school."

He was sitting in a room at the back of the house where the view of a beautiful backyard was just dimming in the setting sun. We introduced ourselves and sat down, Arlene Kaplan nearby. She was graying and plump and wore glasses.

"I've been looking forward to this," Bruce Kaplan said.

"I understand you're an amateur looking into our friend's murder."

"That's right. Dr. Horowitz's granddaughter was my student this year and she and her mother called me."

"What qualifies you to do this kind of thing?"

"A few past successes, I guess. I'm an ex-nun. When I moved into Oakwood after I was released from my vows, I was kind of appointed by the town council to look into a forty-year-old murder to settle a local problem. I didn't know what I was getting into, but I managed to solve it. Since then, murders have just popped up and people have asked me to help."

"Sounds like you've done OK."

"I hope I can do as well on this one. It appears to be one of those cases in which the men in the group are the best suspects, but all the ones I've spoken to seem very nice, very fond of Mr. Wien, and not at all suspicious."

"Well, add my name to the list. I'm a great admirer of Artie, we have all his books—we've even read them—" he said laughing, "and we were as shocked as everyone else when we heard he'd been killed."

"Can you think of anyone who might want him dead?"

"Nobody." He leaned forward in his chair. He had dark hair that was graying and he wore a navy short-sleeved knit shirt with a collar and tan well-creased summer pants. I guessed he hadn't gained more than ten pounds since he left school. His arms seemed muscular, as though he worked out or did heavy work. "Artie was a nice guy. He had a lot of friends everywhere he went. There are people in Hollywood, people with big names, who were his friends."

"Did he ever visit you?"

He turned to look at his wife. "When was the last time Artie and Cindy came over?"

"Last year. They were in New York and we invited them out for a weekend. We had a good time, the four of us."

"Did they sleep over?"

"In our guest room," Arlene Kaplan said.

"Did you ever visit them at home?"

"We sure did. We were in California a few months ago and we saw them. Artie was a generous man and his wife is charming. They took us out to dinner, and the next morning Artie and Bruce played golf."

"Did Arthur Wien ever ask you to help him in any way?" I looked at Bruce for an answer.

"What do you mean?"

"Did he ask you for favors? Did he borrow money from you? Did he ask you to make introductions for him?"

"Introductions." Bruce Kaplan laughed. "He was the one who knew people. Favors, I don't know. Did I fix him up with a blind date when we were younger? Probably. We all did that. As far as money goes, he had plenty of it, or at least he acted as if he did."

"What about at the dinner? Was everyone friendly toward him?"

"Well," Arlene said, "there was the usual musical chairs."

"What do you mean?"

"Artie and Cindy came last and there was a lot of place changing, I remember."

"Someone didn't want to sit next to him?"

"I'm not sure. I think someone wanted to sit next to him and made someone else get up."

"Do you remember who?" I asked.

She shook her head. "Somebody took pictures. Take a look."

I made a note to do just that. "What do you know about Fred Beller?" I asked.

"Haven't seen Fred in at least twenty years," Bruce said. "He doesn't like New York and he doesn't seem to like us very much. Not that he dislikes us. He just seems to get along fine without the group."

"I had lunch with him yesterday."

He stared at me. I was starting to enjoy startling these men. "Where exactly did you see Fred Beller?"

"At the Waldorf-Astoria. I had lunch there with him and his wife."

"I don't believe it."

"He was in town for the last week. He was in town when your group met."

"Impossible."

"He says he ran into Arthur Wien in California a few years ago."

"I think Artie mentioned that. The Bellers were vacationing there. You actually saw him?"

"Saw him and spent an hour with him."

"I wonder if he slips in and out of New York without telling your gang," his wife said.

"Could be. New York's a big place. You could be there a long time and not run into someone who lived a block away from you."

"The men I've talked to all seem to have a fondness for the place where you grew up. Why doesn't Fred Beller feel that way?"

"I could tell you that it's a personal thing with him," Bruce Kaplan said, "that he likes the Midwest, the slower pace, the greener grass. That's probably what my friends have told you. I'll tell you the truth. Fred's mother committed suicide when we were about thirteen years old. She was a disturbed, unhappy woman. I can't tell you much more about it because it was something no one would talk to us about."

"I can understand why."

"Fred came home from school that day and found her."

"How terrible."

"Think about it. She knew he would find her. Think about a woman killing herself and knowing her son would walk into the apartment and find her body."

He was right. It was an unimaginable thing to do. But I could see why the son would want to get as far away from that place, that city, those people as he could. "Did Arthur Wien write about it in his first book?"

"You got me. It's so long since I read that book, I can't remember what he said and what he didn't say."

"You should read it," Arlene said. "It's a good book, and a lot of what he writes is autobiographical."

"I'm going to get it out of the library tomorrow."

"I've got a copy I'll be glad to give you. It's even signed. The last time we saw Artie, I picked up a few copies and had him sign them. They make great gifts." She got up and left the room, returning quickly with a thick paperback that she gave me.

"Thank you very much."

"It's not a first edition, but you know, he won't be signing any more books."

"Who else have you talked to?" Bruce asked.

"Dr. Horowitz on Friday, David Koch and Fred Beller yesterday, and Joe Meyer this afternoon."

"How's Joe doing?"

"He doesn't look very good but he's in good spirits."

"Sounds like Joe."

"They had a terrible tragedy in their family, you know," Arlene said.

"Besides Mr. Meyer's illness?"

"Their daughter was badly hurt in a car crash."

"When did that happen?"

"A couple of years ago. I don't remember exactly."

"Mrs. Meyer showed me a picture of the daughter taking a bow after a performance."

"It's an old picture," Arlene said. "She was badly injured. I don't know whether she'll ever be able to play again."

"How awful."

"I hope she gets her career back."

"Well, what else can we tell you?" Bruce asked. "The names of our teachers? I can still remember a few. How we played stickball on Morris Avenue? Did anyone show you the jacket?"

"Jacket?"

"We had jackets made. On the back it said Morris Avenue Boys and on the front, right here over the pocket, our name. That's half the reason we gave ourselves a name, so we could get jackets."

"I didn't know about the jackets. I toured your old homestead this afternoon with David Koch but he didn't mention them. What I'm wondering—I talked to Dr. Greene last night. He's the only one of the group who doesn't want to see me."

"Ernie's always working, always busy, always going to international conferences. I wouldn't put too much importance on his not meeting with you. He's not a killer; he's a saver of lives. I think sometimes how unbelievable it is that a kid I played ball with in the street grew up to do so much good. Believe me, Ernie may be a little brusque with strangers but he's all good. Of all of us, he's at the top."

"That's quite a tribute. I also haven't been able to reach Bernie Reskin. I assume it's just that he hasn't been home when I've called."

"Keep trying. Bernie'll talk your ear off when you get to him. He's quite a guy. He's another person who's devoted his life to helping other people. Teaching isn't what it used to be, but he gets those kids to learn, he gets them into college, he's really something."

Arlene walked into the room holding a boy's jacket in front of her. I hadn't seen her leave. She was smiling broadly. She turned the jacket around and I saw Morris Avenue Boys in thick light-blue letters on the navy background.

"I love it," I said.

"It's falling apart, but isn't that something?" She showed me her husband's name on the front, then laid the jacket carefully on another chair.

"It's my impression," I said to her, "that women often know when certain things are going on even if their husbands don't. Did Arthur Wien ever have an affair with the wife of one of the men in the group?"

She looked surprised. Her mouth opened but she said nothing. Finally she said, "Who told you that?"

"I heard it had happened," I said.

"I'm floored. Artie and one of the wives? Whoever said that was misinformed or had a grudge."

"Who would have a grudge?" I persisted.

"Nobody. Nothing like that ever happened. And if it did, I don't know anything about it." She looked troubled, whether because something had happened that she had no knowledge of or because of the insinuation, I could not tell.

I turned back to her husband. "Let me ask your advice. I'll be in New York in the next day or two. How awful would it be if I just dropped in on Dr. Greene unannounced?"

"Go for it," Bruce said. "What do you think'll happen? He won't have a temper tantrum; he's not the type. He may not talk to you, but if he does, you can believe every word he says."

"Can I believe you?" I asked.

"Why not? Do I look like a man who has something to hide?"

I assured him he didn't and wrapped up our meeting. I had a copy of the famous first novel of Arthur Wien now and I couldn't wait to get started reading it. And who had wanted or not wanted to sit next to Arthur Wien at the reunion?

10

We sat in the sitting area of our master bedroom suite, a luxury I could not have imagined four years ago when I left St. Stephen's. One nice feature for a careful spender like me is that we put the upstairs on its own heating zone and did the same with the downstairs so we can turn down the rest of the house and keep ourselves warm in the winter and yes, cool in the summer. But the weather was so perfect this June night that we needed nothing more than to open the window and breathe the fresh air.

I had several of the photos from the reunion spread out in front of me on our little table. There was no picture of the whole group, just snapshots of a few here, a few there. I guessed who Cindy Wien was because she was the youngest, and I assumed the man beside her was her husband. To his left was a woman I had not met, but in another picture she sat to the right of Dr. Horowitz. She seemed perfectly happy there. The Meyers were at an end of the table, probably on the other side from the Wiens, and the Koches also seemed to be across from the Wiens. The arrangement didn't tell me much but it gave me something to ask about.

"So you've seen all but two of the likely suspects and you've visited the Bronx," Jack said. "Any leads?"

"They're the nicest group of men and women I've ever

met. If you asked me I would say not one of them could be a killer and I can't think of a reason why any of them would want to kill Arthur Wien."

"Maybe none of them did."

"If none of them did, I've really got problems. I'm going to call Elsie in the morning and see if I can drop Eddie off again. I want to get back to the restaurant before the maitre d's memory fades. I've got a picture of the Bellers, and I want to know if either of them was there on the night of Father's Day."

"You're right. Do it fast."

"And I'm thinking—" I hesitated because the thought of what I was planning made me very nervous. "I'm thinking of just dropping in on Dr. Greene and seeing if he'll give me ten minutes of his time. I can't really exclude him as a suspect if I never talk to him. And I can't accuse him just because I haven't spoken to him."

"Give it a try. If he doesn't talk to you, do what you can without him. But you know, an M.D. probably knows where to put an ice pick better than a guy who hasn't studied the human body."

"I know. And that makes Dr. Horowitz more of a suspect than the others too."

"I see you've got a new book to read."

"This is the great book, Jack, *The Lost Boulevard*, Arthur Wien's first novel. Published before his thirtieth birthday. Can you believe that?"

"Since I'm almost the oldest person in my law class, I can't. Tell me about it as you go along."

"I'm also going to try to talk to the first Mrs. Wien. She lives in Manhattan, over on the West Side. With luck, I'll hit the restaurant, talk to the doctor, and see her—all before I come back. That'll leave the teacher. I'll call him again tomorrow."

"So what've you got? You must have something cooking up there."

"Fred Beller," I said. "I've been springing it on each of the men, that he's here in New York—or was until yesterday— and they're all speechless. None of them has seen him in twenty years."

"Except Dr. Horowitz."

"Except Dr. Horowitz, and I haven't talked to him about it yet. But I'm sure he knows by now that I know. David Koch will have told him. The only other person in the group that saw Fred Beller was Arthur Wien."

"I'm listening."

"And there was something strange about their meeting. They ran into each other when the Bellers were visiting California. The Bellers invited Wien to visit if he was in Minneapolis. Wien did a book signing there and they were supposed to get together, but they didn't."

"And Beller didn't tell you why."

"He said Arthur's schedule was too full. But Marge Beller stumbled when I asked her what happened. Her husband answered for her. There's something weird there, Jack, and Fred Beller admitted he didn't like Arthur Wien."

"Well, I'm glad you came up with something. You've talked to a lot of people."

"And maybe I'll find something in this." I handed him *The Lost Boulevard*. The cover picture was a street that seemed to extend to infinity, apartment houses along either side, a shadowy man's face in the upper left, and an equally shadowy woman's face in the lower right.

"How will you know what's fact and what's fiction?"

"I won't unless I can get corroboration or denial from the men. It certainly looks like there's a love story in it, doesn't it?"

"What else? Who can write a coming-of-age novel without that?"

It was a question I had never asked. I came of age, if that was the proper description, so differently from other people that I could not use myself as a typical example of anything. And I didn't read many books about secular people in those critical years. This book would be an experience in many ways.

"Would you like to visit Elsie again today?" I asked Eddie at breakfast.

"See?" That was his name for Elsie.

"Yes, Elsie."

"See."

"Elsie wants to see you again." I had already talked to her, and she said she had some shopping to do and would be glad to take Eddie with her. "She's going to take you in the car."

Eddie smiled. He was pushing a spoonful of cereal into his mouth, most of it reaching its target. He was wearing pajamas with yellow clowns wearing red hats, and I was trying to teach him the colors, but not at breakfast.

When he was finished and cleaned up, we went upstairs and picked out a pair of brown shorts and a shirt with brown-and-yellow designs on it. I dressed after he was ready and waited for the stroke of nine to call Alice Wien. For the first time, she answered.

I went through my explanation of who I was, why I called, and what I wanted. I wasn't sure how much sympathy to express, since she wasn't exactly on the best of terms with her ex-husband, so I kept it to a minimum.

"We could talk today if you're coming into the city," she said.

I told her that would be great, and we made an appointment. I decided to leave her for last as that would be my longest stop. First I would drop by the institute on the East Side where Dr. Greene worked. I wanted to get that over with because it made me nervous. Then I would go by the restaurant, which I assumed would not be open much before noon. Lastly, I would go over to the West Side and see Alice Wien.

Eddie was happy to be left with Elsie. I knew that might all change one day without notice, but for as long as it lasted, I was happy. If Elsie were my mother, I would think nothing of having Eddie visit her, but she wasn't and I wasn't sure what I would do if Eddie became obstreperous. But today that was not a problem. She waved me away and I drove down to the city.

I found a place to park almost halfway between the two East Side addresses I would visit. Then I walked to the institute, looking in shop windows as I went. It was a beautiful day.

The institute where Dr. Ernest Greene had spent many decades of his life operated under top security. Even if I had known the floor and office number, I would not have been allowed beyond the guards' station. I gave them Dr. Greene's name, admitted he was not expecting me, and waited. A phone call was made, a pair of eyes turned to me as though assessing my veracity—did I really look like a thief or a terrorist?—and the phone was hung up.

"He'll be down in a few minutes. Please take a seat."

The first hurdle was behind me. I sat in a comfortable

chair and took *The Lost Boulevard* out of my bag. I had read myself to sleep last night, caught up in the characters, the story, the intrigues that Wien built in from the outset. Not all the characters were transparent to me. I assumed they would become more so as I read. But I recognized some of the landmarks David Koch had pointed out to me, buildings and businesses and streets and schools. I had read several pages when I heard a man's voice ask, "Ms. Bennett?"

I looked up. A man the age of the rest of the group stood before me. He was wearing a casual shirt and no tie or jacket. I scrambled to get the book back in my bag. Then I stood up and offered my hand. "Dr. Greene?"

"You're very persistent."

"Dr. Horowitz asked me to look into the murder of Arthur Wien. I think it's important that the killer not go free. I need the help of everyone who was at the dinner and everyone who knew him from childhood."

"Come with me."

I followed him to a windowed area of tables and chairs. We sat at right angles and I took out my notebook and pen.

"You seem to be a very young person," he said when we were settled. "What exactly makes you a better investigator than the police?"

I explained briefly how I had investigated the 1950 murder of the mother of a pair of idiot savant twins when I first moved to Oakwood and how people had asked me to look into other murders that were unsolved.

"I'm impressed," he said. "All right. Let's get on with it."

"Your friends say wonderful things about you, Dr. Greene. I don't want to take a lot of your time so let me start asking questions. What was your relationship with Arthur Wien?"

"As I said on the phone the other night, I had almost no relationship with him. I saw him infrequently, usually when we had one of our reunions, and that was all. I went to his first wedding but not to his second. I think I met one of his children once. He lived in California most of the time and I only go out there for medical conferences. There wasn't much of a relationship to talk about."

"Did he ever come to you for favors?"

He studied me. I had the feeling he was looking right inside me, discerning my motives and determining their worthiness. "For a long time, back when we were all younger, Artie Wien was a man perennially without money. To hear him talk, you would think he owed half of California. He borrowed from everyone he knew and that included me. About thirty years ago he came to me and said he was desperate and could I lend him five hundred dollars. I gave him the five hundred. He spent the next two years calling and telling me he would pay it back, not to worry, he was good for it. The long and short of it is that eventually I told him to consider it a gift, that I didn't want it back, with or without interest, and that he was never to ask me for another penny again. He never asked me, and I wrote it off as a bad debt and haven't really thought about it until this moment. But that was my relationship with Artie."

"You said he borrowed from everyone he knew. Did that include the other men in your group?"

"Of course it did. I have no reason to believe that he singled me out. I'm not a rich man, and I certainly wasn't very well off thirty years ago."

"That's interesting because I've asked the others and not one has said he lent money to Mr. Wien."

"I suppose every man's honesty has its limits. Maybe they think that to admit having lent money—and possibly not having it paid back—makes them look like suspects. I haven't been eating my heart out over the five hundred I gave him. I didn't kill Artie, I don't know who did—I'm sure it wasn't any of us—and I'm very sorry that he's dead. He was a talented man; he had a sense of humor; if he made mistakes in his life, well, haven't we all?"

"What was his relationship to Fred Beller?"

"Fred Beller? I haven't seen Fred in—I couldn't tell you when the last time was."

"I had lunch with him on Saturday."

"You flew out to Minnesota to talk to Fred?"

"Fred and his wife were in New York for about a week. They were here on Father's Day."

"What exactly are you saying?" His rather smooth forehead showed an incipient vertical line.

"Just that. I found out by accident that he was here. I called and we arranged to meet for lunch at his hotel."

Dr. Greene shook his head slowly. "And he never came to our party."

"I guess not. Can you think of a reason why he didn't? Was there something between him and Arthur Wien that prevented Fred Beller from being near him?"

"If there was, I'm not privy to that information." He took off his wire-rimmed glasses and set them on the table in front of him. "I'm stunned," he said. "I thought Fred never came to New York."

"Can you tell me anything about his mother's suicide?"

"Just that it was the disaster you can imagine it was. He came home from school one afternoon and there she was. She was a sad woman. In those days ordinary people didn't go for psychiatric help. She might have benefited from it. On the other hand, how could she have afforded it? Our families weren't rich. It was terrible for Fred. I don't blame him for wanting to get away from where it happened and never coming back."

I opened my bag and pulled out the book. As I set it on the table I saw the doctor smile.

"You're reading our life history, I see."

"Mrs. Kaplan gave it to me yesterday. I could hardly put it down last night."

"Artie had a gift. Until that book came out, I had no idea he had been observing us and thinking about our lives. To me the D train was just a subway, but after I read that book, I realized that to him it was a way out. It's an interesting book from many perspectives. It's not the kind of book I ever read, but I can tell you I devoured every syllable of that one, even if Artie took Morty Horowitz and me and made us one rather schizophrenic creature. Or maybe a more accurate description would be a possessed soul and the possessing dybbuk."

"Excuse me?"

"A dybbuk. That's the demon that possesses a person. You need to exorcise it to get rid of it."

"And you see the portrayal of that character that way?"

"Loosely." He smiled and it struck me he was a man that didn't smile much. "It's a graphic way of describing Artie's doctor character."

"Wien seems to love all the boys very much, from what I've read."

"He did. We all did. We were friends in an era when friendship meant something."

"What can you tell me about Bruce Kaplan's troubles?" I asked.

"If you know about it, you probably know as much as I do. He got in trouble. He always struck me as a pretty honest guy. Either he made a mistake, or someone else did and he paid for it."

"I heard Arthur Wien had an affair with the wife of a member of your group."

"I never heard that." It was quick and dismissive.

"At the reunion, was there a problem with who should sit next to Arthur Wien?"

"There's always a seating problem. This one is left handed; that one has to sit next to someone he hasn't seen for ten years. There's nothing new about that."

"Did someone make a fuss that night?"

"I think so. I didn't pay any attention to it."

"As of this moment, I've spoken to everyone in the group except Bernie Reskin. I haven't been able to reach him by phone."

"Keep trying. He'll talk to you. Bernie loves to talk."

"David Koch drove me through the streets in the Bronx where you all lived," I said, coming to the end of my questions and not feeling that I'd learned very much.

"David doesn't drive," the doctor said.

It struck me as a strange response. "He had someone drive us. He showed me where you played stickball."

"And touch football. That was my favorite. Then you must have seen the window of his bedroom that looks out on Morris Avenue."

"I did."

"Did he tell you how we used to crawl through the window in the summer and drag him out of bed?" He was enjoying the memory.

"You were a happy bunch of boys."

"We were that, except for Fred Beller."

"Do you believe it was his mother's suicide that made him feel the way he does about New York?"

"It takes a lot less than that for many people. I think from that day on Fred wanted to get away, physically as well as spiritually. For Artie it was more a spiritual thing, if that's the appropriate word. He knew there was a world out there and he wanted to see it, to become part of it. For Fred, he just wanted to get his tail out of there, resettle in some neutral territory, which he did."

"I gather from the little I've read that Arthur Wien wanted to get his parents out of the Bronx. Was he successful?"

"Not that I know of. I think they lived out their lives there and died in the old homestead. And not that long ago."

"What about your parents?"

"They never gave up their apartment. All our parents were the beneficiaries of rent control. You're probably too young to know much about it, but the rents were frozen during the Second World War and didn't rise very much from the fifties on. It cost my folks so little to hang onto their apartment that they kept it although they bought a co-op in Florida and spent most of the year there. But the Bronx was home, even though the neighborhood changed drastically."

A young woman came over to the table and whispered something in Dr. Greene's ear.

"That's all right," he said gently. "I can take care of things when I get upstairs."

The young woman dashed away, and I realized that before he came downstairs he had asked someone to call him at this moment, to save him from my questioning. Obviously, our conversation hadn't been as bad as he had feared.

"I know you're very busy," I said. "I'm very grateful

that you've given me this much time. If you think of any-thing that might help me, I'd appreciate a call." I had a slip of paper ready with my name and phone number.

"I promise I'll think about it," he said, putting his glasses back on his nose. "You know, there *was* some kind of fuss about the seating. I didn't take much notice of it but somebody in the crowd wasn't happy."

"A man or a woman?" I asked.

"A woman, I think. It could have been Robin Horowitz, but I'm not sure."

"I'll see if I can find out."

He shook my hand, walked me to the front desk, and then nearly flew to the elevator.

11

I had learned one thing: Dr. Greene had lent Arthur Wien money (and assumed all his friends had too). I tried to think how much the five hundred dollars thirty years ago would be in today's dollars. I had heard my mother mention the monthly mortgage payments once, perhaps twenty years ago, and they were a little more than a hundred dollars. So five hundred dollars thirty years ago was a substantial amount of money. I wondered how I would feel if a friend of Jack's, someone who appeared to be making a good living, came to us and asked for two or three thousand dollars. The thought sent shivers through me.

It passed through my mind that Arthur Wien might have blackmailed his friends into lending money to him, money that he failed to repay. But that would assume he had something on all of them. It didn't seem likely. And no one else I had spoken to had admitted to lending him anything more than pocket money.

I walked up to the restaurant where the Father's Day dinner had taken place only to find the door locked. There were lights on inside and I tapped on the glass in the door, hoping to attract someone's attention. Finally, I did.

He opened the locks at the top and bottom of the door, then at the midpoint. "I'm sorry, but we're—" It was the maitre d', and he looked at my face and recognized me. "Come in." He didn't sound welcoming, but he probably wanted to get me inside where no one would see us talking. "What can I do for you today, Ms. Bennett?"

"I'd like you to check your reservations for the evening of Father's Day and see if anyone named Fred Beller had one."

"I just don't see—"

"Please," I said. "It's very important."

He frowned and got the book, turned back several pages and moved his finger down the page. "No one named Beller," he said, snapping the book shut.

I took out the photo. "Do you remember seeing this man—this couple—that night?"

He studied the picture carefully, more carefully than I expected. "They look familiar," he said unhappily. "I'm pretty sure they were here. But that's not their name."

"I wonder if you'd check the receipts for that night. Even if he made the reservation in a different name, the waiter wouldn't know that name and he might have charged the meal using his real name."

"Are you telling me this man could have committed the murder that night? The police have never asked me about him."

"The police don't know he was here."

"Why don't you take a seat? I'll be right back."

There was a small bar in the front of the restaurant and I sat on a stool with my back to the bar. Sitting on a bar stool is not something I've done in my life, ever. Since I dated very few men, and none of them took me to a bar, this was a new experience for me. I didn't find the stool particularly comfortable, but then, I didn't have my feet resting on the rail. Instead, they were on a rung of the stool.

I didn't have much time to think about it because the maitre d' returned quite soon. He was holding a small piece of paper that I recognized as a credit card receipt. Although I don't carry plastic, Jack does, and he generally charges our dinners out and often charges the things he buys in the hardware store.

"There you go," he said. "Fred Beller. Looks like dinner for two. I can tell you what name he used if you give me another minute." He opened the reservation book again. "Olds. F. Olds. The reservation was for six-thirty. He and his guest sat over there along the banquette."

The banquette ran almost the length of the restaurant with tables for two and four spread out along it. If Fred Beller had sat with his back to the restaurant, no one would have seen him. Nor, I thought, would he have seen his old friends as they entered the restaurant. But perhaps he could have seen them after they had passed and were on their way to the back room.

"Thank you very much. I'm sorry to have put you to this trouble, but it's really quite important."

"Should I tell the police?" he asked.

"I'll be telling them if it turns out to be important."

I walked out onto the street. Fred Beller had been there, no doubt about it. Had it been because he wanted to be near his friends or because he wanted to do away with one of them? Surely he would not tell me, and I had no idea who might know. Although these men had varying relationships with other members of the group, it was clear they stuck up for one another.

I found myself in front of a coffee shop and I walked in. This would be as good a place as any to have some lunch before driving to the West Side for my meeting with Alice Wien.

* * *

For me the West Side of Manhattan is principally Broadway and the streets that cross it, numbered streets from the Sixties on up. I had come to know the area a couple of years earlier when an elderly friend of mine was murdered in his apartment in the high Seventies. I spent a week or more talking to his friends, who lived as far north as Columbia University and as far east as Central Park, people who had settled there before and after the Second World War. A divider runs down the center of Broadway; what grass it has is usually weedy. At many corners there are park benches facing the cross street, and mostly elderly people sit there to take the sun and talk to their neighbors.

Alice Wien wasn't my idea of elderly, and indeed, she turned out to be a good-looking woman in her sixties, her hair professionally set and her clothes well cut and in style. She welcomed me, and we sat in her living room, a comfortable room with a beautiful oriental carpet covering most of the floor.

"Dave Koch told me you might be calling," she said. "I don't know what I can tell you because I wasn't at the restaurant the night it happened."

"I think I'm interested in hearing some background from you. When you met Mr. Wien, how long you were married, what you know about his books, especially the first one."

"That sounds pretty easy since I lived through it. Art and I met when I was at City College. We got married after I graduated."

"Were you from the Bronx?"

"I was from Brooklyn. In those days it was practically an intermarriage." She smiled. "He used to take the subway all the way to where I lived to pick me up. What a trip that was."

"The famous D train," I said.

"Art had a real romance with the D train. He saw his little neighborhood in the Bronx as a village, almost like an English village, with the train running through it. He could imagine kids watching that train taking lucky people to London. In his case, the D took him to New York which was the center of the world, and by extension, he could see it taking him across the ocean, maybe even up to the moon."

"So I guess you didn't live in the Bronx after you were married."

"Oh no. We got a darling little place in the Village. I just loved it. My parents thought it was terrible; Art's parents thought it was terrible. But it was the most wonderful place to live you can imagine, right where everything was happening. It was one big room with a little bathroom and a little kitchen. We had a bed and a dresser in one corner, a little sofa in another corner, a table for eating, a little desk for Art to write his book at and a typewriter table."

"Then he was writing his book when you were married."

"He started—let me see—well, he was talking about it the night I met him. He was making notes back then, trying things out, you know, sketches of people and places. He'd think of a good phrase and he'd make a note of it. He lived that book."

"Did he work besides writing?"

"Sure he worked. He taught high school English. He wasn't any slouch. We both worked. But later on, he spent most of his time on the book. And it was worth it. It was a great book. It's still in print, you know."

"I know. I was given a copy last night by Mrs. Kaplan. I started reading it before I went to bed and I could hardly put it down."

"That's how Art wrote. He couldn't stop writing and readers couldn't stop reading."

I was surprised at her enthusiasm. She was talking about the husband who had left her for another woman, for other women, and still she spoke well of him.

"The boulevard in the title is the Grand Concourse. He describes it like some kind of dream."

"It was a dream to those boys. If you were rich, you lived on the Concourse. If you were poor or middle class, you aspired to it. The truth is, if you were rich, you probably lived in Manhattan, but he wrote from the boys' point of view. That was how they perceived the world they lived in."

"He says right from the start he wanted his parents to move there when they became able to afford it. What happened?"

"Well, I don't want to spoil the story for you. Eventually, his folks had a nice income and the kids were gone so they could have afforded a more expensive apartment, but they wouldn't leave the old one. Art was only in his late twenties when he finished writing the book, but the observations he made were sound. He could have said the same things twenty years later."

"Did you know Fred Beller?" I asked without making any transition from what she had been saying.

"Oh Fred." She smiled as though he were a happy memory. "I knew Fred."

"How is that?"

"I met him at City. I knew him before I met Art."

"Did you go out with him?"

"For quite a while. A year maybe."

Somewhere in my memory I heard one of the men say that Fred and Art had dated the same girl. It had not occurred to me that the girl was the one Arthur Wien had eventually married. "Was there—did anything happen to make you switch from one man to the other?"

"We're talking about a pretty long time ago. If my memory isn't sharp, you'll understand."

"I just wondered whether there was some kind of incident that made you break up with one man and start dating the other."

"You might say there was an incident. I was very fond of Fred. He was such a dear thing, so good, so very kind and thoughtful. I would have married him, I'm sure of that, if things had gone along. But one night—it was in the spring, I think—Fred took me to a party down in the Village. It was a big party in a big apartment—I don't know whose it was—and Art was there. Fred introduced us—he was surprised to see him there, I remember—and it was like something you read about. Fireworks, chemistry, bells ringing—it was scary and exciting and overwhelming. Art called me in the middle of the night after I got home. I thought my parents would kill him. He wanted to see me again. I broke up with Fred a week later."

The monologue had deflated her. She seemed exhausted by the memory, by the act of recounting it. I found myself feeling very sorry for her. She had described meeting the great love of her life, a man who had been unfaithful to her, who had left her, who had been murdered only eight days earlier.

"I know this is difficult," I said.

"It's hard to remember such happy times after all that's happened. And an awful lot has happened."

"It sounds like a wonderful relationship while it lasted."

"It was. Art wrote about it in the book. You probably haven't gotten to it yet. It really gave me a great feeling when I read it, knowing what emotions I had stirred in him, and was still stirring."

She rearranged herself in her chair. "I had to make him swear he wouldn't write all of it. My parents—" She blushed suddenly and I saw that it still affected her. "You're quite young. It's awkward saying these things to you, but people who came of age in the sixties thought they had invented sex. I can assure you it was invented at least twenty years before the sixties."

It was my turn to smile. "I suppose every generation needs to feel it's cornered the market on something."

"That's a nice way of putting it."

"Did anything happen between Fred Beller and Mr. Wien when you broke up with Fred?"

"I think so. They talked, but I wasn't there so I can't tell you what was said. I know that the night I broke up with Fred was one of the toughest nights of my life. He really loved me. And he'd had such a rotten life as a kid. His mother—do you know about that?"

"I've been told."

"Imagine doing that to a kid, knowing he would come home from school and find you."

"She must have been very depressed, very unhappy."

"She was. But even so."

"Do you think Fred Beller could have kept a grudge against Arthur Wien for the next forty years?"

"You think Fred killed Art?" It was clear she found the idea incredible.

"I think anything's possible."

"Fred was too good, too kind to hurt anyone. And he never comes to New York so that lets him out."

"He was in New York when Mr. Wien was murdered."

It was the same reaction, disbelief all over her face. "Who told you that?"

"I found out by accident. I had lunch with him and his wife just this past Saturday."

"It seems impossible, but if you say so, then I have to believe it."

"Does that change how you feel? About Fred Beller's being a suspect?"

"Not for a minute."

"Maybe we can talk about the book," I said. "Did you read it as your husband was writing it?"

"Oh yes. I was his first editor. He would finish a chapter and hand it to me, or he would leave it on the table so I would find it when I came home from work. At first I was afraid to make corrections, afraid his ego was so involved that he would be angry at my suggestions. But he wasn't. And I was a gentle editor. I loved the story, I loved the writing, I loved all the people in it."

"I guess you got to know them pretty well."

"Very well. I laughed with them; I cried for them. I read that book so many times that after a while, I could almost recite long parts of it from memory."

"I saw that he dedicated it to you." The dedication had read: To Alice, my great love.

"That's quite a dedication, isn't it? I was almost afraid he would change it after the mess of our divorce."

"Can you tell me what happened?"

"I knew he was unfaithful. Eventually, I told him I couldn't take it any more. The kids were very upset, but I couldn't live with him. So we called our lawyers."

"That sounds pretty civilized," I said.

"Take my word for it, it wasn't. I wanted him to support me. I wanted his estate to support me if he died before I did. I was angry and hurt, and I wanted him to pay. And I also wanted what I believed was mine."

"Which was?"

"The original manuscript of *The Lost Boulevard*. That was a problem."

"He wanted to keep it for himself?"

"Partly that, but the real reason was that he didn't have it."

"I don't understand."

"Art was a man who was always short of funds, or at least he claimed to be. I can tell you I wasn't a spendthrift, but I think he was in ways that I didn't see and didn't always benefit from. Keeping a woman is expensive. Taking people out lavishly costs a lot. And although you hear a lot nowadays about authors' making millions, I can tell you that wasn't the case back in the fifties. But Art wanted a home in New York and a home in California; he wanted people to think of him in a certain way. So he borrowed from friends and paid it back when he could."

"I'm sorry," I said, feeling confused. "I don't see the connection between that and the missing manuscript. Had he sold it?"

"He gave it to someone as collateral against a loan."

"I see."

"Don't ask me who it was; he never told me. But at the time that we were negotiating our divorce, he didn't have the manuscript or the typewritten copy."

"There were two copies?"

"Art wrote in longhand on lined pads using number two pencils sharpened to a fine point. That's the manuscript I edited. He wasn't a very good typist himself. When he was satisfied, I typed the whole thing up for him on his old Royal portable. That was the copy he sent to the agent."

"That's amazing," I said. "All those hundreds of pages written in pencil."

"Nowadays everyone has a computer, and all they have to show for their work is a floppy disk and a printout. His manuscript showed every change, every hesitation, every place where he struggled to find the right word. The manuscript itself is a history of the book. I've had it appraised. If the time ever comes that I need money, I can sell it."

"Is that why you wanted it?"

"Partly. Mostly I felt it belonged to me. It was dedicated to me and my blood, sweat, and tears are on every page."

"I'd love to see it," I said.

"I'd be glad to show it to you, but understand, I can't let it out of my apartment."

"I do understand. Tell me, how does the original compare to the published version?"

"It's quite close. The editor took out a couple of chapters that he felt were weak and didn't contribute enough to the main story. But they're still in the original."

"So how did it work?" I asked. "How did he get the manuscripts back?"

"He probably borrowed more money to pay off the loan, although there was something else going on there, now that I think of it."

"Like what?"

"I'm not sure. Whoever it was didn't want to give the manuscripts back. I don't know any more than that, and at the time, I assumed Art was lying. He'd lied about so many things at that point, I thought this was just another excuse not to give me what was my due."

"How long did it take for him to get the manuscripts back?"

She looked away. "Months," she said. "I don't remember how long, but long enough that our lawyers were screeching at each other."

"Is Fred's mother's suicide included in the book?"

"In a way. Art made it someone's father instead. He didn't want people to be identifiable, not because he thought they would sue but because he respected their privacy."

"Was Fred angry about it, do you know?"

"I don't know. I don't think he was. And that's not the reason he doesn't come to the reunions. He just doesn't like New York and the bad memories. Or I thought he didn't."

"When the book was published, was anyone hurt or angry at his portrayal or the portrayal of some event?"

"If they were, I didn't hear about it. Art did a wonderful job of disguising the real people who were the basis for the characters. You know, he reduced nine to five."

"Yes. One other thing, the man who died, George Fried, did you know him?"

"I met him. I can't say I knew him. He was another one who didn't like New York. In fact, I think Art may have combined him and Fred in the book, but the character is mostly Fred."

"Mrs. Wien, did anything happen when the men were young that might have had repercussions later in life? Some incident which they all participated in or some of them did, which came back to haunt them?"

"You mean something criminal?"

"Possibly."

"I don't know about anything like that and I don't think

such a thing happened. I know what you mean—robbing a bank or accidentally killing someone. They weren't tough kids, Chris. I don't think what you're suggesting is possible, given the men involved. You think there was some kind of blackmail going on and it ended up in Art's murder?"

"I'm looking for a reason why someone walked into that restaurant carrying an ice pick."

"I don't know any reason for what happened. I grew to hate him at one time, but I came through that. He always sent me my alimony payments, most of them on time. He was unfaithful to me when we were married, but after the divorce, he didn't treat me shabbily. I didn't hate him these last years. If anything, I felt sorry that he never felt secure enough to be a happy person. I've made a good life for myself without Art."

"One last thing," I said. "I heard he had an affair with the wife of one of the men in the group. Do you know anything about that?"

"Art? With one of the men's wives? I think you're misinformed. I'm the oldest woman Art ever went out with. He wanted young, not middle-aged or old."

It sounded reasonable. I thanked her and told her I would call if I wanted to read the original manuscript. It was still early afternoon when I started for home.

12

With much of the afternoon still left, I felt it had been a very successful day. I knew that Fred Beller and his wife had been at the restaurant the night of the murder. I knew that Dr. Greene, and possibly others in the group, had lent Arthur Wien money, and in at least one of those cases, he hadn't paid it back. I knew that one person had been so concerned about being repaid that he had held the original manuscripts of *The Lost Boulevard* as collateral. And now I knew that both Fred Beller and Arthur Wien had known Alice and loved her. It was a tantalizing triangle, the young man with the wounded psyche and the confident, possibly even arrogant man with great optimism, great drive, and I thought, probably great sex appeal. I would have liked to see what Alice looked like all those years ago. Her face had aged and softened; there were light wrinkles where smile lines had once been, but she was a good-looking woman now and she must have been very beautiful when those two young men wanted to claim her for their own.

I claimed my little son when I got to Elsie's, arriving as he was waking, warm with red cheeks and a few sleepy tears. Elsie had her usual treat for Eddie, milk and an incredible cookie. Eddie is truly blessed where cookies are concerned. Both Elsie and Mel see to it that he gets the best, and I occasionally manage to benefit from their generosity as well.

When Eddie and I got home, we walked a little, stopping to talk to neighbors. Then we sat behind the house while Eddie played in his sandbox with occasional assistance from me.

I had *The Lost Boulevard* on my lap and was determined to get to the end of it as soon as I could. Unless something had happened quite early in the relationships of these men, I didn't expect to find a clue in the book to who had killed Arthur Wien. But I wanted to see how he painted his friends and his friends' wives, whether I could detect the scent of a deadly sin in his prose, some envy, anger over an old hurt, somebody's lust. There was plenty of lust, but it never seemed to interfere with the men's relationships with each other. These were people who got along with each other, who supported each other.

The theme of convincing his parents to move out of their old apartment ran through the book like a drop of water making its way across a sloped plane. The Arthur Wien character seemed to sense that the old neighborhood would decline before his parents would. What he wanted was not so much that they leave the Bronx but that they find an apartment on the Grand Concourse. There the buildings were more refined, the men went to better paying jobs, the women dressed better, the children went to expensive colleges, colleges with reputations that extended beyond the five boroughs and the Hudson River.

But his father felt he would get less for the rent he would pay and his mother said it would be a longer walk to the stores she shopped at. They liked where they were.

For the Wien character the Concourse was a dream. It

had elegance and class, neither of which was apparent in his neighborhood. But for himself, the Village became the center of his life. He made friends with poets and writers who lived there or who, like him, spent their time there. He met girls who admired him and who, eventually, had sexual relationships with him although finding a place was always a problem. He lived at home, and most of the girls that he met also lived at home, although occasionally one lived in a dormitory at Barnard or New York University. They became adept at finding people who were going away, friends with an extra room they would not need till after midnight, at which time they would drag themselves out of bed and sleepily find the nearest subway. He would take her home and then work his way over to a D train stop and go home himself.

I had the sense that everyone lived in a permanent state of exhaustion. As a person who throughout her twenties got up daily at five in the morning, I could not imagine surviving the kind of affairs Arthur Wien described. But his character thrived on that life, even did well in school, got raises at work, and seemed to hold together in his personal life.

I became aware, as I was reading, that Eddie was crying. He had gotten tangled in a toy and I went over to extricate him and sit on the grass beside the sandbox and help him play. I had made a good dent in the book, but besides enjoying it, I had learned nothing that would lead to Arthur Wien's murderer. I wondered if it was worthwhile sitting in Alice's apartment and turning the pages of the original to see if something had been excised that might be telling. But before I did anything else, I thought it was time to call Dr. Horowitz and confront him with what I knew about Fred Beller.

* * *

When Eddie was down for the night, I called Morton Horowitz. He must have known when he came to the phone what my first question would be because he pre-empted it.

"I understand you've met with Fred Beller," he said.

"I had lunch with him and his wife on Saturday. From what he said, I gather you saw him last week."

"I did. We all got together. I know you think I should have mentioned it to you when we spoke the other day."

"Is there a reason why you didn't?"

"It didn't seem relevant."

"Dr. Horowitz, the Bellers were at the same restaurant that your group was at on Father's Day."

There was a silence. As his friends had been shocked to hear that Fred had been in town, he was shocked to find out Fred had been at the restaurant.

"He was there at the same time that we were?" he asked.

"Approximately. I've confirmed it with the restaurant. He used his credit card to pay for his dinner."

"I didn't know."

"Well." I started feeling guilty about confronting him with this information. "That's one of the surprises I've had since we've spoken. I've seen all the men now except Mr. Reskin. He hasn't been home when I called. I hope to reach him tonight."

"He'll be there eventually. Chris, about Fred Beller, if he used his credit card at the restaurant, that would tend to clear him if you were thinking he might have killed Artie."

"That's true, but it took a lot of digging to find out he was even there. He used another name to make the reservation. I only found out because his wife gave me a picture of the two of them and I was so surprised they were in town that I went back to the restaurant this morning and made them check."

"I can't fault you. It sounds like you're doing a very thorough job. Have you learned anything else?"

"Nothing that points me toward a killer. All the men have been very cooperative except Dr. Greene. When I called, he refused to talk to me, but I went to his lab this morning and he came down and was very pleasant once we got together. He told me he'd lent money to Arthur Wien a long time ago."

"I believe it. Ernie's very generous."

"He also said many of the men in your group lent money to Mr. Wien, but no one else has admitted it."

"Maybe because they felt it wasn't significant. I once gave him fifty dollars and I don't think he ever repaid me, but until this moment, I haven't thought about it for years. People forget these things. They don't kill over them."

"What do they kill over?" I asked.

"I wish I knew."

"Someone told me Arthur Wien had had an affair with the wife of someone in your group. Do you have any idea who that might be?"

"With one of our wives? I don't think so. Artie liked them young."

That was what Mrs. Wien had said. "I talked to Alice Wien this afternoon."

"I hope you're not going to tell me she was at the restaurant too," he said lightly.

"I didn't ask. She told me she had dated Fred Beller before she met Arthur Wien."

"Well, that was a famous switcheroo, I can tell you, one of those unlikely crossings of paths. It happens. Fred was very unhappy at the time, but he met Marge and Marge was the right woman for him. They've been married for over forty years."

Too long to carry a grudge, I thought. "Well, I'm going to talk to Mr. Reskin as soon as I can arrange it, and I may look at the original manuscript of *The Lost Boulevard*. Alice Wien has it, and she'll let me see it if I read it in her apartment."

"Alice has it," he said with surprise. "Interesting. He dedicated it to her, you know."

"It was very important to her. She requested it as part of the divorce settlement."

"I don't blame her. It's probably worth a fortune."

"Dr. Horowitz, I'm having a difficult time finding a motive for this murder. Everyone says nice things about Arthur Wien, but underneath the surface I find that he cheated his friends and his wife. It sounds to me as though he made a practice of borrowing money and not returning it. He was unfaithful to Alice. He met Alice when she was practically engaged to Fred Beller and he destroyed that relationship. And there's a possibility that he had an affair with the wife of one of the men in the group."

"Chris, you're painting a very dark picture of a man who wasn't as bad as you make him seem. Half the people I know met their wives or girlfriends when they were going out with other men. That's not a calamity; it's life. So he borrowed money and forgot to return it. Forty years later you don't kill over fifty dollars. There has to be something else and it has to involve someone outside the group."

"I'm still looking," I said.

I didn't feel very satisfied after talking to him. I had made a report, which I felt was due at this time, but I was left with the sense that everyone I had spoken to, with the possible exception of Alice Wien, had been holding back. Was a man who lent the victim fifty dollars forty years ago afraid the finger of justice would point at him if he admitted the loan? I had asked all of them or nearly all of them whether some event had happened when they were young, something they would all want covered up, and all of them had assured me there was nothing. In fact, as I thought about it, sitting in the family room with my notes and my recollections, even Alice Wien had said such a thing was not possible, although she would know only from hearsay if she met her husband while in college.

I went back to the kitchen and dialed the number for Bernie Reskin. This time a woman answered on the second ring.

"You must be Chris," she said when I started to explain why I was calling.

"That's right, Chris Bennett."

"Mort said you'd be calling. We've been out a lot the last few days. When would you like to talk to us?" She sounded almost eager.

"Anytime starting tomorrow. Whatever's convenient for you."

"Let me check with Bernie."

The conversation with her husband took only a minute and then she was back. "Bernie gets home at one tomorrow. Anytime after that."

I asked if after dinner would be all right. Then Jack would be home to baby-sit. She said it was fine.

I wrote down her directions and hung up. If the Reskins didn't come up with something new, I wasn't sure what my next step would be. Everyone wanted the killer to be someone outside the group, but I didn't see how that was possible. I wondered if the police, when they responded to the call on Father's Day, had questioned everyone in the restaurant. I wondered, too, whether Fred Beller had been there when the murder occurred. He had had a fairly early dinner reservation. How many hours could two people sit at a table after they had finished eating? For a moment I thought that might clear him. The party in the back had lasted hours but Fred Beller had arrived at six-thirty. Even with lingering over dessert and an after-dinner drink, they should have been ready to leave by nine.

I thought about it. Say he gave them his credit card, signed the receipt, and disappeared into the men's room while his wife went outside. That would make her an accomplice. He could have waited in a stall with the door locked till Arthur Wien came in. Not that it was a sure thing that Wien would visit the men's room, but it was a pretty good bet. If Fred were waiting in the first stall, he could see through the crack who was there. He could have come out, plunged the ice pick into Arthur Wien's heart, and walked out of the men's room and on out of the restaurant to join his wife, who would, of course, swear they had left together much earlier if she were asked, which was unlikely.

But I needed a motive, and if Fred had killed his old friend and had had the cooperation of his wife, the motive could not have been that Arthur Wien broke up an almost engagement to another woman forty years ago.

I knew I would have to call Fred Beller at home in Minnesota before I was done, and I didn't look forward to it. I now knew something he had gone to some lengths to keep secret, and even if I didn't threaten to tell the police, he was smart enough to know the threat existed.

This was a part of the job I found distasteful. It isn't fun to threaten people, especially when you know that of all the suspects, only one is guilty. And at this moment, I had no idea who that one might be. I had started out thinking that the embezzler was my man, but nothing pointed to him any more than to anyone else. He had been friendly and open, his wife had given me a signed copy of *The Lost Boulevard*—which certainly made it seem that they were friends with Arthur Wien—and he had added very little to what I already knew.

I pulled out the snapshot of the nine little boys and looked at them again. Dave Koch who had taken me to the old neighborhood was a successful lawyer, an apparently very nice person, best friend to Morton Horowitz. Bernie Reskin was still unknown. Ernie Greene, a research doctor, didn't want to talk to me but was gracious when I forced the issue. He had lent Arthur Wien five hundred dollars when that was a small fortune. Morton Horowitz, successful, hard-working doctor, discovered the body of his friend and lent him fifty dollars forty years ago. Bruce Kaplan, convicted of embezzlement, friendly, had been friends with Arthur. Fred Beller was a tough one—lots of questions. George Fried was dead. Joe Meyer, ill and with a life of music, successes, and honors, admired Arthur Wien. Someone in that group or one of their wives had made an issue of sitting next to Arthur Wien at the reunion.

I looked at the list of addresses and phone numbers that Dr. Horowitz had made up for me. I had checked off all but Bernie Reskin, whom I would see tomorrow, and Pamela Fried, George's widow. I looked at my watch. The address was San Diego, which made the time difference three hours. If it was four-thirty in San Diego, Mrs. Fried might be home now. I didn't know what I could learn from her.

She was George's second wife so she knew nothing about the group of men firsthand, but she was a source and I knew better than to leave anyone unquestioned.

The phone rang three times and then a man with a deep voice answered. That put me in a tizzy; if Mrs. Fried had remarried, I had no idea how to refer to her.

"I'd like to talk to Pamela Fried," I said, "if that's her correct name."

"That's her name. She's not here now and I'm not sure when she's coming back."

"Well, maybe I'd better call again. This is long distance and I don't want to put her to any expense. Who am I talking to, please?"

"This is George," he said, "her husband."

13

For the first time, my voice refused to operate. I swallowed while he asked if I was still there. "You're George Fried?" I said finally.

"The one and only. Who are you?"

"My name is Christine Bennett. I'm calling from a town near New York. Mr. Fried, I was told you were dead."

"I'm *what*? Oh, you're in New York. Listen, Chris or whatever your name is, in New York I *am* dead. You're talking to a ghost. Do me a big favor and don't blow my cover. I don't want those guys in my life. It's easier if they think I'm dead."

"You mean this was all a big ruse?"

"If you want to call it that. I have a nice life here, I have no interest in the people I grew up with, and we're all better off if they don't know the truth."

A hundred questions were racing through my head. I pulled one out and asked it. "Were you in New York last week? The weekend before last?"

"Weekend before last in New York? Yeah, I was there. We were on a trip, and we landed at JFK and spent two days in the city just to rest up. I hate New York. It's filthy and I can't stand the people. Except for that, it's a great place."

"What days were you there?"

"Saturday and Sunday a week ago."

Father's Day. I had another suspect. "Did you see any of your old friends?"

"They think I'm dead, honey. Why would I see them? Pam and I went to a hotel, we slept late, we ate a couple of good meals, and we went home. What's the purpose of these questions?"

"I'm looking into something for Morton Horowitz."

"Morty. How is he?"

"He's fine and working hard. I would like to talk to you for a while if I could. I'd like to ask you about the group, the Morris Avenue Boys."

"I can do that but not now. My wife is coming home soon and we'll be going out. Maybe tomorrow morning? I'll be here until about eleven."

I did some figuring. "I'll call you at ten."

"Ten it is. California time, right?"

"Right."

"I'll sharpen my memory."

I couldn't believe I had had the conversation.

"The guy they told you was dead is alive?" It was only five minutes since I had spoken to George Fried. Jack had just set down a carton full of stuff from his desk at the Six-Five. His move was imminent and he had begun clearing out his locker.

"They didn't just tell me he was dead. They believe it. His wife called them years ago and said he had died ten days before, the funeral was over, and that was it."

"So the whole thing was a cover-up." He looked the way I had felt when the voice on the telephone had identified himself.

"I think he just wanted to be rid of them. If they thought he was dead, they wouldn't bother him to come to reunions and they wouldn't call if they were in town."

"But he answered the phone."

"He's supposed to have died years ago. By now he probably feels it's safe to answer. I'll ask him when we talk tomorrow. Come in the kitchen and let's get started on dinner."

I had put some hamburgers on the grill when his car drove up the driveway. He went out and flipped them, putting a slice of cheese on top of each and opening the buns onto a shelf to warm them. On the table I had quarters of a fragrant cantaloupe and we started eating as soon as he came back inside.

"This is really good," he said. "Where'd you find it?"

"I went to the farm. They didn't grow it, but they knew where to find good ones. When I smelled it, I was almost overcome."

"That's the way to do it. Can we get back to this dead man who's turned up alive?"

"That's really all I know at this point. I made an appointment to call him tomorrow afternoon at one our time. But he hasn't seen any of these people for a long time so I don't know what he can tell me."

"He can tell you about when they were kids."

"That's about it. And maybe if he doesn't like these men, he'll be more apt to tell me things they've been keeping to themselves."

"That's the way to do it, find someone who doesn't like them to spill the beans. He may exaggerate a little too, so you've got to be careful."

"I can always talk to one of the others and check up on

what he tells me, but this is so amazing. I've really learned something the others don't know."

"A guy playing dead and living in the open. It'll be interesting to see what he says."

"And after we eat tomorrow night, I'm off to the Reskins'. They're the only couple I haven't met yet, and I've been told he loves to talk."

"Let me check on the burgers." Jack went outside and I cleared the cantaloupe rinds from the table.

I took the potato salad, coleslaw, and pickles out of the refrigerator and put them on the table. I had become something of a regular at Melanie's delicatessen, a cross-cultural jump for me but a very pleasant one. I had to agree with her that the potato salad was the best I'd ever eaten although Jack has occasionally made coleslaw and it's as good as it gets. The sour pickles were a new experience for me. My eyes had watered the first time I'd tried them, but I had persisted and come to like them very much.

Jack came in with the cheeseburgers and rolls, his eyes lighting up when he saw the salads. He's as cross-cultural as they come, having lived in Brooklyn for his entire life and having sampled just about every kind of food you can find in New York. I'm still learning that you don't ask for a corned beef sandwich on white bread if you don't want to be laughed out of the deli.

"What's in the carton?" I asked when we were doctoring up our cheeseburgers with relish and other things Jack finds indispensable.

"You wouldn't believe what I've saved all these years. I have letters thanking me for this and that from people in the precinct, snapshots that I must've just tossed into the locker and forgotten about, a pair of the filthiest sneakers

I've ever seen in my life, and a lot of notes on cases that I can't bring myself to toss."

"You and every detective I've interviewed over the last few years. As far as I'm concerned, it's great that you all keep them. When someone like me comes along, years after a homicide, you've got the information I need right at your fingertips, even if you're long retired."

"You say that now, but when you start stumbling over these cartons, you'll get grouchy. On second thought, you don't get grouchy."

I laughed. I always enjoy Jack's opinion of me, which is usually a much better picture than the truth. "I'll look before I stumble," I promised.

"You know, I'm nervous as hell about this change of jobs."

I knew he meant it because I remembered his problems early on in law school, when he was sure he didn't have what it took to make the grade. I also knew I was likely to be the only person in the world he would confide his fears to. And it always amazed me that a man who carried a gun, who occasionally had to draw it in a dangerous situation, could be nervous about taking on a new job. "You know you'll work into it," I said.

"I know. It's just those first few days, that first week, when the phone rings and somebody has to know something and I have to find it and it has to be right."

"It won't be as hard as the first semester of law school."

"Yeah. I didn't think of that. You're probably right, as usual. Should that make me grouchy?"

"Not tonight. At least you'll be dealing with the living. I have a dead man to talk to tomorrow. This group of sweet, innocent boys from the Bronx has turned into something else."

"Don't they usually? One of them's a killer. Why should you expect them to be telling you the truth?"

Because I expect it of people, I thought. I tell the truth and so should they. "I've worked out a scenario where Fred Beller could have murdered Arthur Wien even after he paid his bill and his wife left the restaurant. I just don't have a motive."

"That means any one of them could have done it."

"There's even a possibility that the dead man, George Fried, could have done it. He and his wife were in a New York hotel on the night of Father's Day."

"I like that."

"But he would have had no way of knowing where the group was meeting. Since he's dead, they don't send him announcements."

"Right. You have to keep remembering that he's dead."

"I'm going to read as much as I can of *The Lost Boulevard* tonight and tomorrow, but as far as I've gone, I don't see anything promising."

"How about Arnold? Have you asked him if he knows the lawyer in the group?"

I looked at my watch. "I haven't, but you're right; that's a good idea. I'll call him before we have our coffee."

"I made a call today, Chris, to a guy I know in the Nineteenth Squad, the one that has jurisdiction and is handling the homicide. The autopsy didn't tell them much they didn't know, but they've interviewed several of the people at the reunion a couple of times. And they talked to everyone who was in the restaurant when the body was found. No one named Beller on the list. And Wien's kids seem to be in the clear. They've got detectives in California asking questions too, but so far nothing's developed out there. But he told me something." He looked troubled.

"This doctor you're working for? Morton Horowitz? They really like Horowitz for the killer."

I felt as though I'd been knocked down. "Can you tell me why?"

"Something about his wife and Arthur Wien."

That left me almost gasping for breath.

"Must be time for Jack to start acting like a lawyer," Arnold said when I greeted him. Arnold has been a defense lawyer for most of his long life. He met Jack not long after I did, and he has been a real mentor to Jack through his law school years.

"It's happening in a couple of days. It's nail-biting time around here."

"He'll do fine. He's as conscientious a man as I've ever met. He'll find it's easier than he thinks it'll be, and he's smarter than most of the people he'll be dealing with. Believe me."

"I'll tell him you said so. I'm actually calling to see if you know someone I've met recently in the noble profession."

"Give me a name."

"David Koch."

"Dave Koch. I know him. Smart guy. Got a good head on his shoulders; thinks right. You can put your trust in him. The difference between Dave Koch and me is that he's rich and I'm not."

"You're rich in spirit, Arnold."

"Doesn't pay the bills. And there's something else."

"What's that?"

"He's a Bronx boy; I'm from Brooklyn. You have to take a lot of guff from him about the Yankees. It's that Bronx arrogance. I know where the best baseball in the world was played."

"Where's that?"

"Ebbets Field, long departed, a pox on Walter O'Malley. What brings you and Dave Koch together, Chris?"

"A friend of his, the writer Arthur Wien, was murdered a week ago yesterday—"

"And you're in on it?"

"Through a student of mine. A doctor friend of Dave Koch is her grandfather and he's asked me to look around for a killer. The police think he may have done it because he found the body."

"Sounds like the way the cops would think. You report finding a body, you have to have killed it." Arnold has never had much of a love affair with the NYPD.

"There are some other things too. I've talked with the doctor and also with the Koches. Mr. Koch drove me up to the Bronx yesterday to show me the old neighborhood where all these men grew up and went to school. They're a group of originally nine boys who still get together for reunions."

"Sounds like my wife's cousins club. I read about the Wien homicide. He was pretty well known, wrote a lot of books."

"Someone put an ice pick in his heart on the evening of Father's Day."

"You check his kids out?"

"The police did. As far as I know, they weren't in the restaurant where the party was. But it's an interesting case. I'll tell you about it next time we get together."

"Can't wait. Your cases are much more interesting than mine. I wish I could tell you more about Dave Koch. We're not what you'd call friends, but he strikes me as an honorable man."

So were they all, I thought, all honorable men.

14

After we'd had our coffee, Jack spent some time going through his carton of treasure and trash and I pulled out my copy of *The Lost Boulevard* and resumed reading. As I began a new chapter, I realized I was approaching the suicide of Fred Beller's mother/father. Even knowing the outcome, I felt my insides tighten up as the boy left school and started for home with his friends. The father in the story was a baker. He awoke early in the morning and left the apartment before anyone else was up. When the son came home from school, it was the father who greeted him, who sat at the kitchen table with him and talked to him. The mother had a job that kept her away till after five.

The boy pressed the buzzer at the side of the door to the apartment and pressed it again when no one answered. He had his own key and he used it to get inside. The boy called and there was no answer. There was the kind of silence that means emptiness and loneliness. The boy felt frightened. His father was always home when he got there. He looked in the kitchen for a note but there was none. He looked in the living room, then walked to his parents' bedroom. My heart tightened with every step he took. The father hung from a thick rope looped through the heavy metal ring attached to the ceiling lighting fixture. The double bed had been moved to the side so that his feet would not reach it.

I wondered how much of the description was true and how much Arthur Wien had made up. Not that it mattered. It was a terrible scene, a terrible episode in the lives of the boys. The family was religious and the funeral was the next afternoon. They were spared an autopsy. Except for the son himself, none of the other boys attended the funeral. Funerals were not for children, their mothers told them, although they were technically all men by this time, having reached their thirteenth birthdays and been bar mitzvahed. But being a man in the eyes of God was one thing; being a man in the eyes of your mother was quite another. Several of the mothers went, however, and even a couple of fathers took time off from work to go. The narrator's father was one of them. That night was one no one would ever forget.

The bereaved family, the boy and his mother and several aunts and uncles who lived in the city, sat shiva for the rest of the week. Each of the boys in the group put on his best suit and went to the apartment with his mother to pay their respects.

It was a turning point in all their lives. This wasn't war; it was peace. This wasn't Germany; it was the Bronx. This wasn't a sick man or an old one; it was a man with his health and with enough of his youth that he could have expected to live for decades. And he was gone.

I had lost my father when I was younger than Fred Beller, and my mother when I was slightly older. Perhaps it was those twin events in my life, those two catastrophes from which I had never completely recovered, that made me feel so deeply for the child in the book. I read on, how the boys were embarrassed when their friend returned to school after the mourning period, how long it took for things to creep back to a kind of normality.

I pressed on in the story. The death weighed heavily on the narrator but life continued. A semester ended, a season changed, a holiday was celebrated. They were getting ready for high school, applying to the special high schools that required high marks and entrance exams, doing things that occupied their time and their thoughts. Even so, death had entered their lives and had affected them. They had changed.

Jack had everything from the carton organized by the time I put the book down. He had thrown out the sneakers and a few other things, but some of the contents that were left surprised me. People in the precinct had written him letters thanking him for his help over the past years. Some were beautifully typed, as though by secretaries, others handwritten on fine paper. Many of them were scrawled in pencil or ballpoint on lined yellow or white paper in marginal English. I picked up several and read them.

"You never told me about these," I said.

"I just chucked them in the locker." He sounded very offhand.

"You have to save these to show your son. You never talk about these letters. You did wonderful things for these people."

"Every cop does, Chris. Every cop has a lockerful of nice letters. There are others, too, you know, the nasty ones. I just toss them."

"Let me put these away somewhere." I started gathering them up, smoothing them. "These are real love letters."

"I guess you could say so. I never thought of them that way."

Real love letters, thanks for getting my father to the hospital in time, thanks for getting the social worker to come and help me, thanks for finding the guy who killed my brother, thanks and thanks again. I wondered, as I made a neat pile of them, what color ribbon would be right to tie them up with.

"I've been avoiding asking you this," I said. We were in bed, and my energy, what was left of it, was fading fast.

"Ask before you fall asleep."

"You said the police think Dr. Horowitz did it because of a relationship between Mrs. Horowitz and Arthur Wien."

"That's what they told me."

"How do they know, Jack?"

"She visited him at his apartment in Manhattan."

"Do you know when?"

"The detective I talked to didn't say. Not recently. But she was there several times."

"How do they know? How do they know it was Mrs. Horowitz?"

"The detective said they showed a bunch of pictures to the doorman. He identified Mrs. Horowitz."

I closed my eyes. Mrs. Koch had said one of the wives. David Koch and Morton Horowitz were best friends. That meant that their wives knew each other well and might well be friends on their own, maybe even confidantes. "Jack, none of these women could have been considered suspects in the murder when it happened. Where do the police get pictures of them?"

"Let me tell you how it works." He pushed his pillow up and sat. "When the detectives arrive at the scene, like the night Arthur Wien was murdered, they've got a group of people who are potential suspects, the people at the party. But you don't get anything out of people if you treat them like suspects so what you do, you tell them they're possible witnesses and you need everything they can remember to help you find the killer. And you treat them very politely. You try to convince them that they are the most important witness and anything they can remember is golden. You say things like, 'It could help to catch your friend's killer.' You divide them up, keep them apart, and talk to them separately. I'm sure they had several detectives over at that restaurant to do the job.

"By the time the detectives are finished, they've figured out a few things about the victim. He's an older guy with a trophy wife; he spreads money around. Chances are good he's a womanizer. Could be he had an affair with one of the women in the group and the husband got wind of it. They find out Wien has an apartment in New York, and they go over and talk to the doorman. New York doormen know everything that goes on in their buildings. The doorman tells them, 'Yeah, Wien had women visit him. Some of them came around a lot.' So they start by getting pictures of the wives of the men, and the best place to get them is Motor Vehicles."

"I see."

"They're not great pictures but if a doorman says, 'Yeah, I think I remember this one,' they're on their way."

"It doesn't fit," I said.

"Why?"

"Mrs. Horowitz is in her sixties."

"You never saw a good-looking woman in her sixties?"

"Sure I have, plenty of them. But Wien liked them young. Look at his wife. She's probably half his age."

"That's who he married. Doesn't mean he didn't have the hots for Mrs. Horowitz."

And Mrs. Koch knew it and spilled the beans. And at the party, Mrs. Horowitz had asked someone to move so she could sit next to Arthur Wien. "Then she could be the killer," I said. "It doesn't have to be her husband. He might not even know. Maybe she's been dying of jealousy since Wien married Cindy Porter."

"Could be. Murder is an equal opportunity business."

"Do you think the Horowitzes know that he's now a suspect because of this?"

"I doubt it. I think the police are being careful, gathering their evidence so it looks good when they make an arrest."

"Do you mind if I talk to her? Mrs. Horowitz?"

"Go ahead. Just so long as you didn't get it from me."

"I didn't," I said, scrunching down in bed. "I got it from someone in the group. I don't like this at all."

"It's murder. What's to like?"

I had a busy and possibly complicated day on Tuesday. I had to be home at one to call George Fried, and I wanted very much to talk to Mrs. Horowitz before the police got to her. That meant I could see her in the morning if I could make the arrangement or I could drive over after Eddie woke up, in which case I'd have to have something for dinner that didn't take a lot of preparation. But that shouldn't be too difficult, I thought, now that grilling season was here. In a pinch, I could do a steak or some fish or pick up some lamb chops. That gave me more flexibility.

I called Mrs. Horowitz's daughter, Lila Stern, a few minutes before nine to make sure I would get her before she left the house. It was Janet who answered, and she got her mother to the phone as soon as I asked.

"Chris?" Lila Stern asked.

"Yes, good morning."

"I've gotten little messages here and there that you've been very busy. Do you have anything?"

"Not much, but I need to talk to someone and I'd like you to arrange it for me."

"Of course."

"I'd like to visit your mother."

"Let me call her and I'll get back to you. What's a good time?"

"This morning or this afternoon about four."

"I'll call you right back."

I wasn't surprised that the return call didn't come for twenty minutes. Mothers and daughters always seem to have a lot to say to each other. I've been at Melanie's when her mother has called, and they seem to have more to say to each other than old friends who have not seen each other for years.

Lila said her mother was home this morning and anytime I came would be fine. I asked if I might bring Eddie with me, and she said she was sure her mother would love it. It was a little unsettling, the prospect of taking my little child to the home of a possible murder suspect, but I didn't really think Mrs. Horowitz had killed Arthur Wien, not that I knew who else had.

Lila offered to come with me, but I told her it would be best if I spoke to her mother alone. The last thing I needed was to confront Mrs. Horowitz with evidence of an old love affair in front of her daughter. Lila gave me very good directions, and Eddie and I started out.

The Horowitzes lived closer to New York than we did,

and it took only about half an hour for me to get to their home. It was a house that had been lived in for a long time. The trees were tall with heavy trunks and leaves that shaded the lawn. Eddie toddled up the walk, pointing to things, and by the time we got to the door, Mrs. Horowitz had opened it.

We spent a little time getting to know each other and getting Eddie situated on the floor of the family room where he could play with the toys I had brought, look out a floor-to-ceiling window, and carry on a conversation with the Horowitzes' dog who was on the patio on the other side of the window watching Eddie with as much interest as Eddie showed for him.

I watched him for a minute and then turned to the unpleasant task at hand. My quick appraisal of Robin Horowitz was that she was no beauty but a fine-looking woman who would not be mistaken for a woman ten or fifteen years younger than her true age.

"This is hard for me," I began.

"I don't understand. I thought you just wanted to hear about Artie Wien and the Morris Avenue Boys."

"I need a little more than that. I have heard something that I want you to explain. I believe you used to visit Mr. Wien at his apartment in New York."

She stared at me. "Can you tell me how you know this?"

"I can't. But I believe it to be true. I'd like you to tell me about it."

"I can't." She had beautiful large eyes which looked directly at me. Her hair had crossed from dark to gray but there was still plenty of dark in it. She had worn glasses when she opened the door, but she had taken them off when we sat down. "It was a private matter."

I didn't want to press her. I looked away, watching

Eddie for a moment. He was sitting on his haunches in that maddening way that little ones have, his knees sticking up, and he was giggling at the dog whose tail was wagging furiously.

"Do you think the police will find out about it?"

"I expect they will."

"You don't think I had an affair with Artie, do you?"

"I don't know what went on between you, but I think it may have some bearing on his murder."

"I don't really know," she said as though she were thinking of it for the first time.

"If you could tell me about it, Mrs. Horowitz."

"I can't. It was something very personal and I cannot break a promise. Are you going to tell the police about this?"

"I will not."

"Thank you."

"Does your husband know about these meetings?"

"No!" she said, raising her voice. Eddie turned and looked at her, and she smiled and said, "I didn't mean you, honey. You're doing just fine."

The dog barked to regain Eddie's attention and the love affair resumed.

"This is just terrible," she said. "I can't believe this is coming back to haunt me this way."

"You know how this looks, don't you, when a woman goes to meet a man at his apartment several times?"

"You think Artie and I were having an affair?"

"It certainly looks that way."

"Well, if people want to misinterpret events, there's nothing I can do about it."

"Please think about the consequences," I said. I didn't

want to go into detail. It was easy enough for her to think the situation through without my assistance.

She looked at me as if the word *consequences* had just sunk in. "They're going to think Mort killed Artie because I was having an affair with him, is that it?"

"It's a possibility."

"How can this have happened?" She said it to herself.

"Would you tell me something honestly, Mrs. Horowitz? Did you have an intimate relationship with Mr. Wien?"

"I did not."

"I was told that one of the wives of the Morris Avenue Boys did have an affair with him."

"Well it wasn't me, and I couldn't guess who it might have been. Artie was an attractive man, especially when he was younger and thinner. He had plenty of girls interested in him, always. And he encouraged it. But I wasn't one of them, and I'm not going to break my word and tell you why I met with him to prove it."

"I also heard that you insisted on sitting next to Mr. Wien at the reunion dinner."

She looked almost confused. "I did sit next to him. There was a vacant chair and I took it."

It wasn't the way Arlene Kaplan had described it. "Thank you." I stood and looked over at Eddie. He was bouncing from his squatting position, laughing, steaming up the glass where his nose pressed against it, marking it with his hands. On the other side, the dog was trying to lick him through the glass. All in all, the window was a mess.

I took a diaper out of my carryall and went over to fix things up.

"Don't bother to do that," Robin Horowitz said. "It'll

take care of itself." She went over to Eddie. "Would you like to touch the dog, Eddie?"

He stood and smiled at her. She opened the glass door and the dog bounded in. He didn't need to be invited to nuzzle Eddie, who laughed gleefully.

"She's an old dog," Mrs. Horowitz said, "and she's wonderful with children. Just watch she doesn't knock Eddie over in her enthusiasm."

It was good advice. I let them play for a couple of minutes, then told Eddie it was time to go. He knew how to say no and he said it with feeling. When I finally got down and picked him up, he cried bitterly and kicked. To make matters worse, the dog barked at me. I felt I had made everyone in that room unhappy, including myself.

"He'll get over it," Mrs. Horowitz said comfortingly.

"The trouble is, I won't. I never dreamed anything like this would happen. I feel as if everyone's life has been ripped apart. And I don't know who can sew it back together again."

We walked through the house to the front door and she came outside with me. "What did you know about George Fried?" I asked, largely to change the subject to something less inflammatory.

"Oh George," she said dismissively. "He was a bore. He died years ago. I never blamed Iris for leaving him."

"Iris?"

"His first wife. She was a fool but she came to her senses finally."

I put Eddie down on the walk. His tears had stopped, but they remained in streaks on his face, reminding me of how I had deprived him. He walked toward the car, pointing at it. When I got the back door open, I picked him up and put him in the car seat.

"You come visit me again, Eddie," Mrs. Horowitz said. "You can play with the dog, OK?" She reached in and gave him a loving pat. When I had closed the door she said, "I didn't have an affair with Arthur Wien," and she turned and strode back to the house.

15

We got home in plenty of time for Eddie's lunch, my lunch, and a short breather before I had to call George Fried. I was very troubled about my conversation with Robin Horowitz. She seemed as believable as all the rest of them, but it was obvious that she was hiding something that could bring her or someone else great embarrassment. It might also result in the arrest of her husband.

I knew exactly what Jack would say if I told him she had denied having an affair with Arthur Wien: What else could she say? And it was true. Whatever had taken her to his apartment was very private and sensitive enough that it was still a secret from her husband. It would come out, I knew, as soon as the police decided to move in and arrest him for the murder. It made me feel that I had to get to the bottom of this before that happened, assuming the doctor was innocent.

Eddie was fast asleep when I finally dialed the California number and heard George Fried pick up on the first ring. He had been waiting for my call.

"So what can I tell you?" he said when the formalities were over. "You know I haven't been involved with the boys for a long time, and unless you've told them, they think I'm dead, which is how I'd like them to think of me."

"Why is that, Mr. Fried?"

"They're a boring group of people. I just don't want to spend three hours asking them what they've been doing since the last time I saw them. I don't care what they've been doing, and I don't think they give much of a damn what I've been doing. And the last thing I want is people dropping in on me and telling me stories about guys I haven't seen in twenty years."

"But telling people you're dead, it seems so extreme."

"OK, you're right. I got a bug in my head and did something crazy, but it's done. Let's leave it."

I agreed. "What can you tell me about Fred Beller?"

"Freddy had a tough childhood. He had a mother who was depressed and eventually took her life. Then he met a girl he really cared about, and Artie Wien batted his eyelashes at her and she left Freddy for Artie. It wasn't a pretty situation. Besides, who would live in New York if he had a choice?"

"Not you, I guess."

"Not me and not Freddy. Not Artie either, from what I hear. He bought himself a house in California."

"He kept an apartment in New York too."

"Well, what do you expect? He's a big shot author. He's got to play the intellectual scene; gives him points with important people or so he thinks."

"Mr. Fried, do you know that Arthur Wien is dead?"

"To tell you the truth, I didn't know till yesterday. His obituary didn't make the local paper. My wife picked up a magazine and saw a notice."

"Did he ever ask you to lend him money or do favors for him?"

"He could have." He said it as though he attached no importance whatever to it. "It couldn't have been much because I didn't have much in those days. Why? Is his estate paying back his debts?"

"I don't know about that."

"I'll put in a claim for two dollars, how's that?"

"That's pretty reasonable. What I'm interested in is the relationships of the men to each other, of their wives, that kind of thing."

"You a detective?"

"An amateur with experience. I'm looking for a motive."

"OK, Chris. That's your name, right?"

"Yes, I'm Chris Bennett."

"I'm off to Chicago this afternoon on business. On Thursday I'm flying to Newark Airport. I've got business in a town in Jersey. You want to meet me at Newark Airport for an hour and we'll talk? I'll try to think up all the dirt I know on the flight."

"That would be great—sitting down with you."

He gave me his flight number, and we agreed to meet at the baggage carousel at noon on Thursday. He began to describe himself, but I told him I would make a sign with his name on it, as if I were a taxi driver picking up an incoming passenger. He laughed and said that was a good idea. When I got off the phone, I went looking for Jack's shirt cardboards.

That left me with a free day tomorrow after having spoken to everyone in the group and most of the wives. I called Alice Wien and asked if I might come into New York in the morning and spend as much of the day as I needed to look through the original handwritten manuscript and the typewritten copy that she made from the original.

She said that would be fine, and she would be ready for me at nine-thirty or nine forty-five although I didn't think I'd make it till ten. I decided I would ask her to send out for lunch for both of us, my treat, so I could get as much work done as possible before leaving for home. I checked with Elsie, and she said she'd take Eddie both Wednesday and enough of Thursday so that I could meet George Fried at the airport and have an hour's conversation with him.

Then I sat for a while and thought about my next call. Ellen Koch was the only person who had indicated there might be an affair between Arthur Wien and one of the wives. I was sure she and Robin Horowitz knew each other well. Their husbands were best friends and the couples would surely spend much time together. If Robin Horowitz had confided in Ellen Koch, would Ellen tell me? I didn't think so, but if she saw that I had figured it out, maybe she would add something that might be useful.

"Chris," she said when I identified myself, "are you getting any closer?"

"I've learned a lot but I don't know if I'm closer. I wanted to ask you about that tantalizing nugget you tossed out on Saturday."

"What was that?"

"That one of the wives of the Morris Avenue Boys had had an affair with Arthur Wien."

"Oh yes, that."

"I have reason to believe that Robin Horowitz is the person you were referring to."

"Robin?" She spoke the name as a simple question, with no surprise or shock, no anger, no derisive humor.

"Yes."

"What can I say? I told you I didn't know who it was."

"Would you be likely to know if it was Mrs. Horowitz?"

"Only if she told me, and she hasn't."

"Do you think it's a possibility?"

"I don't know what to say. Anything is possible but I don't think that's probable. Robin and Mort are a happy couple, they have a nice family, they live enjoyable and satisfying lives. I can't think why Robin would have an affair with anyone."

"Can you think of any reason why she would visit him by herself and keep the visits a secret?"

"None."

"I'd appreciate it if you wouldn't mention to her or to anyone else that I asked you these questions."

"They didn't lead anywhere," she said. "I have no reason to mention them."

"Chris," Melanie Gross called as I pushed the stroller by her driveway. "You going anywhere?"

"Just going," I called back. I leaned over to Eddie and said, "Look, there's your friend Mel."

He returned her smile and wave and said something which I recognized as his version of Mel but which I could not reproduce myself.

"Let's walk." She came to the curb. "We never do our morning thing any more and my muscles miss it."

"So do I. Where are your kids?"

"Doing after-school things. I'm a free woman for the next hour and I really feel the need of a walk. And I want to hear about the case."

I started by telling her that the dead man was alive.

"Chris, how do you find these things out? That's incredible."

"I just called the number, he answered, and he owned up to who he was."

"Why haven't the others in the group found out?"

"Because they've never called his number. He thought they were pretty boring, and I gather they thought the same of him. Why would they call his widow, who was his second wife and no one knew her very well if at all? What would there be to talk about?"

"I see. So he lives out in the open and no one sees him."

"That's the way it looks to me." I brought her up to date and then said, "Tomorrow I'm going through the pencil manuscript of *The Lost Boulevard*."

"Pencil, gee. Do they still make pencils?" Mel laughed.

"I guess they did in the fifties."

"What do you expect to find?"

"I don't know. Maybe a line that didn't get printed that says something telling about someone."

"Chris, that'll take you days, weeks."

"Well, I'll start by glancing at every page. Something may leap out at me. There should be things he crossed out, things that never got in the final manuscript. Maybe those were sensitive things that it would be in bad taste to publish."

"You really have quite a job cut out for you." We turned a corner and kept moving. "I hope it all comes together."

"They all know things they're withholding, Mel. I talked to a woman this morning who visited Arthur Wien at his apartment several times a couple of years ago, and she denies they had an affair but won't say what the visits were about. She said she gave her word to keep it secret."

"So there really have been things going on."

"Oh yes. And Wien borrowed money that he didn't return. One lender insisted on having the manuscript as collateral."

"So they knew his reputation."

"But they all say nice things about him anyway," I said. "They stick up for each other."

"Sounds like one guy didn't."

"But which one? Come, let's give Eddie a run for his money."

16

Jack is, of course, the best baby-sitter I have, except for the first time I left him with Eddie, when Eddie was very young and Jack very inexperienced, even more inexperienced than I. Now I rely on him completely. Although he doesn't get to see Eddie in the evenings as we are a morning family, rising early, he sees him every day from getting out of bed till leaving for work, a couple of good hours. That will change in the next few days when Jack's schedule changes with his new assignment, but I know their relationship will not suffer.

Anyway, I dashed out of the house for my evening meeting with Bernie and Marilyn Reskin as soon as we had finished dinner. These were the last people on my list, and I had been told that they were gossipers so there was still hope I could get something new and useful out of them.

Marilyn Reskin opened the door and greeted me with great enthusiasm. She was a small woman wearing a colorful cotton skirt, a short-sleeved shirt, and sandals, comfortable clothes that were far from showy. Her husband appeared as we were walking toward the back of the house, and he greeted me just as warmly. He then introduced me to a tall young man who was apparently a student and who was now leaving.

"I hope we've got him straightened out," he said when he joined us on the enclosed porch where we had seated ourselves. "That boy is right on the line. If he tips the right way, the world is his."

"This is Bernie's life," his wife said and I could feel pride emanate from her.

"I hope you're successful," I said. "It must be very hard for you when the scales tip the other way."

"Harder than you can imagine. I've visited boys at Riker's Island. I don't recommend that to anyone."

Having made one visit to Riker's myself to see an inmate, I could only agree with him. "I'm afraid I'm here to talk about something that's also quite painful."

"Artie's death, I know. Morty said you were working on it, and I know he's worried because the police think he could have done it."

"Why would they think that?" I asked as unassumingly as I could.

"He found Artie. They figure he killed him, then walked out and told us he'd found a body. Morty couldn't kill anything. He's a healer in the truest sense of the word."

"Someone killed him," I said.

"Sure, someone killed him. Maybe someone in the restaurant walked into the men's room while Artie was there, and they got in a fight."

"And the other person just happened to have an ice pick in his pocket?"

His wife leaned forward. "Bernie and I have been through this a hundred times. These men are friends, many of them since kindergarten. Why would one of them kill Artie?"

"You tell me."

"How far back do you want to go?" Bernie asked.

"That's an interesting question."

"Well, everybody knows that Artie took Freddy Beller's sweetheart away from him. That was over forty years ago, and Fred is married to a wonderful woman and lives in Minnesota. You think that's too far back?"

"I don't think it's too far back. I think it's not a motive."

"OK, that sounds reasonable."

"Do you think Fred Beller could have resented the use of his mother's suicide in *The Lost Boulevard*?"

"I can't see that," Bernie said. "First of all, Artie made it a father, not a mother. And he was very sensitive in how he portrayed it. I thought he did a great job with that book."

"And Fred Beller hasn't been in New York in years," his wife added.

"Even so," I said. It had occurred to me that since Fred had married happily, he might be considered off the hook for the murder if it ever came to light that he had been in New York that weekend. But he might have had another motive, one the police might not be aware of. "For the sake of argument, let's consider Fred Beller among the group of suspects."

"Which includes me," Bernie said.

"And everyone else at the dinner."

"OK, so Fred's a suspect even if he was a thousand miles away."

"Did you know that he and Arthur Wien were supposed to get together in Minneapolis once and something happened and it didn't work out?"

"It doesn't surprise me," Bernie said. "Artie was a friendly guy and he did a lot of traveling, you know, promoting his books. If a get-together didn't jell, well, some of them don't. Who told you about this? Cindy?"

"I found out another way. Let me ask you about the most mysterious member of the Morris Avenue Boys, George Fried."

"George? George is dead."

"I know that." But I knew, too, that being dead meant no one would ever mention his name as a suspect. Being dead seemed to me like the best cover a killer could have. "I just want to know more about him."

"He's a little guy who turned out to be a big guy," Bernie said. I knew he was referring to the old photo in which George was in the front row and Bernie in the back. "I'm a big guy who turned into a little guy."

"Did you like him?"

"We liked everybody. We were a great bunch of kids. We all had a mission. We wanted to grow up and be somebody, do something. And thank God, we all did."

"Who did the best?" I asked, knowing it was an unfair question.

"Bernie and Ernie," Marilyn said quickly. "Bernie helps kids become good people, and Ernie helps people live when their bodies want them to die."

"I would pick Artie and Joe," Bernie said, "a writer and a musician. Think of how many lives they affect. Artie's books sold in the millions, I heard, and when Joe played before an audience, thousands of people heard him. When you add radio and television, my God, it's millions."

"What did George Fried do?"

"He was in business, made toys, I think. His son probably runs the company now."

"Bruce Kaplan is also a businessman," I said.

"Bruce Kaplan is a very sad story," Bernie said, "a very,

very sad story. He went to jail for doing something that's not so different from what the kids I work with try to do. It's called stealing."

If he had been trying to shock me, he succeeded. All the other members of the group had ridiculed the possibility that Bruce had done what he had served time for. This man's view was the exact opposite: Bruce was guilty as charged. "I was led to believe he had taken the rap, so to speak, for someone else."

"You can believe that," Bernie said. "I think a lot of people believe that. The story is that his father-in-law stole the money and Bruce accepted responsibility. I don't think that's true. His father-in-law wasn't even going into the office in those days. Bruce did it. Why don't you ask him?"

"Because it must be very embarrassing to talk about. And if he's covering for someone, I don't expect he'd tell me that that person did it. So what I'd hear is that he did it. If he even agreed to talk about it."

"That doesn't make him a killer, you know," Bernie said.

"I know. I'm still looking for a motive. Did Arthur Wien ever borrow money from you?"

Marilyn laughed. "I have to hold Bernie back from giving money to stray dogs and cats. I don't let him out of the house with more than he needs to get home. How could he lend money to anyone?"

"I was told Mr. Wien borrowed from his friends."

"Could be," Bernie said. "But it wasn't from me."

"Or me," his wife added.

"I heard something else," I said, deciding at that moment to talk about it. "I heard one person who lent him money kept the manuscript of *The Lost Boulevard* as collateral."

Bernie smiled and looked at his wife.

"Sounds like a shrewd lender," she said.

"Must have been some sum of money," he said.

"Was it either of you?"

They both spoke at once, denying it.

"Who might have done something like that?" I asked.

"Got me," Bernie said. "But I love it."

"What I was thinking was that perhaps Bruce Kaplan took money from his business to lend to Arthur Wien."

"That's ridiculous," Bernie said. "Bruce isn't a soft touch, not for a lot of money. There'd have to be one hell of a reason that Artie needed a lot of money for Bruce to do something like that. And I don't believe it happened."

It was, of course, possible that Alice Wien had made the whole story up. "Why did you pick Father's Day as the time for the reunion?"

"Because there wasn't another weekend on the calendar," Marilyn said. "You would not believe the phone calls that went back and forth till we got that date. Nobody wanted Father's Day. But someone had a wedding the weekend before, someone else had a wedding the weekend after, there was a graduation, a convention. You wouldn't believe what we had to contend with."

"Who arranged the dinner?" I asked.

"We did, Bernie and I. No one ever wants to do it so we do it."

"Then you must stay in touch with everyone."

"We do," she said. "We keep it all together."

"Then you probably know more than anyone else the state of Joe Meyer's health."

"Terrible," they said, almost in unison.

"For a wonderful guy, a guy who never hurt anyone in his life, a guy who only made the world a better, happier place, it's a terrible way to go," Bernie said.

"Not to mention what happened to their daughter," Marilyn said.

I looked at her.

"She cracked up her car, and her body. What it did to Joey and Judy, you can't imagine." She took a deep breath and looked down at her lap. A tear dropped on her hand. It was as if she were talking about her own child.

"How did it happen?" I asked

She swiped her fingers across her cheeks. "She was in her car, somewhere here in the New York area. I don't really know the details because they never said and I couldn't ask, but there were a lot of broken bones and I don't know if she'll ever play again. You have no idea how talented she was."

"They showed me a picture of her bowing onstage, holding a bouquet of roses."

"At least they have the memories."

"They never said there'd been an accident," I said.

"How can you talk about that kind of thing? It breaks your heart. I don't know how Joe survived it."

"They're tough people," Bernie said. "We're all tough people. No one's life is easy. What about yours, Chris? Do you have an easy life?"

"I do now," I admitted. "I'm very lucky. But when I was fifteen, things were very different."

Bernie smiled. "I'm glad things are better for you. Are we telling you anything that's going to help? I have a feeling we haven't."

"Actually, you've told me a few things I didn't know. Now I'm going to ask you a hard one. I heard that Arthur

Wien had an affair with the wife of one of the men in the group."

They looked at each other as though each wanted the other to come up with a name. Then Bernie started to laugh. "Artie and one of the wives?"

"That's right. The question is, which one?"

"I don't know. That's crazy. Was it you, Marilyn? I remember once you came home late from a meeting. Were you having a fling with Artie Wien?"

"God forbid." She looked at me. "I never heard of such a thing. Who told you this?"

"I'd rather not say. I thought you might have heard a rumor."

"I wish I had," Bernie said. "Artie and one of the wives. I'd sell what's left of my soul to find out who."

"If it happened," Marilyn said. "If it happened."

Which was the way I was starting to think. "I guess you can't help me there. Do you know if any of the wives might have been a kind of confidante of Mr. Wien? Someone he'd talk to if he had a problem?"

She pursed her lips, he shrugged.

"The only two people connected with the group that I haven't met yet are Cindy Wien and Dr. Greene's wife. What can you tell me about them?"

"Cindy's very sweet," Marilyn said. "She's smart. She's pretty, but that goes without saying. Artie wouldn't spend time with someone who wasn't. She dresses beautifully and she has the right figure to show it off."

"Any reason she might want her husband dead?"

"None that I know. I'm sure she was sitting at the table when Morty found the body."

"Are you sure of anyone else?"

She shook her head. "There was a lot of moving around.

If I was looking to my right and someone on my left left the room for five minutes, I wouldn't know it."

"What about Mrs. Greene?"

"Mrs. Greene is also Dr. Greene," Marilyn said. "She's a psychiatrist, been practicing as long as we've known her. She's a quiet, intelligent woman, raised three nice kids. It's a great marriage. You're too young to remember, but there was a time when doctors married nurses. Nowadays I'm happy to say, doctors marry doctors. Ernie and Kathy were ahead of their time by about thirty years. I've always admired him for that."

"I wonder if Arthur Wien ever saw her as a patient?" I suggested.

"I doubt it," Bernie said. "Artie often said he wouldn't trust his head to a shrink. Thought it would ruin him as a writer."

"When the dinner started, did someone make a fuss about where they were sitting?"

"Robin did," Marilyn said right away. "An uncharacteristic fuss. She *had* to sit next to Artie. She moved from wherever she had been and sat next to him."

"Where had she been?" I asked.

Marilyn shrugged. "The other side of the table, I think. Maybe next to the Koches. But I'm not sure."

"How often are these reunions?"

"Every so many years when we can schedule one. The last one must have been three years ago at least."

"Then I guess that's it." I thanked them and they said they'd call if they thought of anything that might pinpoint the killer, but it was clear they were just saying what they thought I wanted to hear.

I drove home to read *The Lost Boulevard*.

17

Alice Wien opened the door for me with a smile. I had arrived before ten that Wednesday morning and parked my car in a garage a few blocks away so I would not have to run out periodically and feed a meter. She offered me coffee but I refused. I just wanted to get to work.

It was an apartment in an old building, one with a foyer big enough to double as a dining area. Alice had pushed aside the centerpiece that decorated the table, a large, heavy cut-crystal vase filled with dried flowers, giving me a work area as far as I could reach. In that space lay two open boxes, each filled to the top with paper. The one on the left had a plastic-covered sheet of lined paper on top with some handwriting in smudged pencil. The other box had a typed sheet that read *The Lost Boulevard* with the name Arthur A. Wien centered two lines beneath it.

"There's no title page on the original," I said.

"Art didn't think it was necessary. We both knew what the title was and no one but us would ever read it. I've covered the acknowledgment page to keep it from smudging and tearing."

I lifted about half the manuscript carefully out of the box and set it where I could reach it easily. Then I did the same with the typewritten copy. "And there's no dedication," I said, finding the first page of chapter one directly below the acknowledgments.

"I have it framed," she said. "Do you want to see it?"

"That's OK. Maybe later," I added, not wanting to hurt her feelings.

"It was very important to me, that he wrote it in his own hand. I wanted to preserve it."

I was touched by her memory of love. "I understand," I said. "I think I'll get started."

"Let me just show you. On the handwritten manuscript, if Art wanted something deleted, he just crossed it out, like here." She flipped to a page where the entire page had a huge *X* across it and the word *OMIT* scrawled across the top. "Sometimes he inserted a paragraph or more, and he marked the place where it belonged and then used a fresh piece of paper to write the insert itself. Those are usually held together with a paper clip." She looked at the top of the stack, found a paper clip, and showed me.

"The typewritten copy is a lot thicker than the original because wherever the editor made changes, I retyped the page. We saved the original with the editorial corrections. They're all at the back in order. Also, where the editor cut a few pages or a chapter, we saved what was cut with the edited sheets. So if it's in the original and not in the typed copy, it's because the editor removed it.

"And one thing more. You see these blue pencil marks? That's from the copy editor. Mostly that's punctuation and that kind of thing."

"OK, I think I can find my way now. I've brought my copy of *The Lost Boulevard* with me. I haven't finished reading it yet but I'm on my way."

"That should be exactly the same as the typewritten copy with all the copyediting."

I went to work, aware that Alice Wien was standing nearby, not quite looking over my shoulder. Finally, she walked quietly away and then I heard soft music from another room.

The book felt like an old friend. It was only days since I had read the beginning, hours since I had read the middle. I have to admit I was fascinated with the changes Wien made, substituting one word for another, in many cases replacing what I thought of as a perfect word with one that seemed no better. I didn't want to get caught up in this aspect of the work; I wanted to find a clue to Wien's murderer, but as I progressed, it seemed less and less likely that I would. True, there were wholesale omissions, three and four pages at a time crossed out with the huge *X* that he drew freehand, but on looking through them, I had to agree they added nothing to the book and slowed down the action.

I went through about a hundred handwritten pages, comparing them quickly to the typescript to my right, flipping pencil to the left and type to the right. There was nothing extraordinary, nothing suspicious, no red flags or flashing lights. I stopped and put my head in my hands, closing my eyes. It isn't easy reading penciled words and I felt drained. I was about to go back to work when Alice appeared from the living room.

"You look exhausted."

"I am."

"I've just put some coffee on. I picked up some Danish this morning before you came. Can I entice you?"

"Absolutely. It sounds like just what I need. But I'll work till it's ready."

I went back, turning this page, then that—junior high

school, admissions test for high school, the Yankees, the D train, the Grand Concourse.

Alice called and I joined her in the kitchen. Propped on the chair across from mine was a picture frame with a sheet of unlined paper behind the glass. I leaned over and read the dedication, in Wien's scrawl, signed "Art." "That's very nice," I said. "It's a happy memory."

"It is," she said, pouring the coffee. "You know, when you start a book, you don't begin with the dedication and the acknowledgments or even the title. You may not know what the title is at the beginning; you may not know to whom it's dedicated. You have no idea at that point who the people are who will give you information. That comes later. You just put a one at the top of a sheet of paper and start writing: 'Once upon a time there were nine boys who lived on Morris Avenue in the Bronx.' "

I knew she was speaking metaphorically about the first sentence but I got the idea. "But he always knew this book was for you."

"Not really. For all the years that he wrote it, I thought he'd dedicate it to the Morris Avenue Boys. When he wrote that," she pointed to the picture frame, "I was completely overcome."

We sipped our coffee and nibbled our Danish, which was very good. After a minute she said, "Have you found anything yet?"

"Nothing. Every section that he crossed out seems genuinely irrelevant. And the tightening up improves the book."

"He was a careful writer. And I followed his directions to a T."

"I guess what I was hoping was that there would be a

section that referred to an event, to a person, to a grudge, something that he decided not to publish."

"If there is such a thing, you'll find it. It's either crossed out in the pencil copy or removed to the back of the typed copy."

I finished my Danish and sipped the rest of my coffee. "I'm looking at every deletion, no matter how small." I glanced at my watch. "Time to go back to work."

> *Ma, you know that building on the concourse you always said was so nice looking? They've got an apartment for rent. I'll go over and look at it with you.*
> *Talk to your father.*
> *He'll say no. He always says no.*
> *Then let it be.*

That was the way it always was. Whenever the narrator talked to his mother about moving, she found an excuse to say no. I never got the impression that where they lived was anything less than acceptable, only that he wanted to ascend the social ladder, taking his parents with him, and the first step was moving to the Concourse.

I thought a moment, then pushed aside the original manuscript and drew the typescript closer. I removed the section that was still in the box and found the place where the book ended and the pages with changes and deletions began. Then I began to work my way through them. I was aware that I was looking at pages that had been created before the advent of Wite-Out and other liquid deleters, that back in the fifties, if you made an error typing, you erased it as well as you could and typed over or you did the page over from scratch. These were small technological developments, to be sure, but the time saved was enormous.

And now, with computers and word processors, all these changes could be made in the blink of an eye.

I went through page after page with small and large deletions and corrections, none of them particularly interesting from my point of view. When I reached the last of these pages, I looked at my watch and saw that it was lunchtime. I got up and found Alice.

She seemed pleased that I offered to treat us to lunch and made a few suggestions. I picked the one I thought was most elegant, rejecting Chinese food and pizza as too mundane and, frankly, too cheap. She went to the phone and called in our order. In the half hour it took to be delivered, I returned to my work, thinking that I didn't have all that much time left, that I had to hurry if I was going to accomplish my mission in one day.

We took our lunch break, eating quite a good meal that Alice insisted on putting out on pretty dishes. I found I liked her and I listened to her stories about her children and grandchildren with interest. All her children had been out of the New York area at the time of the murder; she knew this because she had spoken to each of them on the phone that Sunday evening as she usually did. So much for my theory that Father's Day had been picked by one or more of Wien's children as a payback. I knew Alice's phone number and could have her bill checked, with the help of my husband, if need be.

Finally, just before I went back to work, I said, "I have to ask you this. Where were you on the evening of Father's Day?"

"Right here," she said.

"With anyone?"

"No." She thought a moment. "I talked to my children that night. I may have called my sister too. I didn't kill Art.

I didn't know where the party was until the next day, and I told you, the anger is gone. I'm my own person."

I went back to turning pages, reading less and less, just looking at deletions, notes in the margins. It was really a huge manuscript, a long book, too much to do in one day. I knew I would have to come back, finish it another day. It was hard knowing there was a little boy who would wake up in Elsie's house before I got back.

Page after page. Two o'clock and counting. I was now further along in the manuscript than in the published book I had been reading. The narrator was in college; the boys were on various campuses, although most of them were in the city or the New York area.

I came to the place where the narrator met the woman I guessed was the fictional Alice. I could see that he came close to describing their sexual relationship or at least alluding to its existence but avoided it tastefully. It struck me as a bit odd that he did. The book was published long enough ago that such descriptions were much rarer than they are today and might have encouraged sales. Then I remembered Alice had mentioned when we spoke on Monday that she had prevailed on him not to be explicit for the sake of her relationship with her parents.

I looked at my watch. I would have to leave soon, even if I hadn't reached the end. There were at least a hundred pages to go in the pencil copy and words were starting to blur before my eyes.

I turned a page and something peripheral made me stop. I looked up at the top of the page where the number 418 was written. I flipped back to the previous page. 413. I closed my eyes, opened them and looked again. Four handwritten pages were missing.

I got up and found Alice. "Would you look at something?" I said.

"You look demolished."

"I feel that way."

We went back to the dining room table. "Look at this," I said.

"That's funny." She paged forward, looking for the missing sheets. "I don't understand."

"Could he have thrown them away?" I asked.

"I guess it's possible." She didn't sound convinced. "But then why didn't he renumber? I mean, if he read it over and thought it was terrible and threw it away, he could have crossed out these numbers," she pointed to 418 and 419, "and changed them. Or just erased them. It was pencil, after all." She looked bewildered.

"You don't remember typing these pages and finding missing numbers?"

"It's so long ago. I need a minute to think."

I opened the paperback that lay near my left hand, found the chapter we were looking at, and located the place that concerned us. The text went smoothly from the material on page 413 to that on page 418 but included paragraphs that must have come from the missing pages. It looked to me as though he had removed the four missing pages from the pencil copy after the manuscript had been typed.

I reached for the typescript and located the chapter, turned pages until I found the equivalent of 413 in the pencil copy. Four pages were missing here too but in a different way. At the top of page 451 in the typescript—the typed copy was about ten percent longer than the original—someone had drawn a dash and then written 454. Four pages had been removed and a blank sheet had been used, most probably to retype part of page 452 and part of page

455, to make a smooth transition to cover up what had been left out. I handed the page marked 451–454, page 455, and page 456 to Alice.

"Well, let's see what was omitted," she said, reaching for the material at the back of the typescript while I stood by. She flipped through the pages quickly and I noticed she went beyond the pages numbered in the four hundreds. "It's not here."

"Let's think about this. It's clear from the numbering that the pages missing in the original were typed before the pencil copy was thrown away. Am I right?"

She nodded. "Right." She seemed dazed. "It had to be typed."

"It looks to me as though Mr. Wien made a decision after the book was typed to eliminate something, some event, some character. He threw away the pencil pages and doctored up the typed pages so that it reads smoothly without whatever had been there."

"And threw those pages away too," Alice said.

"Why would he do that?"

She moved her shoulders, her hands. "I don't know. He never said anything to me. If his editor told him to get rid of it, why aren't the deleted pages in the back of the manuscript with all the others? And why would he go back to the original and pull those pages too? No one was ever going to see them."

She had asked every question that I had wanted to ask, and if she didn't have the answers, how could I? "He didn't want to leave a trace of whatever he pulled. Maybe he thought he'd offend someone or make someone mad."

"Or get sued. But I don't think he really worried about that too much."

"Let me go quickly through the rest of the pencil copy

and see if there are any more missing pages. This mysterious character or event may have been mentioned again
later."

"I'll do the same with the typed copy," she said. She
pulled out the chair next to mine and sat down. Then we
both began turning pages, looking only at the numbers at
the top.

"Here's one," I said. "Two. Pages 445 and 446."

"They're missing here too, at least I assume they're the
same pages. The numbers in this copy are larger."

We laid our pages on the table and inspected them. They
corresponded almost exactly. And once again, in the typed
copy a single page represented two pages and had only
a couple of paragraphs on it.

We kept going and found one more missing page in both
copies.

"I am just stunned," Alice said.

We had finished our quick run-through of the manuscripts. My head was probably spinning as much as
Alice's but with different questions. "Did you type these
pages that bridge the gaps?" I asked.

She looked at them carefully and I could see her head
shaking as her finger moved down the page. "Not me," she
said. "Not any typist with experience. Look at all these
strikeovers, look at the erasures. This is a hunt-and-peck
person doing his best, which isn't very good. I wouldn't be
surprised if Art typed these pages himself."

"Which means that after you prepared the final manuscript, he removed the missing pages and retyped the inserted pages himself to get rid of something he didn't want
published."

"Something I must have read," she said. "I read the
whole pencil manuscript. If there had been any omissions

or gaps, I would have seen them. And he didn't want me to know he was doing it."

"And nothing struck you as harmful or libelous or just plain discourteous to someone in the group?"

"I have to think about it." She got up and walked away from the table. "My original is ruined now, isn't it?"

I realized this meant more to her than a missing episode or maligned character. It meant her prized possession had lost some of its value. "Maybe a little," I said, hoping to diminish the hurt.

"I can't believe this has happened."

"Alice, something in those pages may give us a clue to the person who killed Arthur."

"How is that possible? This was written forty years ago. We've all lived two-thirds of our lives since then."

"I'd like you to try hard to remember what was in those pages."

"It's impossible. I can't do it."

"You don't have to do it now." I stood. The time for me to leave was right now. Alice needed to be alone, needed to calm herself and restore her self-confidence. "Just think about it. No one knows that book the way you do. You lived and breathed it. You told me yourself you were able to quote pages of it at a time."

"Yes."

"Maybe you can read over these last hundred pages or so and the missing incident will come back to you."

"Maybe, yes." She pulled another chair from the table, the chair at the head, and sat down. "I'm sorry, Chris. This is so upsetting for so many reasons. You've been very nice and I know what you're doing is important. I can't explain how I feel. It's as if Art cheated me and I've just found out about it."

"He didn't cheat you. I think before the book was submitted he called the person that he wrote about and said, 'Do you mind if I put in that time that you did so-and-so?' And the man said, 'Don't you dare.' That's what happened. And for whatever reason, he didn't tell you."

"He didn't want me to know. That's why he didn't tell me." She was half angry and half hurt.

"Did you ever read the book after it was published?"

"No. The last time I read it was when I went over the galleys with Art. He read them first and I read them afterward. I was a better proofreader then he was, and I picked up typos he had missed."

"And you didn't notice these missing passages."

"The editor had taken a lot of things out. Whatever this was, it was just one of those things to me, something that slowed the story down or wasn't relevant."

"I'm going to go now." I started to put the pencil manuscript together when she stopped me.

"Leave it. I'll read at the table tonight. I'll do it."

"You're the only one who can," I said. "No one but you and Arthur read those missing pages. You're the only person alive who knows what was in them."

"Except whoever he wrote about," she said. "Did you think of that?"

I had, and I wanted to find out who he or she was.

18

Jack came home with another carton, this one containing the last of the things he wanted to preserve. The blue-covered notebooks that he kept as a detective would be returned to his lieutenant on his last day. They were the property of NYPD and would be retained virtually forever. If any questions arose at some future time about a case that Jack had handled, they could not only read the D.D. 5s in the file but also look at his original notes, the source material that he had used to type the 5s. Even closed cases were occasionally reopened and the detectives who had worked on them called back to testify.

While he was sorting through his things, I called one after the other of the Morris Avenue Boys. I asked each of them if Arthur Wien had written something in *The Lost Boulevard* which they preferred not be published and which he had deleted from the final manuscript.

To a man they seemed confused. Not one of them, and I managed to reach all of them except Fred Beller and George Fried, would admit that he knew what I was asking about. I didn't call Fred because I decided I'd made enough calls for one night, and I made a note to ask George Fried when I met him at Newark Airport tomorrow.

But I was sure I had stumbled on something important, perhaps important enough to account for the murder of Arthur Wien forty years later. And Jack concurred.

"That's good detective work," he said. "Think of how many years those two documents have been around and no one picked up on the missing pages."

"It's not the sort of thing you go back to," I said. "For Alice it's a potential financial disaster. That pencil copy was like the family jewels stashed away in a safe, waiting for a rainy day to be sold. I don't know anything about original manuscripts, but these omissions must diminish the value considerably."

"But that's her problem. For you it's a real opening in a case that looked impenetrable."

"While you were going through your souvenirs, I called all the men I've spoken to and asked if there was something they didn't want Arthur Wien to publish."

"And they all said no."

"Not surprisingly, they all said no. But maybe one of them knows that I'm onto him. And maybe he'll do something or say something that will give him away."

"What about that guy in Minnesota?" Jack asked.

"I haven't called him yet. And tomorrow I'll ask George Fried."

"Your dead man."

"My dead man, right."

"And then it's off to see Sister Joseph."

I smiled. "I think it's time for a visit. The convent will look beautiful and Eddie will have a good time running around."

"Let me know how your interview with the dead man goes. It's something I've never done."

* * *

The interview went very well. I got to Newark Airport about twenty minutes before his flight from Chicago arrived and parked my car in the hourly lot. I had my silly sign with me, G. Fried in big black letters obviously drawn by an amateur. I went to the carousel his luggage was arriving at and stood outside the perimeter among a group of men holding signs better lettered than mine and a handful of friends and family of the incoming passengers.

He was a big man with a big smile, pulling a black weekend-sized suitcase on wheels. "This I like," he said, taking the G. Fried sign from me. "Nice to meet you, Chris. I'm George."

We went upstairs to a restaurant and sat at a table near a window. He ordered a Scotch and I asked for a Coke. Then he turned to me. "Start asking. I gotta be in New Brunswick in a couple of hours so get what you can while there's time."

"Where did you meet your first wife?" I asked.

"That's an interesting question. What does that have to do with Artie Wien?"

"I don't know."

"It was a blind date. Somebody fixed us up."

"When did you meet her?"

"After college. Artie I think was already married. Why?"

"Had she dated anyone else in your group?"

"Iris? I don't think so. I didn't see too much of them after I left the Bronx."

I had thought perhaps Iris had been the girlfriend of someone else in the group, but that didn't look productive. "How long were you married to her?"

"Too long. Maybe thirty years."

"Whose idea was it for you to 'die'?"

"It just came to me one night. I had a new wife, a new home. I was just trying to make my life a little easier."

"Did you stop answering the phone after you were supposed to have died?"

"Yeah, I did. We put the phone in Pam's name. I never answered the phone anyway. It wasn't that big a deal. A few of the guys wrote notes saying what a great guy I was. They didn't mean it, but it was a nice thing to do. I'm sure they forgot me after a month or two."

"Have your read Arthur Wien's first novel, *The Lost Boulevard*?"

"I started it, I remember. I don't know if I finished it."

"Did Mr. Wien ever ask you whether it would be all right to publish something in that book that pertained to you?"

"Like what?"

"I don't know. I just wondered if he ever called you and described some event and asked how you felt about it. Or maybe you heard from another member of the group that he was planning on publishing some embarrassing fact or incident." I waited. "Do you remember anything like that?"

"You mean like if I wet my pants or something when we were kids?"

"Actually, it would have been something that happened when you were all in your twenties."

"Doesn't ring a bell."

So it was still unanimous. "Did you know about Bruce Kaplan's embezzlement?"

"I heard about it. I heard he was covering for someone else."

The waitress had put our lunch in front of us while we were talking. I picked up a triangle of my turkey club sandwich and took a bite. "I heard one of the wives of the men in the group had an affair with Arthur Wien."

"No kidding! Which one?"

Not exactly the answer I had hoped for. "I'm trying to find out but no one seems to know."

"Well Iris thought he was pretty cute, but I don't think we were around him long enough for anything to happen. He married young, you know, in his early twenties. A lot of them did. Ernie waited till after medical school, but he had a big hassle with his folks."

"Why?"

"His wife isn't Jewish. Our parents' generation couldn't handle that. My generation doesn't like it, but we know it's happening. I think he married a pretty nice girl."

"I understand she's a psychiatrist."

"Something like that. They met in medical school."

"He sounds like a very busy man. He didn't want to take the time to talk to me, but I dropped in on him at his research center and he was very gracious."

"Ernie's a nice guy. They're all nice guys. I told you, I just got bored with the whole business. It's nothing personal."

"Have you seen Fred Beller in recent years?"

"I haven't seen anyone. I'm dead, remember? And I hope you'll let me stay dead."

"I will," I promised, "unless it turns out you killed someone."

That got a belly laugh.

"George," I said, "let me be honest with you. I'm looking for dirt. I'm looking for a reason that one of those men would have murdered Arthur Wien."

"I wish I could help you. I told you, they're a boring crowd. Boring people don't commit murders; interesting ones do. I sit in the same room with them, I fall asleep. This one did this, that one did that, over and over. You tell me one of the wives had a fling with Artie? Maybe she got bored out of her skin."

"Was Arthur Wien more interesting than the rest?"

"He had something the others didn't have. Maybe it was imagination."

I must have looked a little lost because he said, "I'm not helping you, am I?"

"Nothing seems to lead anywhere," I admitted. "I can't find any reason why one of those men would want Arthur Wien dead."

"Well, maybe you're looking in the wrong place. Maybe it wasn't one of the boys. Maybe it was this wife he was having an affair with."

"That's a possibility. But I can't figure out which of the wives that could be."

"Well, Artie was pretty friendly with the Meyers, Joe and Judy, the musicians."

"What's the motive?"

"Who knows? Then there's Morty's wife—what's her name again?"

"Robin."

"Robin, yeah. She was a beautiful girl, a very beautiful girl."

"Was she friendly with Arthur?"

"I couldn't tell you. I didn't hang around long enough to find out."

"Well," I said, disappointment in my voice, "if you think of anything . . ." I handed him my scrap of paper with the necessary information.

"I'll be the guy who doesn't leave his name."

19

I drove home feeling disappointed. About all I had learned from George Fried was that he found the Morris Avenue Boys boring and that boring people didn't commit murders. It was an interesting thought, one that I tended to agree with as long as we were talking about a murder planned for a long time, which I thought this probably was.

The other thing was his comment that perhaps it was a wife, not a husband, that had killed Wien. This idea had been growing in me for some time. It was a little sticky, considering that the event took place in a men's room, but the location didn't rule out a female killer. She could have watched to see that no one was in the men's room and darted in and out, the ice pick in her bag. Even a small evening purse would hold an ice pick.

But which one? Only Mrs. Horowitz had a provable relationship with Arthur Wien. I had spoken to all the wives except Kathy Greene. I suppose I am subject to many stereotypes and the beliefs that go along with them, but I had a hard time believing that a psychiatrist would murder her husband's old friend.

The other wife I hadn't spoken to was the present Mrs. Wien herself. I had the address of their New York apartment as well as their California home. I didn't know where she was, but a phone call would tell me. I was down to my last possible suspects now and I couldn't leave anyone out.

Eddie was in a giddy mood when I got him home. We played together outside after I checked my phone messages. There was one from Alice Wien and I wanted very much to call her back and see if she remembered what the missing pages had held, but I had been away from my son much of the day and decided to wait and call her later. As it turned out, Eddie wore himself out in the remaining light hours of the day and went off to bed without a whimper before Jack got home.

It was more or less the dinner hour, a time that seems to vary from family to family, but I called Alice anyway.

"It came back to me," she said.

"The material in the missing pages?"

"Yes. It was nothing, really, nothing that involved Art."

"But it must be important, Alice. It must have bothered or angered someone."

"It was a love affair, a brief fling that one of the men had with another man's wife."

"Well I can see why the participants wouldn't want it published. Do you remember who they were?"

"I really don't. I've thought about it all day. I almost have the feeling he made it one couple first and then changed it. The truth is, the book is better off without it."

"But it isn't the book we're talking about; it's the people represented in it. Maybe one of the lovers was angry enough when he or she heard the affair was going to be in the book that they forced Arthur to pull it."

"It couldn't have been a she," Alice said. "Art wouldn't have talked to any of the wives about the book. He used to call the men once in a while to check something, you know, the name of a particular teacher or a Yankee game they'd gone to. The women couldn't have told him anything. They weren't there."

It sounded reasonable. "Then it was a man. But which one?"

"I can give you eight names, but you know them already."

"Alice, I've been trying to figure out since last Sunday which of the wives Arthur may have had an affair with. Maybe my information was wrong. Maybe it wasn't his affair but someone else's. Maybe he knew about it and was blackmailing someone."

"Does anyone care about a forty-year-old affair?" she asked.

"I don't know. Perhaps not. Look, I appreciate your putting so much time into this. If you wake up in the middle of the night remembering anything, please call. I just want to ask you one more thing. I haven't talked to either Cindy or Kathy Greene. What's your opinion of them?"

"Cindy's a little ditzy. Art always went for that kind of girl. She's been with him for a while although they weren't married until a couple of years ago. I don't know why she'd want to kill him. And with Kathy, you're barking up the wrong tree. She and Ernie are two very cerebral people. I don't think they had anything in common with Art except that Ernie and Art grew up together."

"I see."

"You're out of suspects?"

"I never really had any. It was just my hope that I'd turn up a jealous husband or someone that Arthur owed money to. But I guess if he owed money, there wasn't much of a chance he'd pay off after he died."

Alice laughed. "Hard to collect from a dead man if you don't have a piece of paper."

"Well, let me know if you think of anything."

I left it at that till after dinner. Jack came home a little late—he still had a lot to clear up—and I told him about the dead man I'd interviewed. He seemed very taken with my discovery of the second life of George Fried, even if it had yielded little.

"He could be right," Jack said over dinner. "It could have been a woman who killed Wien. I know you have no motive, but you don't seem to have a motive for any of the men."

"Except Dr. Horowitz."

"NYPD's favorite. You know, they may not get their man every time, but they're not bad."

I smiled. "I know. And what you told me about Mrs. Horowitz's seeing Arthur Wien came from them. I didn't dig it up myself. So I'm in their debt."

"If it leads anywhere."

"I'm going to see Joseph tomorrow."

"Well, that should do it," Jack said with a grin. "She'll see something you didn't and she'll pull out the killer."

"I hope you're right. I'd like to see this settled, especially if the police are about to move on Dr. Horowitz."

Joseph had never quite "pulled out a killer," but she had the knack of seeing things that were right in front of me that I somehow failed to see or failed to take seriously. I've learned that there's a great value in presenting information to an intelligent and perceptive human being who is interested in the intellectual challenge as well as wanting to get a killer off the street. Rather than point to a suspect, she tended to ask questions that I had overlooked or not thought worthy of asking. Of course, she entered every case after I had done the bulk of the information gathering, whereas I began with nothing. But even if it all came to naught, an hour or two in her company was a bonus in my life.

When we had finished our dinner, our coffee, our talk about tomorrow's being Jack's last day at the Six-Five, I pulled a chair over to the kitchen telephone and dialed Cindy Porter Wien's number. She had a pleasant voice, and she seemed to know that I was looking into the murder of her husband.

"I know this is a difficult time for you," I said after some polite conversation, "but I'd really like to know if you have any sense of who in the group might have had a falling-out with your husband."

"I don't know them that well," she said. "I've read Art's book, of course—I've read all of them—and I feel I know them better from the book than from real life. He never said anything to me that might indicate an argument or a grudge or anything like that."

"Did anyone ever try to borrow money from him?" I asked, reversing my usual question.

"Not that he ever told me. I think all the men do pretty well, don't you?"

"They seem to. Did your husband ever talk about the men to you? Tell you about love affairs they might have had?"

"That sort of thing didn't interest him after *The Lost Boulevard*. He set those memories aside when he went on to his second book. He was a person who always wanted to try something new, write something unique. The group was always there, but he didn't talk about them, not in any negative way. He loved those men. It's hard for me to believe—" She faltered and I heard her take in her breath. "I don't know what to think. The police sound as if they believe that Mort Horowitz did it. It's absurd. He's a lovely man."

"Did your husband have a special friendship with Dr. Horowitz and his wife?"

"Special in what way?"

"Did he see them when he was in New York? Did he invite them over? Did he go out with them?"

"We did that once in a while, with the Kocnes too and the Meyers until Joe's illness got worse and it became hard for him to go out at night. It was too tiring."

"When did that happen?" I asked.

"A couple of years ago, about the time we were married. But I had met them many times before that."

"Anyone else in the group he was especially friendly with?"

"I think that's it."

"Did he ever mention Mrs. Horowitz as a special friend, someone who might have helped him through a troublesome time?"

"Not to me."

"Did your husband ever talk about the manuscript for *The Lost Boulevard*? Did he ever show it to you?"

"Oh that's a story. Alice demanded it as part of the divorce settlement. It was dedicated to her, you know, and she felt it was due her. They hadn't been married long when it was published. Art couldn't find it. He went through everything in his mother's apartment, everything he had in storage. And Alice got antsier and antsier about it. She wouldn't give him the divorce until he found it and gave it to her."

"Did he eventually find it?" I asked somewhat disin-genuously.

"Oh yes. And they settled right away."

"Did you ever see it?"

"No. It all happened before I met Art. They've been di-vorced for quite a while."

"So he gave it to her after all."

"Of course he did. The marriage was over and he had agreed to it. He was a man of honor."

Except that he had lied about where the manuscript was. "The night of the reunion, was there any discussion about who would sit next to your husband?"

"I think we were the last ones to get there and there were two empty chairs, but people started getting up and moving around. We were hugging and kissing people so I don't remember what it was all about. We sat down and that was that."

"Well, I appreciate your time. If you think of anything, Mrs. Wien . . ."

"Yes, I know how it goes. I'll call the police."

"Or me. I'm really very interested in finding his killer."

"That makes two of us."

I talked to Jack about it. I had no doubt Alice's story was the true one. Arthur Wien had put a positive spin on the story for his new love, but he couldn't get away with that kind of lie to Alice. She knew him too long and too well. A tale of digging in his mother's apartment and a storage bin might satisfy young Cindy after the fact, but he had been forced to tell Alice the truth. It wasn't much of a lie and Jack agreed it didn't make much of a difference, but it re-inforced my feeling that money might be at the root of the murder.

I went back to the phone and called the Greenes' number. The woman who answered turned out to be Dr. Kathy Greene.

"I hear you waylaid my husband the other day," she said with humor in her voice.

"I really needed to talk to everyone in the group," I said. "I hope I didn't keep him away from his work too long. He was very kind and spent a lot of time with me."

"He was glad to meet you. Do you have something else to ask him?"

"Actually, I'd like to talk to you."

"As a suspect or an informant?"

"I have no suspects. Everyone's an informant at this moment, and I have to tell you, they all tell me the same thing."

"They love each other and no one could have killed Artie."

"That's right."

"Well, I think they feel that way."

"How do you feel?"

She uttered a breathy "Hmm. I think one of them must have killed Artie," she said carefully, "but I couldn't tell you which, and whoever it was, when I find out, I'll be shocked and surprised."

No help there. "I heard that Mr. Wien was having or had had an affair with one of the wives. Had you heard that?"

"Artie and one of the men's wives? That sounds incredible."

"Why?"

"Artie went out with young women. Look at Cindy. She must be thirty years younger than he. And there were others before her, probably even while he was seeing her."

"Do you know whether he had what we might call a friendly relationship with any of the women?"

"Friendly? You mean sitting and talking about books and music? I think he had that kind of relationship with the Meyers. Why do you ask?"

"I'd rather not say. I don't want to break a confidence. Did you know Fred Beller and his wife?"

"Haven't seen them for years. But Fred always struck me as a very nice person, thoughtful and kind. He lives somewhere in the Midwest."

The same thing over and over. "Thank you, Dr. Greene. If something comes to you—"

"We have your number. Have you spoken to the Kaplans?"

"I have. Mrs. Kaplan gave me a copy of *The Lost Boulevard*."

"There's something strange there. I assume you know by now that Bruce served time for stealing money."

"I know."

"Something about that was never right. I would tell you more if I knew more, but I don't. And I have no idea whether it involves Artie."

And that was that. Were they all covering for each other or did they truly not know each other's secrets? Except Robin Horowitz. She knew something and wouldn't tell. I lay awake for a long time that night trying to figure out how to get her to tell me what she knew.

20

It was good to get out of the house and drive the pleasant drive to St. Stephen's. Eddie sat in his secure seat in the back, and I narrated the trip until I realized he had fallen asleep, whether because my rendition was so boring or because the movement of the car simply induced sleep, I did not know. This was the trip I had made every month from the time I bought my car until I left St. Stephen's to move into Aunt Meg's house on Pine Brook Road in Oakwood. The purpose of those monthly trips was not so much to visit Aunt Meg but to visit her son, Gene, who lived at Greenwillow, the home for retarded adults that was then in a neighboring town. Gene and I had grown up as best friends, and it was he who named me Kix when he couldn't pronounce Chris properly. He is fascinated by Eddie, and Eddie loves visiting him and playing with his collection of miniature cars. They do a lot of zooming together.

The moment I wait for as I drive north along the Hudson River is when I first see the steeple of the chapel at St. Stephen's in the distance and then the top of the Mother House, a building that resembles a fortress more than anything else. It did no good to tell Eddie. He was fast asleep; this was OK with me. He would be bright and awake when we got out of the car, ready to charm the nuns, who hadn't seen him for a while and would be delighted to be my baby-sitters while Joseph and I were talking.

In fact, his eyes opened as I shut the car door and came around to his side. He was a little weepy so I held him on my shoulder away from the sun and patted him gently for a few moments before reaching in and pulling out the paraphernalia that comes with motherhood, the toys, the snacks, the food, the diapers, the tissues, the can of juice. Laden on both shoulders, I made my way from the parking area to the Mother House and was barely halfway there when Sister Angela burst out of the stone building and ran toward me, probably leaving the switchboard unattended, but it wasn't exactly the busiest switchboard in the county.

"Chris, Chris, it's so good to see you. And my baby. Let me see my baby."

Obstinately, Eddie refused to budge his cheek from my shoulder. Angela dashed around to look at him from behind me.

"You are the sweetest," she said, "the most wonderful, the most adorable thing I have ever seen. Would you take your thumb out of your mouth just for one second? One little second?"

"Eddie," I said to the weight against me, "this is Angela. Do you remember Angela? You saw her last time we were here."

He giggled suddenly, and I knew Angela had done something to elicit it. As we got into the cool dark foyer of the Mother House, he allowed her to take him from me but refused to remove the thumb.

"He doesn't take orders very well," I admitted. "I worry about spoiling him, but it's probably too late to worry."

"Oh a thumb doesn't matter. I just hope he doesn't eat it up."

We got ourselves settled, and Angela called Joseph who came downstairs to see Eddie before she and I got together. Seeing her is always a bright moment. Joseph is a tall woman, now well into her forties. Little of her hair shows from beneath the veil and she has worn glasses for as long as I've known her, which is nearly twenty years. The habit, which all the nuns wear, is the brown, long-sleeved Franciscan dress that comes to midcalf, and the brown veil. On her left wrist she wears a large round watch whose numbers can be seen from a distance. Her hands are very beautiful, strong with long, slim, unadorned fingers. She is distinctly uncomfortable around babies and small children, preferring people with whom she can converse on an equal footing. She met Arnold Gold the Christmas after Jack and I were married, and they ask after each other frequently, having enjoyed each other's company enormously.

After we greeted each other, she went to the table on which Eddie was sitting somewhat precariously, courtesy of Angela, and talked to him for a while. "I know you hear this all the time, Chris, but what a difference a month or two makes in the growth of a little child like this one."

"Eddie," I said, "this is Joseph. Remember Joseph?"

He pointed at her and smiled. "Doess," he said. "Doess."

"Well, he's getting there," Joseph said. "Pretty soon there'll be a second syllable."

"I'll work on it," Angela said. "Come with me, Eddie. I've got the loveliest cookie in the whole world waiting for you in the kitchen."

Cookie was a word he knew well. His face lit up, and he

scrambled to go with Angela as Joseph watched, shaking her head and smiling.

We then went up the wide stone stairs to the second floor and on to her office, which was at the far end of the hall. The ceiling sloped along one long side of the room, and there were windows on the sloped side as well as the back of the room where Joseph keeps her desk. As usual, we sat at the long heavy table that takes up most of the room, one of us on each side, as though this were part of the ritual of our talks. On Joseph's side lay unlined paper and several pens and pencils. I knew that lunch would be brought up on a tray for both of us when the time came, and as always, I looked forward to sharing the meal with her.

"Well, I am absolutely trembling with anticipation, Chris. It's so many months now since I visited you and Jack on Fire Island last year when you were working on that interesting situation and I found myself part of the Chris Bennett investigating unit."

I laughed at the description. "I've done a lot of leg work on this one. I've talked to what feels like countless men and their wives, and most of them say exactly the same things."

"Leading you nowhere."

"Exactly."

"But some of them have said some things that were different."

"That's true, and I've discovered a dead man who's alive."

"Well, if that isn't a miracle, I don't know what is. Start at the beginning." She pulled the paper in front of her and picked up a pencil.

So that's what I did, going back to the phone call from

Janet Stern over a week ago and the lunch with her and her mother at Maurice's. I tend to tell Joseph what I have learned in the same order in which I learned it. That way, I don't inadvertently stress something that has impressed me. I want her to listen and make up her mind without my influence. And I listen carefully to her questions, which often point to facts I haven't realized were missing or to incidents that need elaboration.

These retellings of mine tend to take a fair amount of time, and this was no different. I showed her the snapshot of the little boys, told her what each of them was doing now, how he had spent his life professionally, who his wife was. I handed her the photographs of the Father's Day dinner and paused while she went through them, attempting to identify each person.

Then I started with my lunch with Dr. Horowitz at his office and my subsequent visit to the crime scene, the restaurant where the murder had taken place. I didn't tell her at that point that the Bellers had been in the restaurant, saving that for my lunch with them the next day. I related my first conversation with Dave Koch, in his apartment, at the end of which I had met his wife, Ellen, who had sprung the mysterious rumor on me, that one of the wives had had an affair with Arthur Wien.

"Well, that's interesting," Joseph said. "I suppose it's possible that this woman, whoever she is, resented his marrying the new Mrs. Wien."

"Anything is possible," I said.

Joseph laughed. "You sound as if you're near the end of your wits over this."

"Very near." I continued with the lunch with the Bellers at the Waldorf-Astoria, a place I had never imagined entering, much less dining in.

"Very elegant," Joseph commented.

"And tasty. It was really good food." I made sure to tell her about the Bellers' meeting with Arthur Wien in California and the subsequent visit in Minnesota that never took place, Mrs. Beller's sudden silence when I asked what had happened to prevent it. I took out the photo of the two of them at that point and handed it across the table.

"A pleasant looking couple," Joseph said. "They look like they're enjoying themselves."

I went on to relate the trip to the Bronx, the business street cut in half and the noisy highway below, the old homestead—apartment houses and school and shops—that no longer included a kosher butcher or a delicatessen but was the heart of all the memories of the Morris Avenue Boys. I told her about that afternoon I had visited the Meyers, and that night the Kaplans who mentioned the fuss over the seating arrangement.

"And what did Mr. Kaplan say about the alleged embezzlement?"

"I didn't ask," I admitted.

"But it might be important, Chris."

"It was too embarrassing." I felt embarrassed to say it.

"That's understandable, but if nothing else points to a killer, I think you'll have to do some more digging there. It would be interesting, at the least, to hear what he has to say about it."

I wrote a note for myself, knowing this was going to be one of the hardest things I had ever had to do. Then I moved on to Monday and my talk with Ernest Greene at his research institute followed by my discovery that the Bellers had indeed been at the restaurant the night of the murder.

"That's quite a discovery, Chris. Are the police aware of it?"

"I doubt it. They may not even know Fred Beller exists."

It was Joseph's turn to make some notes.

And then there was my first meeting with Alice Wien when she told me the circumstances of her meeting with her husband while she was nearly engaged to Fred Beller. I watched Joseph's eyebrows rise and saw her nod. And then there was the story of *The Lost Boulevard*'s being used as collateral for a loan.

I had shown her my copy when I talked about the Kaplans. Joseph opened it and noticed that it was signed, and I explained that Mrs. Kaplan kept several such copies around for gifts.

"It certainly sounds as if Arthur Wien and the Kaplans were on good terms."

"It does, yes. I imagine a writer would be very happy to have someone stock his book to give to friends."

I then told her how I discovered that George Fried was still alive.

"Chris, this is amazing. You know something that no one in the group knows."

"That's right. I don't think it's worth very much, and I don't intend to give that information to Dr. Horowitz or anyone else unless I find out that Mr. Fried was somehow involved in the murder. It sounds as though he just wants to be rid of them as friends and this is how he chose to do it."

"Well, go on. This is very interesting."

My next fact was from Jack: Mrs. Horowitz had been seen visiting Arthur Wien several times at his New York apartment. This was followed by my meeting with her and her denial of any affair and her refusal to explain the visits.

Later that day I had spoken to the Reskins. Bernie Reskin was the first person I talked to who thought that Bruce Kaplan had actually stolen the money that he went to prison for stealing.

On Wednesday I had gone through the pencil manuscript and the typescript of *The Lost Boulevard* and found pages missing.

"Well," Joseph said. "Finally."

"Finally what?"

"Finally something concrete, something that isn't hearsay. I imagine Alice Wien was quite shocked."

"Quite shocked, yes. Very shocked. This was her prize, Joseph, her reward for being married to Arthur Wien. This was her children's inheritance and her husband ruined it for her. Not only that, he did it in a deceitful way, probably when she wasn't home, removing the typewritten pages from the manuscript and typing them over with so many mistakes she could see immediately that she hadn't done it herself. He didn't bother rewriting the pencil edition because it didn't matter. I suppose one day when she carried out the garbage, she was disposing of her most treasured possession."

"That depends," Joseph said.

I looked across the table. "On what?"

"On when those pages were removed from the pencil manuscript."

"The typed pages had to have been removed before he submitted the manuscript to a publisher. He could have disposed of the pencil pages at the same time, or however many years later, he could have pulled them when his creditor insisted on holding the book as collateral."

"That's one possibility," Joseph said distantly. "Do you have more for me?"

"A little." I told her about my lunch and conversation with George Fried at Newark Airport, including my shirt cardboard with his name on it so that I looked like a limousine driver waiting for a passenger. That had been yesterday, and when I had gotten home, there was a message on the machine from Alice.

I told Joseph about what the missing manuscript pages had probably contained.

"A love affair between a different man and one of the wives," she said. "That's the stuff of blackmail, isn't it?"

"Probably."

In the evening I had spoken to Cindy Wien, who also had no suspects, and with Kathy Greene who thought there was something strange about Bruce Kaplan.

"Then you must call him, Chris. Whatever Kathy Greene meant, she's a person whose perceptions are useful in her work. I know this will be painful, but please give him a call."

"I will," I promised. "And that's the last thing I have in my notes. We got up this morning and I packed Eddie in the car and here we are."

"Give me a moment." Joseph turned her sheets over to the first one, leaving me surprised at how many notes she had taken. She went through them, picking up a red pen and marking some places. "Everything I'm going to suggest will cause you embarrassment, I'm afraid," she said apologetically. "You're going to have to ask people things they don't want to talk about, and if they refuse to answer, I think your duty will be to take what you have to the police."

"I know I have to do that." I scanned my notes. "You want me to press Mrs. Horowitz on her visits to Arthur Wien."

"That's one. Another is Fred Beller. You must find out why they didn't meet Arthur Wien when he went to Minnesota."

I had guessed that was coming simply because I had thought of it myself and declined to make the phone call.

"And Bruce Kaplan, as I've already said. And I'm afraid you really need to get back to Mrs. Koch and press her on the tantalizing information she volunteered to you. Am I to believe that someone told her a woman she knew and a man she knew were having an affair and she forgets not only who the party to the affair was but also the name of the person who told her? I can almost believe she could have forgotten the source of the information—I do that myself from time to time—but she knows who the woman was."

"Do you?"

"I may, but I'm not speculating."

"I've sprung this on many of the people I've interviewed and not one of them thinks it's credible. Everyone says Arthur Wien liked his women young."

"That may be. But the wives weren't always middle-aged. Now let's get back to those missing pages. I agree that Arthur Wien threw away the typed pages before the manuscript went to his editor or agent or whoever was the recipient of the unpublished book. And he went to some lengths to hide what he did from his wife. But I think there may be another explanation of what happened to the missing pencil pages."

"I don't understand."

"I would think that an author, especially one who wrote in the days before computers, would have a sentimental attachment to his first draft, especially to the first draft of his first book, a book that went on to be very successful."

"I agree."

"And since no one was likely to read those pencil pages for many years, possibly until after his death when he wouldn't care any more who knew what, I think he kept the pencil manuscript intact."

"Until he gave it to someone."

"Suppose he gave it to one of the people involved in this allegedly fictional love affair."

"The person he borrowed money from."

"Exactly. And that person removed the pages."

"Did Arthur Wien know the pages were removed?" I asked.

"I'm not sure. There are several possibilities. One is that the person removed the pages and returned the manuscript without telling the author what he'd done. It never occurred to Wien that anything was missing so he didn't check. Another possibility is that the person refused to return those pages, to ensure that the affair would never be revealed. And the third possibility is that the person simply didn't want to return the manuscript under any conditions."

"So that he could sell it for a tidy sum himself."

"Perhaps. If the second explanation is the correct one, then the dickering wasn't over the money Wien owed or how much extra he was being coerced into paying, but just getting those pages back so the manuscript would be intact."

"And Wien lost. He got the manuscript back without the pages and he never told anyone."

"He couldn't tell his first wife. She might have gotten a warrant to find the pages, feeling they properly belonged to her husband and then to her."

"Do you think this person still has the pages?"

"I think it depends on the reason they were withheld."

"Money or keeping a secret."

"There might be a third possibility," Joseph said thoughtfully, and I knew enough not to press her.

"So you think the person who had the manuscript is the killer?"

"I'm not at all sure of that, but it's possible. I would very much like to know what Mrs. Horowitz was seeing Arthur Wien about. And I think you should try to put together all the times in this case, Chris. When did Arthur go to Minnesota? When did Mrs. Horowitz visit Arthur Wien? When did Mr. Wien marry his second wife? When did George Fried 'die'? When did Bruce Kaplan allegedly take money illegally?"

I was writing furiously. "Anything else?"

Joseph smiled. "There is one other thing, an event you mentioned rather quickly, almost as an afterthought. Think about it. It might be important."

That is Joseph's way. I knew I had my work cut out.

21

Our lunch was delivered while we were still talking and we put aside the Wien homicide to enjoy it and talk about other things. St. Stephen's, like other convents, uses the talents and skills of its nuns to best advantage. I never learned to cook, and I was rarely asked to prepare a meal, only when no one else was available. And then I wasn't asked again for a long time.

In my honor, today, several of the sisters living in the Villa, the home for retired nuns, had whipped up a fine lunch that included fresh biscuits and still warm cookies, a specialty of Sister Dolores. I knew there would be a bag of them downstairs for me to take home and I hoped Eddie wasn't overdoing it on sweets, but these visits were far from frequent and I wanted everybody to be happy we had come.

When Joseph and I had finished, we went downstairs where Eddie was sleeping in his stroller in a shady spot outdoors, one of the older nuns crooning a lullaby as she sat in a chair beside him. Since both my son and his sitter were quite happy to remain where they were, Joseph and I took a walk across the convent grounds and the adjoining campus to admire the new plantings and get a good dose of the fresh air of upstate New York.

It's difficult to communicate a love of place. I have not traveled much in my life and very little outside the New York, New Jersey, and Connecticut area in which we live. I have managed to drive through a good deal of New York State and dip into Pennsylvania, but aside from that, there is most of the country and a whole world that I have not seen. And yet I am certain that if I am fortunate enough to visit the many wonders of that world, places of great interest, beauty and charm, I will still return to this place and feel that its beauty and its peace are unchallenged. Joseph knows how I feel because she feels the same way.

So our walk was satisfying and refreshing, the scent of grass almost overwhelming, the quiet blissful. The college semester had ended and the students were gone. It was the way I liked it best.

Joseph's main concern was the dearth of future nuns. The convent was down to a few novices, one of whom she had doubts about. I could not imagine this wonderful place closing forever as a convent although I knew of other convents that had merged or dissolved. Joseph was hoping to avoid either fate, and I could not have wished her better if I tried.

Back at the shady side of the Mother House, I found my little son still fast asleep; the nun in the chair beside him had fallen asleep herself. When she awakened, I took the stroller and walked to the Villa to say hello to the elderly women who lived there and thank them for the sumptuous lunch. They whispered to let Eddie sleep, and then we walked away and chatted in normal tones. A nun I had known since I was fifteen had died during the past year, and a tree had been planted in her memory. We walked outside to admire it, to feel her presence in the strong green leaves.

And then it was time to go. Eddie stirred as I lifted him into his seat, but he went back to sleep after a whimper. Angela came out for a last hug and Joseph came to see us off.

The last thing she said to me was, "Remember it was Father's Day."

Eddie woke up cranky while I was still driving. I gave him a pretzel which ended up thrown on the front seat beside me, but the second time I offered it he thought better of it and took it. When we got home, I marinated some beef cubes for shish kebab and then, taking Eddie with me, went out to the backyard to pull some weeds. My vegetable garden was starting to look good; the little seedlings I had nurtured through the cool spring were now a darker green with buds promising flowers and fruits. I may not do well in the kitchen, but I have managed to become an estimable vegetable gardener. I was hoping that this year Eddie would grow to love cherry tomatoes off the vine as I did.

Today was Jack's last day at the precinct he had worked at for many years, and I knew he would be in a precarious state when he got home. I was pretty sure the detectives would throw him a party this afternoon so I didn't call. We could talk about everything later.

I gave Eddie his dinner and his bath and read him a story. He was in blue summer pajamas that his grandparents had given him, and he looked as adorable as they had intended. I was about to put him to bed when I heard Jack's car drive up. I said, "Here comes Daddy."

Eddie ran to the window overlooking the driveway and stood there smiling till Jack got out of the car, looked up and saw him, and waved. When Jack came upstairs, he put his hand in his pocket and pulled out a small box, which he handed to me. Then he went over to Eddie and picked him up.

I opened the box. In a soft, suedelike pouch was something made of metal. I pulled it out and gasped. It was a gold key ring with a gold disk that had a raised scales of justice hanging from it. Engraved on the back was his name, rank, and the date. He was a lawyer all right. Even his colleagues had acknowledged it.

"Did you know they were giving me a party?" We were eating a melon whose name I have forgotten, sweet and small, while the shish was grilling.

"Nobody told me but I guessed they would. Who was there?"

"Everyone in the house who could avoid work. It was at O'Boyle's down the street. That's some gift, isn't it?"

I had teared up when I looked at it. "It's wonderful, Jack. And all your keys will fit on it."

"I think I'll save it for a while."

"Nothing doing," I said with more insistence than I usually projected. "You will pass these exams in the fall, and you're not waiting for that to happen to use this beautiful gift from your friends. You're starting a new job Monday as a lawyer, and you're going to have that in your pocket when you leave the house."

"Well, that's reading me the riot act."

I grinned. I was very happy and I felt I was right. I wanted him to enjoy everything that was there for him.

We started eating—the marinade was Mel's and the cooking courtesy of a great barbecue, leaving little to my ability to massacre a meal—and talking first about his day and then about mine.

"You were up at St. Stephen's today, weren't you," he asked, as though he had just remembered it, "seeing my favorite people?"

"And talking about the Arthur Wien murder."

"Sister Joseph pull it out for you?"

"Not exactly. What she did was tell me I have to call a number of people back and ask every embarrassing question that I was afraid to ask the first time around."

"Like 'did you go to jail for something you did or were you covering for somebody?' "

"You knew I'd have to ask him, didn't you?"

"Hey, for all you know, that guy — what's his name?"

"Bruce Kaplan, and he's a very nice person."

"Bruce Kaplan, and maybe he is and maybe he isn't. For all you know, he took money that didn't belong to him to lend to Arthur Wien and he never forgave him for it. Maybe Wien didn't pay it back in time and an audit found it missing."

"I think I'm going into early retirement," I said, not entirely facetiously.

"Nobody likes to ask questions like those," Jack said sympathetically. "Nobody gets a kick out of humiliating another person. Do your usual best. He'll know you're not doing this for fun."

I went through the rest of Joseph's comments, all of which I had taken down, some legibly, some in an almost unreadable scribble that I would never have accepted from a student. He agreed that almost everything she suggested was relevant and therefore necessary, except calling the Bellers. I asked why not.

"Fred Beller didn't like Arthur Wien. That was clear

early on. When you found out that Wien had taken Beller's girlfriend away, that said it all. Beller didn't want anything to do with Wien, whether he was in Minnesota or New York or anywhere else. I don't blame him. But make the call. Sister Joseph is better at these things than I am."

So I made that call first. Mrs. Beller answered and listened to my request.

"You're making a mountain out of a nothing event," she said, happily mixing metaphors. "Art was very busy when he came to Minneapolis. They wined and dined him. That's all it was."

I didn't believe her. "Do you remember when Mr. Wien made that trip to Minneapolis?"

"I'd have to think about that. It was after our trip to California because that's where we ran into him the first time. We took that trip—let me see—" She said "Mm" a couple of times while I waited. "I think it's three years since California so it's less than that, maybe two and a half?" She said it as though I could give her the answer.

"OK," I said, writing it down. "Mrs. Beller, if you decide to tell me what really happened when Arthur Wien came to Minneapolis, I'd appreciate your calling me."

"I've told you." She sounded almost plaintive.

I had thought about letting her know that I knew she had been at the restaurant the night of the murder, but I couldn't bring myself to threaten her. "Please," I said. "Whether you liked him or not, he didn't deserve to die."

"I'll talk to my husband," she said and hung up.

That struck me as progress. Then, just to see if I could come up with some answers through the back door, I dialed Cindy Wien.

"Do you have something?" she asked almost eagerly.

"I have a couple of questions. How long were you married to Mr. Wien?"

"We were together a long time."

"About how long?"

"Seven years, maybe a little longer."

It occurred to me that she might have been in her twenties when they started going out. "And when were you married?"

"Two years ago. We just had our second anniversary."

"Were you with your husband when he visited Minneapolis?"

"To publicize his book? No, I stayed in California. He said those were dreadful trips, being whisked from one place to another with hardly enough time to grab a sandwich."

"Did he mention to you that he might see the Bellers there?"

"Fred and his wife? You know, he did. He had bumped into them in California and they had invited him to visit if he ever got to Minneapolis."

"Do you know what happened when he got there?"

There was some silence. "He didn't see them, I know that. He said they pulled out at the last minute."

"They pulled out?"

"Yes. He was going to take them to dinner. They said something else had come up unexpectedly and they couldn't make it. I'm sure of that. He told me when he came home."

I thought about it after I hung up. Another lie by Arthur Wien? Or had the Bellers decided they really didn't want to spend an evening with him? Among the living, only Fred and Marge knew the truth.

*   *   *

I saved the call to Bruce Kaplan until after Jack and I had had coffee and the wonderful cookies I had carried home from St. Stephen's. To say they were a success is to downplay his reaction by decibels. There were so many in the bag, I didn't need to remind him to leave some for Eddie for tomorrow. They were loaded with chocolate chips and were absolutely huge. The bag they had given me had contained half a dozen biscuits as well, and we had eaten them for dinner.

Finally, having put it off long enough, I called Bruce Kaplan. Arlene answered, and I thanked her for the book, of which I had already read three-quarters. We chatted for a few minutes as though I had called merely to exchange literary opinions. Finally I asked to speak to her husband.

"Yes," he said when he came to the phone. "Got some more questions?"

"Mr. Kaplan, I'm feeling very uneasy asking you this, but I've heard that you were convicted of a crime. Would you tell me about it?"

He let his breath out as though he had to prepare himself for an ordeal, which he probably did. "It was a very simple thing. I took money that didn't belong to me, money I intended to pay back to the company, and it was discovered before I had a chance to repay it. I went to trial and ended up serving what you might consider a short sentence but that was the longest sentence of my life."

"When did this happen?"

"It's over twenty years, twenty-five. I've put it behind me. I did something I shouldn't have, I paid the price, and I've moved on."

Twenty-five years. It seemed a long time to carry a grudge, if that was what it was. "I've heard someone else actually took the money and you paid the price for it."

"There are people who find it hard to believe that someone they've known since childhood could commit a felony, and they spin tales to make the situation look better. I was solely responsible for what happened."

That seemed as definitive a confession as one could find. "Did you lend any part of that money to Arthur Wien?" I asked.

There was total silence. "Did I—" In the background, I could hear his wife's voice. "No, I didn't. What would make you—"

"I heard he borrowed from friends."

"He may have."

"Did he borrow from you?"

"An inconsequential amount."

"Did he pay you back?"

"I believe so."

"When did he borrow from you?"

"I couldn't tell you within a ten-year period. It was very casual and it wasn't a lot of money."

"Did you ever borrow from him?"

After a pause he laughed. "From Artie? You were lucky if he'd pick up his half of a dinner check. Artie was a classic cheapskate. Doesn't mean I didn't like and admire him, but he'd be the last man in the world I'd go to if I needed money."

I was about to finish the conversation when I decided to ask one more embarrassing question. "The money you took, can you tell me what you used it for?"

"I used it for something personal. I didn't gamble it away; I didn't drink it or shoot it up my arm. I used it for something that meant a lot to me."

I knew there was nothing more I could ask.

* * *

Jack had walked outside for a breath of fresh air while I was on the phone. I followed him through the door in the family room. It was dark now, a week after the longest day of the year. Jack had turned on the outdoor lights that theoretically allowed us to give parties and entertain in our backyard on summer nights but in practice we had never used. The lawn looked very green and healthy in the glow, our plantings stronger and taller than a year ago. I had fought myself for every dollar we had spent, worrying that we were overdoing it, that some catastrophe would render us impoverished. Jack had known that we could afford both the addition to the house and the landscaping that followed, that we, and especially I, would enjoy both the extra rooms and the shrubs and flowers that beautified our property and enhanced our life. The great thing about marriage is that our individual strengths and weaknesses lie in different areas, and we had learned to support each other and to accept that support.

"I called him," I said, moving to his side and putting an arm around his waist.

"I know. That's why I came outside. How'd it go?"

"He didn't do it, Jack. He was my first suspect, because he was convicted of a felony and I was ready to accept that a thief could be a murderer. He's a good man. They're all good men. I don't think any of them did it, and if one did, I don't even want to know who."

"And the wives?"

"I don't know." I didn't want to think about it. "These are nice people, good people. I don't have a motive and everyone at the party had opportunity. I looked over the photographs taken at the Father's Day dinner. The women's purses are lying on the table. Most of them are small evening bags. Any one of them could have carried an ice pick in her purse."

"With a cork to keep it from sticking through the fabric."

"Right."

"And no motive."

"Mrs. Beller is lying to me. She said at first that Wien had canceled their meeting because he had so much to do. When I pressed her, she said she would talk to her husband."

"So there is something there."

"There's something. I can't make her tell me, Jack."

"You know something about them they don't know you know."

"I really hate this."

He wrapped me up in his arms and held me tight. He was starting a new job on Monday and he was nervous. I had to call people and ask them the kinds of things polite people don't talk about, and I didn't want to. But here we were in our own backyard, under our own lights, with our own little boy upstairs in his crib. It was almost enough to make me forget everything else.

22

I read *The Lost Boulevard* before I turned off the lights. I fell asleep pretty quickly, and then something woke me, a noise or a feeling, I wasn't sure. I put my slippers on and went into Eddie's room. He was sleeping soundly in his little blue pajamas, the light cotton blanket kicked to the bottom end of the crib.

I watched him for a moment, then left the room. I didn't feel sleepy so I tiptoed back into our bedroom and got *The Lost Boulevard* from my night table. My bookmark was near the end, and I really wanted to see how it all came out, whether the Koches married each other, whether the musicians married each other, whether the doctor made of two separate human beings would work out the problems he had with his family and marry the woman he loved.

I took the book downstairs, turned a light on in the family room, and snuggled into my favorite chair. It was the fifties and the lives were moving forward, the blind dates yielding relationships that became marriages and families. It was interesting that the George Fried character had been combined with the Fred Beller character, the distinctive characteristic about the two men that they disliked New York and wanted to get away. It didn't seem very distinctive to me; half the people I knew disliked the city enough that they refused to go there alone. I had always liked it myself, going back to when my wonderful father took me in to meet the people at the small company he worked for in downtown Manhattan.

I looked hard for some indication of a temptation, two people meeting accidentally or clandestinely, or almost. There was none. The young man who wanted to get out of New York was perceived as a misfit while the doctor who had fallen in love with a non-Jewish woman was seen as admirable, as though disappointing his parents gave him a certain panache in the eyes of the narrator. It was hard, really, to put the name of a real person on a character. Wien had done a good job of fictionalizing them. With a sure hand, he had made them go the way he wanted them to go.

When I finally became too tired to read, I had only a chapter left to go and I was still without a motive for murder.

I never heard Jack get out of bed in the morning and when I finally opened my eyes, I couldn't believe I had slept till almost nine. I dashed into Eddie's room, but he was gone, probably eating a better breakfast than his mother would have made for him.

"That's a first," Jack said as I walked into the kitchen. "You get up in the middle of the night?"

"Something woke me, and I decided to sit downstairs and read Arthur Wien's book."

"Well, we've been having a good time here fixing breakfast and eating. Care to join us?"

I did. Eddie pointed out the glass, the cup, and the muffin. "Not bad," I said. "You're a regular vocabulary builder, Daddy."

"You bet. Need a good vocabulary if you're going to communicate."

Jack joined me for another cup of coffee. Coffee seems to be the lifeblood of police officers; they can never get enough of it. Eddie was tired of sitting at his feeding table and Jack had sprung him loose. At the moment he was in the family room and I had my eye on him.

"That information you got on Robin Horowitz," I said. "Do you have any idea when she made those visits to Arthur Wien's apartment?"

"Got the dates." He got up from the table and came back with a piece of paper. "No one kept a record, you understand. This was just the doorman's recollection. He was able to place the time because he filled in for several months for the daytime doorman who had some surgery and it happened during that period. It was only weekdays because he didn't work weekends and the weekend guys didn't pick up on the picture. He's sure there were three visits but there could have been four or five. They were made more than two years ago and less than two and a half. He thinks about two and a quarter."

"Was Cindy Wien living in the apartment?"

"There was no Cindy Wien. They hadn't gotten married yet. Miss Porter wasn't there. She didn't always accompany her boyfriend to New York."

"That's why they met in the apartment," I said. "If Cindy had been there, they probably would have met somewhere else and we'd never have known about it."

"That's why we ask, because sometimes we get lucky."

"So these meetings were a few months before the Wiens married."

"You sure of that?"

"I talked to Cindy last night. She said they'd just had their second anniversary."

"OK." Jack nodded, got up from the table and came back with a sheet of blank paper, which he folded twice in his usual way and started to write on. "So Mrs. Horowitz and Mr. Wien could have been involved in last-ditch negotiations on their future together."

"Or apart."

"Which is the way it turned out. You gotta press her, Chris. If she doesn't have a better story to tell than what it looks like, either she or her husband is in big trouble."

"She follows Wien out and kills him and then her husband goes to the men's room and finds the body—an unfortunate coincidence."

"It's certainly the closest thing you have to a motive."

"I'll give her a call," I said, feeling very unhappy.

I reached her later the same morning.

"I have nothing further to say to you," she said. "Please consider the matter closed."

"It isn't closed, Mrs. Horowitz. It's very open. The person who saw you go into Mr. Wien's building is an employee there. He has been talking to the police."

"I don't believe you."

"I'm telling you the truth. You were seen going to Mr. Wien's apartment at least three times about twenty-seven months ago."

She said nothing.

"Can we talk about this?" I asked.

"Not now."

"I think the sooner we talk about it the better off you will be."

"Just a moment."

She put the phone down, and I waited, wondering if she was looking through an appointment book and assigning me a time next week when her husband might already be in jail.

"Two o'clock," she said, startling me.

"Today?"

"If you can make it. Do you know where Neiman Marcus is in White Plains?"

I gulped. The very idea of Neiman Marcus made me tremble. "Approximately," I said.

"I'll be on the third floor, in the gift department. It's a small store. We'll find each other."

Before I could say anything else, she hung up.

"Why don't you treat yourself to something special?" Jack said when I told him.

"Please," I said. "I'm already a nervous wreck just thinking about walking through an expensive store. Remember 'Lead me not into temptation'?"

"Chris, maybe it's time you let yourself be tempted."

"I can't afford it."

"Sure you can. Buy yourself a lipstick. How much can that be? I bet they put it in a nice bag."

I shooed him away. "I'll be back as soon as I can. If Eddie gets up—"

"I know, I know. Calm down. You're more nervous about where you're going than what you're going to do."

It was true. I looked at my watch, grabbed my bag, and started for the door.

"Open a charge account," Jack called after me.

The store had told me on the phone how to get there, and I made only one wrong turn that led me astray. I was in their parking garage by a quarter to two and on the escalator to the first floor a few minutes later. I didn't want to be early so I got off and walked through the men's department. There were beautiful ties on a table in an array of colors. That would make a great gift for Jack, a tie that would tell the world he was an attorney-at-law. I picked one up that had mostly blues in a neat pattern and turned it over. The tag said sixty dollars. I swallowed, the tie still aloft in my frozen hand. Did I live in a world where men's ties cost sixty dollars?

Carefully, because I knew how valuable it was, I put it back where it came from and moved slightly away from the table. I had never bought Jack a tie in the nearly three years we were married although we had shopped together several times and I had helped him select some.

"May I help you?"

I looked toward the voice, a youngish man in a dark suit with a beautiful tie against his white shirt. I shook my head. "No thanks," I managed to say. "I have to be upstairs in three minutes."

"Come back when you have time."

I wondered if I would ever have time for a sixty-dollar tie.

I rode the escalator up to three and found myself looking at what I supposed was the gift department. There were large hand-painted plates in wonderful colors, shimmering crystal vases and plates that looked almost too heavy to lift, place settings of china framed by shiny silverware, and beautiful table linens. Most of what Jack and I used had belonged to Aunt Meg and I had never thought of replacing it. If ties were sixty dollars, what must these household articles cost and how could anyone afford to get married nowadays?

I shook my head to clear it of these irrelevant and expensive thoughts and walked around till I spotted Robin Horowitz. She looked up from a table of pottery and saw me. I walked over.

"Where's the baby?" she asked.

"He's home with his father. It's his nap time."

"Oh." She seemed disappointed, as though she had made the appointment just to see Eddie.

"Please tell me why you visited Arthur Wien in his apartment."

"It was a personal matter that concerned only Arthur and myself."

"And someone else?" I asked.

She looked very concerned, her forehead lined, her mouth set. "Perhaps."

"The wife of one of the Morris Avenue Boys?"

"You don't know what you're talking about."

"Have the police questioned you about this yet?"

"No."

"It isn't worth getting into trouble with the police over this," I said.

"A confidence is a confidence. And what makes you think that everything I do concerns my husband's friends? I know plenty of people outside that group, many more than I know inside it."

"People who also know Arthur Wien?"

"I am a member of a library support group. What makes you think I wasn't asking him to speak to our group?"

"Then what's the secret?" I asked. "And why several visits to his home? Don't you make arrangements like that on the phone?"

She picked up a piece of pottery and held it in front of her, as though appraising it. "It's a room with a lot of beige and pale yellow. How would that be on the wall?"

"Lovely," I said. "It's a beautiful piece."

"I think so too."

"Mrs. Horowitz."

She laid the large plate on the table. "I served as a mediator," she said. "There was a problem between Arthur and another person. It was impossible for them to talk about it face to face or any other way. I helped arrange a settlement."

"Was it a woman he had had an affair with?"

"I've said all I'm going to say. You know as much about it as I'm going to tell you. Arthur is dead but the other party is still alive. That's it."

"Why you?"

"Why not me? I've done counseling for years; I suppose you didn't know that. I knew the parties involved, I liked them, I wanted to save their feelings for each other as much as was possible. When I was asked, I stepped in." She picked up the plate and looked around, signaling a saleswoman who was nearby. "I'll take this," she said. "I'll need it gift wrapped." She took out a credit card as the woman took the plate from her.

"That's it, Chris. I'm done here and we've spoken for the last time."

"What will you tell the police when they ask?"

"I haven't thought about that yet. Probably nothing. I know nothing that can help them." She looked at her watch. "Kiss the baby for me."

On my way out, I avoided the men's shop.

23

"What do you pay for your ties?" I asked Jack later that afternoon when the three of us were outside, Jack rolling a ball to Eddie across the grass and Eddie attempting to return it, giving Jack most of the exercise.

"I don't know. Depends what I'm going to wear it for."

"What do you mean?"

"I spent a lot for the tie I wore to our wedding. I spend a lot less for ties that I wear around the squad room."

"I saw a tie for sixty dollars at Neiman Marcus."

He grinned at me. "Well, it's a pretty pricey place. I've never spent that. You feel better?"

"I don't do much comparison shopping. If I need something, I go and get it. I didn't know men's clothes were so expensive."

"I guess you pay for a tie now what you used to pay for a suit."

"I see."

"My dad always says you pay for a car what you used to pay for a house."

"It's scary. I realized that when we shop together, you never let me see the price tags."

"I hate to shake you up. I remember when you told me

228

you used to leave the convent with fifty cents in your pocket."

I thought about it. "I bet they need a dollar now."

He came over and gave me a kiss. "I told you to stick with lipsticks."

I wanted to call Ellen Koch and press her about Robin Horowitz and her relationship to Arthur Wien, but I didn't. She had been pretty definitive the last time we spoke that she knew nothing about such a relationship and she had nothing further to tell me. I had managed to alienate the two women who seemed to know more than anyone else in the group, which meant I had to come up with new information or I was finished. But aside from Marge Beller, I just didn't know where to look.

Since I had nothing scheduled, I called Greenwillow and arranged to pick up my cousin Gene tomorrow morning for mass and to bring him home with us for dinner. Jack gave up playing ball and went out to shop for tomorrow's dinner since he's the weekend cook by mutual agreement.

While Jack was gone, I took Eddie for a walk, stopping to talk to neighbors, lingering for a while at Mel's, where I updated her on the case. Sometimes Mel has very good ideas about where to go next or even where to go first, but today she agreed that I had hit a wall. I promised to keep her posted and we toddled home to wait for Jack.

On Sunday morning we drove to Greenwillow and picked up Gene who scrambled into the back to talk with his friend Eddie. They giggled together while we drove to church. Gene and I sat halfway down the pew while Jack sat at the edge next to Eddie. If Eddie became rambunctious, they would go outside and wait for Gene and me. For a while Eddie squirmed, but a few minutes later, I looked down at him and he had fallen asleep, his head on Jack's lap. When mass was over, we all got in the car and drove home.

The answering machine was beeping and flashing. Jack pushed the play button as Gene and Eddie went into the family room.

"Hello Chris," a man's voice called, as though I were faraway. In the background were the noises of a place with a lot of people. "I made a mistake. It wasn't Horowitz; it was Koch."

Jack looked at me. "That's my dead man," I said. "He must have called from the airport."

"But what did he mean?"

"I have no idea." I got my notebook and read through our conversation. He had met his first wife, Iris, on a blind date. He didn't think she had dated anyone else in the group. There were some notes on why he "died." Arthur Wien had never asked his permission to publish anything personal. He had never heard of any of the wives having an affair with Wien. Ernie Greene was mentioned, Joe and Judy Meyer, and no one else unless it had been something apparently so unimportant that I had not written it down.

"He never talked about either Dr. Horowitz or Dave Koch. There's nothing in my notes."

"It'll come to you. Some favor he asked one of them or they asked him, something like that."

" 'I made a mistake,' " I repeated from memory. " 'It wasn't Horowitz; it was Koch.' Who did what?" I asked rhetorically.

"Don't think about it. Your brain'll worry it up."

I knew I couldn't reach George Fried today if he was on an airplane, and since I didn't know where he was going, I didn't know when he would be home. I went to the family room where Gene and Eddie were sitting on the floor, playing with Eddie's toys. Gene reached over and patted Eddie's curls. I smiled and backed out to the kitchen, hoping my brain would do its duty.

It was while we were having dessert that something came back to me. "He said Wien was friendly with the Meyers," I said to Jack.

"Your dead man?"

"Mm-hmm. And then he said something about Mrs. Horowitz, that she was a very beautiful girl."

"So Wien could have had an affair with her thirty, forty years ago."

"But he's wrong and I knew it when he said it. Mrs. Horowitz isn't beautiful and I don't think she ever was. She's kind of a plain woman with a good figure who dresses well and loves babies."

"OK." I could hear the expectancy in his voice.

"Mrs. Koch is beautiful. She has short gray hair, thick, beautiful hair, and the face of a girl, a beautiful girl."

"Then that's what Fried meant; it wasn't Horowitz who was beautiful; it was Koch."

"Ellen Koch is the wife who had the affair with Arthur Wien." I felt a rush of excitement. Suddenly an impossible case had become less impossible. My head was whirling with ideas. "She was talking about herself when she told me a wife had had an affair with Arthur Wien."

"Sounds like you've got something."

"I have to talk to her." I took another taste of ice cream. "Excuse me, everybody. I have to make a phone call."

* * *

"Yes, Chris. Hello."

"We have to talk, Mrs. Koch."

"I've told you everything I know, and so has Dave."

"I don't want to talk to your husband. I want to talk to you, alone. I know who had an affair with Arthur Wien."

"Really? Who was it?"

"We both know, Mrs. Koch. That's why I'm calling you. There are some other things we have to talk about too, things that Alice Wien has an interest in."

"My husband is out till seven," she said.

"I'll get there as soon as I can."

Jack said it would be fine; he would take Gene back to Greenwillow and get Eddie ready for bed later in the day if I wasn't back. I worried about his not studying for the bar, but he said he was sure he'd have time every day on his new assignment to do that, that this was more important. I didn't argue. I kissed everybody and ran.

I pulled into the underground garage and ran for the elevator. Ellen Koch was waiting for me at the open door, my first impression of her confirmed. She was an exceptionally beautiful woman with firm skin and a girl's fine features. She was wearing a black skirt and a short-sleeved pink shirt with a necklace of black beads. We walked into the beautiful living room and I stopped to take in the view.

"Make yourself comfortable. We don't have a lot of time. Dave may be early."

"You're the wife who had the affair with Arthur Wien," I said.

"What makes you think so?"

"The sum of all I've learned in the last ten days."

"That doesn't sound like convincing evidence."

"You have a piece of Arthur Wien's pencil manuscript of *The Lost Boulevard* in your possession."

"What if I have?"

"It belongs to Alice Wien."

"Not if he gave it to me it doesn't."

"You held it for ransom, Mrs. Koch."

"I don't think anything you know can prove that."

"You're the one who lent him the money and took the manuscript as collateral."

"That sounds like a story Alice told you."

"Alice told it to me because Arthur told it to her."

"Art didn't always tell her the truth, you know."

"Why don't you tell me the truth?"

She crossed one slim leg over the other and fingered the black beads. "Art and I fell in love sometime in the fifties. He was already married to Alice, and I think I had just married Dave. I told myself there was nothing we could do. If we both divorced and remarried, there would be more than hell to pay. There were four sets of parents that would never understand. Divorce wasn't common and wasn't easily accepted. What we'd done would have been perceived as adultery. Getting a divorce in New York State was almost impossible, and besides all that, I didn't really want a divorce and I think Art didn't either. I love Dave very much."

"Does he know?"

"No."

"Alice doesn't either."

"I didn't think she did." She looked troubled now. I could imagine she might never have talked about this affair with anyone except her lover, that there was no one alive now who even knew. "It was as crazy a relationship as I could ever have imagined. It just went on and on. We were always there for each other. I don't know what else I can tell you about it."

"How long did it last?"

"I suppose it must be forty years by now. Hard to believe, isn't it?"

"Tell me about the manuscript."

"The book was dedicated to me. I know you don't believe that. I'm sure Alice has shown you her framed dedication. The one I have isn't framed, but it's written in his hand and it says more and it means it. I told him I wanted the manuscript. It was the only thing I ever asked for in all those years and he gave it to me."

"When?"

"I can't give you a time because I don't remember. It was after the book was published, I know that. I put it away where it was safe, where it was mine to treasure. And then, a long time later, Art and Alice separated and Alice demanded the manuscript as part of the divorce settlement."

"What happened then?"

"I said I wouldn't give it up. It was mine. It was a book my lover had written, dedicated to me, and given to me. Why should I give it to the woman who was going to be his ex-wife?"

"So he paid you for it."

She gave me the kind of stare that was surely meant to inflict bodily harm. "How dare you even suggest such a thing," she said calmly.

"Then you tell me what happened."

"What happened is that we quarreled over it, for months. I didn't want to give it up. I knew he would never tell Alice who had it. It would have enraged her. She would have been driven to ask for much more than she was asking. Eventually, I just caved in, I guess. I gave it to him."

"Minus several pages."

"I knew he wouldn't go through it to check. It was in the same box it had been in when he gave it to me twenty years earlier. He took it and gave it to the court, which gave it to Alice. I gather she never looked through it either."

"She didn't, or I think she would have gone after him for the missing pages. Why did you keep them?"

"I took what was mine, the parts that were about me. He had asked me before the book was published how I felt about those sections. He had disguised our relationship, pretended it happened between two other people. I told him either he wrote the truth, which I knew he wouldn't, couldn't without getting an awful lot of flak from my husband and his wife, or he had to take it out altogether. So he took it out."

"But he only pulled the pages out of the typewritten version," I said. "He left it in the original."

"And that's what I kept."

"Forgive me for harping on this, Mrs. Koch, but no money passed between you for the return of the manuscript?"

"Not a cent. I did lend Art some money once, but that was much later."

"And there was no collateral?"

"Love is the best collateral there is."

"I see."

"Are we finished now?"

"There are still a lot of unanswered questions. When did your affair end?"

She looked toward the windowed wall and fingered the

beads again with her left hand. She didn't want to answer that one. "Around the time he married Cindy."

"Two years ago?"

"About that."

"Can you tell me why it ended? It had survived one long marriage, and you must have known he was unfaithful to Alice."

"Of course I knew. I knew everything." She looked as though she might cry. Her face had lost its natural brightness; her eyes were full. "And he'd had Cindy around for years at that point. I guess I just didn't want to live through another marriage of his, another time of his being exclusively someone else's. While they were seeing each other, they were often at opposite ends of the country. Art would come east and stay in his apartment, and Cindy would stay in California. It gave us time together."

"Did you meet him at his apartment?"

"Never. I know about doormen. I didn't want to walk in one day with my husband and have the doorman greet me like an old friend. We met in other places."

"How did it end?" I asked, my voice a shade lower.

Her eyes could not hold the tears any more. "We're civilized people," she said. "We had loved each other longer than most people are married, longer than some lives are lived. We didn't hate each other or dislike each other. We just knew we couldn't continue our relationship any more. We didn't part enemies and we didn't part friends. I suppose we parted lovers. We just saw each other one last day, one evening." She drew in a shaky breath, "One night."

"Did anyone—" I hesitated, "did anyone act as an intermediary?"

Her face broke into a sad smile. "Do you mean did we arbitrate the end of our relationship like labor and management in two separate rooms? The answer is we didn't need to. Our feelings for each other were very deep and very real, and they helped us through to the end."

I had only one question left and I knew I had to ask it. "Did you kill him, Mrs. Koch?"

She shook her head, the stains of tears marking her cheeks. "How can you ask me that after what I've told you?"

"I need an answer. You're the only one with a motive."

"What motive?" she asked plaintively. "I've just told you that I loved him."

"And that he essentially left you for another woman."

"I did not kill Art," she said, looking me straight in the eye. "I did not ever think of killing him. I loved him."

"Thank you." I stood and put my notebook in my bag. I wasn't sure I believed her but I couldn't think where to go.

"I hope you won't make this public," she said, standing and smoothing her skirt.

"I won't, unless I find you're lying."

"Then you won't make it public."

"There's just one thing I don't understand. Why did you tell me last week that you had heard that one of the wives had had an affair with Arthur Wien?"

"I can't explain it. Maybe something inside me wanted to confess. I knew as soon as the words were out of my mouth that I had made a terrible mistake, but there was no taking it back. It was done."

"I would never have guessed," I said.

"Well, now you know."

I shook her hand and went out to the elevator, feeling the weight of her confession throughout my body. I could not imagine such a deep and pervasive relationship's being kept a secret for so many years. I could not imagine a woman filling the roles of wife and lover with two different men and feeling happy in both roles. I had not asked her about guilt, but how could she have avoided it?

There was so much I could not understand, and yet I knew that human beings were more complex than most of them appeared to be on the surface. Today I had broken through that surface in a woman I liked, a woman I would never completely understand.

This time when I picked up my car, they handed me a bill.

24

"That's some confession," Jack said when we were sipping coffee later in the evening. "Forty years with two men. Hard to believe."

"I think she killed him," I said. "She looked me in the eye and said she didn't, but there's a motive now. She wanted him for herself. And I'll bet it bothered her that his new wife was half her age."

"So how do we prove it?" Jack asked.

"I don't know. Mrs. Horowitz has to be involved in this somehow. Her meetings with Arthur Wien must have something to do with the breakup. But I don't think she'll tell me or anyone else."

"How do you figure it?"

"I bet there was a lot of less-than-loving discussion between Ellen and Arthur for a long time. She was jealous of this younger woman. She didn't want him marrying again. Maybe she threatened to talk about their relationship and he asked Robin Horowitz to try to prevent that. I'm sure Cindy Porter wouldn't have been any too happy to find out that her lover of seven years, soon to be her husband, had been fooling around with another woman."

"But if you can't crack Horowitz—"

"I know. It's hopeless."

I got up and found the envelope of pictures Lila Stern had given me ten days ago. I went through them again, looking carefully at the faces of the people, at the evening purses on the table, at the seating arrangement. There was a beautiful picture of the Koches, his arm around her, both smiling. The other couples also had pictures of themselves and everyone looked happy, even the Meyers who must have known this was the last reunion they would attend together. No one looked like a killer. Cindy Wien glittered both literally and figuratively. Arthur looked like a man who had a few more books yet to be written. If there was anything to be learned from these pictures, I was unable to see what it was.

I looked at my notes again. Joseph's suggestion that I find out when events had happened had been a good one. Two years ago Cindy and Arthur had married. Two years ago Ellen Koch and Arthur Wien had dissolved their decades-long relationship. That was a nice fit. But two years ago or a few months more, Robin Horowitz had visited the Wien apartment at least three times when Cindy wasn't there. What was the connection?

If I was right and Ellen Koch had lied to me, she had harbored a grudge so deep and hurtful that she had planned to kill her former lover at the next reunion, which was Father's Day. She had gotten nothing tangible from the murder, no money, no memorabilia. But she had the satisfaction of knowing that Cindy was Arthur's last wife and last woman. If I could only figure out what Robin Horowitz's role had been. The pictures yielded nothing, but my time line fit all the facts.

I gave up thinking about it. This was an important night in our lives. Tomorrow Jack would drive to One Police Plaza for the first day of his new assignment. It was a nine-to-five job, at least at the beginning, which was an hour earlier than he had started work for years. That meant our lives would have to adjust to a different schedule. I never have difficulty waking up early. For the fifteen years I lived at St. Stephen's, I had awakened daily at five, but at the other end of the day, I had turned in between nine and ten.

We went upstairs early and I didn't read the last chapter of *The Lost Boulevard*. It was a kind of epilogue and I felt I had gotten from the book whatever the substance was. Whoever had killed Arthur Wien almost forty years after the publication of the book had not done so for anything that happened when the Morris Avenue Boys were boys. And if I was right about Ellen Koch, it was something that had happened only a couple of years ago that had given her life a murderous turn. I slept well.

Jack left earlier than he had to, but I understood his need. Traffic is unpredictable, especially during rush hour, and he was anxious to be early to find out where everything was located. I wished him luck, asked him to call if he got a chance, and watched him give Eddie a big kiss. Then Eddie and I went back to the kitchen and I tidied up after breakfast.

At nine I called Joseph and told her what I had learned over the weekend.

"I thought she might be the one," Joseph said when I told her about Ellen Koch. "It seemed strange that no one else knew about this mysterious relationship."

"But she looked me in the eye and said she hadn't killed Arthur Wien."

"That's possible."

"She also said she hadn't used the manuscript as collateral for a loan. She acted insulted that I would suggest such a thing."

"A woman of strange principle. Do you have anything concrete to tie her to the murder?"

"Nothing, I'm afraid. I don't even know what kind of concrete thing I should be looking for. The police have the ice pick. If there were prints on it, they would have made an arrest."

"I'm sure you're right. I don't think you'll find anything of that kind, Chris. I think eventually you'll know who did it and why, but I have no idea whether you or the police will be able to bring that person to justice."

I had told her about my meeting with Robin Horowitz. Now I asked whether she thought Robin might know the truth.

"She may have her suspicions, but like so many cases that you've worked on, this will probably be circumstantial, unless you get a confession."

After we spoke, I called one of the mothers in our little play group and she invited us over. I told Eddie we would be visiting Eric, but the news didn't seem to make much difference to him. Our invitation was for ten until eleven so we drove over a little before ten.

It was an uneventful hour. The two little boys, who were almost exactly the same age, played in Eric's sandbox and swung on Eric's swings while Eric's mother and I gossiped about town events. At eleven, after the boys had had juice and a cookie, Eddie and I went home.

The answering machine was making its usual annoying noise. The message it was keeping for me was short. "This is Marge Beller. I'd like to talk to Chris."

I put Eddie safely in his playpen and called her back. I had almost forgotten that I had not heard from her.

"I talked to Fred," she said. "He didn't want me to tell you, but there are some things you don't know and I want to stop speculation before it starts."

The things I didn't know were probably things she didn't think I knew, like their being at the restaurant the night of the murder. "Go on," I said.

"There was a reason why we didn't get together with Arthur Wien the night he was in Minneapolis. It was our decision to renege."

"I see."

"What we didn't tell you is that when we ran into Arthur in California three years ago, we were there with our daughter. Art invited us all out to dinner and we accepted."

"Was Cindy with you?"

"No. We didn't meet her on our visit. The next day Art called at our hotel and offered to take Melissa to one of the movie lots. He's had several books made into movies so he knew his way around. Melissa thought it was a great idea and he picked her up before lunch. Fred and I went around by ourselves. When we got back to the hotel, there was a message that Melissa would be back after dinner so we took off for dinner without her. She came back much later and called our room to say she was back. I went down the hall and knocked on her door." She stopped.

"Was something wrong?"

"A lot was wrong. She opened the door and I took one look at her." Marge's voice had become agitated. "She looked like a teenager who had been making out with her boyfriend in the back of a car."

"What had he done, Marge?" I asked, feeling unsettled.

"Oh he hadn't raped her. She saw to that. But he had

treated her like a girlfriend. He was her father's age, exactly Fred's age. She wasn't a child; I don't mean to say that she was. She was about twenty-five at the time. She's our youngest and there's a big gap between her and the next oldest. I probably sound like an overprotective mother, which I'm not, but I found the whole thing sordid. Imagine a man in his sixties coming on to a young girl in her twenties."

"I understand why you were so upset. Did he see Melissa again?"

"Not on your life. He had the nerve to call the next day, but Fred talked to him and said we were busy for the rest of our stay. We had argued about whether Fred should talk to him about it, but finally Fred listened to me and didn't. I didn't want a scene and there was nothing to gain. We would never see him again, and there was no point in leaving with bad words between us."

"How did Melissa feel about what happened?"

"She said he had taken her by surprise, that she didn't know how to stop him. She said she had thought of him as a father figure, and when he started kissing her, she couldn't quite believe what was happening."

"And then he came to Minneapolis."

"That was about a year later. He hadn't married Cindy yet, I know that. He called when he got here and asked if he could take the three of us to dinner."

"He included Melissa."

"Very definitely. And we said something had come up and we couldn't make it. That was the last time we spoke to him."

"I see why you didn't want to discuss it, Marge," I said. "And I thank you for telling me."

"I wouldn't want you to think that I wished him dead."

"I don't think that."

"It's one thing to be a philanderer, but when you go after girls less than half your age—"

"It's very hard to take," I said. "I appreciate your call."

So many things were going on in my head it was impossible for me to decide what to do first. Marge's story had triggered a memory, something that had seemed unimportant, but as I thought about it, all the little unexplained events and pieces of information began to come together. Robin Horowitz had had her part in it and so had Ellen Koch, although they may not have known at the time what was to come and may not have known of each other's involvement. I needed one fact and I knew the people who could give it to me, but would any of them do it?

I looked in on Eddie and got his lunch going. Robin wouldn't tell me anything, she had made that very clear. She was protecting friends. Ellen had been involved, but had she known exactly what her involvement was? I might have to go to the source and I didn't relish the conversation.

I took out the Manhattan phone book and looked up a couple of numbers. When you're dealing with a common name in New York, there can be pages of them, including those with initials instead of first names. It's very daunting. I copied down several that might be the one I needed and then got Eddie and gave him his lunch. He had had a busy morning, and he was half asleep when he finished his milk. I carried him upstairs and put him in his crib and then did a lot of thinking over my tuna salad sandwich.

Jack called while I was thinking and eating. He sounded more relaxed than he had been over the weekend so I assumed no one had called with an unanswerable legal question between nine and noon. He gave me his new phone number and I wrote it down in my book. I was glad he had called. I told him quickly what I had learned and what I thought it meant, and he agreed I was likely on the right track.

Finally I called one of the numbers I had taken down. When a man answered, I said, "Joshua?"

"Yes, who's this?"

"My name is Christine Bennett. I'm trying to reach your sister, Marsha."

"Is this connected to her music?"

"It's connected to it, yes," I said.

He gave me the phone number and I thanked him. "Is she usually home in the afternoon?"

"Sometimes. Give her a call and see."

I did. A machine picked up on the fourth ring and I hung up. It didn't mean much. She could be out now and back soon. I decided to take a chance. I called Elsie and asked if she could come over. Twenty minutes later I drove into New York.

The address was in the Village and I couldn't find a place to park. The Village is mostly old buildings without underground parking so I drove around till I found a lot, then walked back to the address I had found in the phone book. It was one of those fine old buildings that had been refurbished and had an elevator. I rang the bell of 4E and announced my name to the staticky voice that responded. I assumed I sounded equally staticky, but she buzzed me in and I rode the elevator to the fourth floor.

"I'm Chris Bennett," I said when she opened the door. "I've met your parents. I need to talk to you about something. May I come in?"

She frowned but she let me in. She was about my age,

the same beautiful young woman of the picture I had seen, but she walked with a cane and her hands were unpleasant to look at. I followed her into the small living room where she sat in a firm chair.

"What is this about?" she asked.

"The accident," I said. "Who was with you in the car?"

"I can't talk about that."

"Why not?"

"There was an agreement."

"You were given a sum of money to keep quiet?"

"I was given a sum of money so that I could live and also so that I could get therapy and maybe play the cello again."

"And also to keep you from telling who was in the car with you."

"For the record, I was alone."

"But you and I know someone was with you."

She didn't answer. She had a beautiful face, a perfect amalgam of her parents' faces, but she was better looking than either. At this moment she looked very sad.

"It was Arthur Wien, wasn't it?"

She didn't answer.

"He was a friend of your parents, wasn't he?"

"Yes, he was."

"You grew up knowing him."

"That's right. And many other friends of my parents."

"When did he start taking you out?"

She sat without speaking.

"Were you in love with him?" I asked.

Tears ran down her cheeks. "I wasn't in love with him. I was never in love with him."

"But you went out with him."

Silence.

"Were you driving when you had your accident?"

"I was alone in the car so I must have been driving."

"What happened after the accident? Did he run away and leave you? Did he get help? Did he make you promise while you were sitting there in pain that you would tell no one what had happened?"

She put her head in her hands. I walked over to her and patted her back. "I'm sorry to ask you these things," I said, feeling sorrier than I could express.

"Then please don't ask. Just go away. I've told you all I can. There isn't any more."

"I think there is. I think Arthur Wien was in the car with you. Maybe he was driving. I think he left you after the accident to protect himself. He got married not long after that, but I'm sure you know that. Your parents were his friends. They admired him because of his writing. He visited your parents' apartment, and he knew you when you were growing up." As I spoke, it all seemed right, the facts and suppositions blending into one easy story that had ended in disaster. "I suppose you threatened to sue him after the accident, but someone who knew him and knew your parents helped to mediate an agreement. Someone else lent him the money to pay you."

"What?"

"I don't know the sum, but I know he borrowed from an old friend. And part of the agreement was that you would never say he was in the car with you the day of the accident."

She looked at me with a tearstained face. When she smiled, it was a bitter, sad smile. "You came here just to tell me a story?"

"I came here to ask you if you killed Arthur Wien."

A shiver went through her. She looked at her right hand. The fingers were bent and gnarled. "How could I have killed him? I can hardly hold my bow any more."

25

I knew I was right. And I knew Joseph was right too; it was circumstantial. Without a confession I could prove nothing. I drove uptown and parked at a meter on Broadway in the Eighties. From there I walked to the Meyers' building and rang the bell. Judy answered and let me in. I felt sick to my stomach as I walked down the hall to their apartment.

"Hi," Judy called. "Come on in."

Joe came into the living room as we sat down. He smiled and greeted me, then sat in the chair near the windows.

"You don't look so good," Judy said to me. "Can I get you something?"

"No thanks." I was sitting where I could face them both. "I know about Marsha's accident," I said. "I know that Arthur Wien was in the car with her. I know he paid her to keep her quiet. I even know where the money came from."

They both looked too surprised to speak. Finally Joe said, "This is a little too much too fast. Who told you these things?"

"Almost everyone I talked to contributed, but they said small things and it's taken a while for me to put it all together. I know Arthur Wien dated young girls. Your daughter wasn't the only one. I can't tell you how terrible I feel about what that accident did to your daughter and the life she loved. You felt he had to pay for it, and you got your opportunity on Father's Day."

Joe looked down at his lap and Judy got up and walked toward his chair. "We were friends," he said finally. "Friends don't do those things to friends."

"There's nothing to say, Joe," Judy said. "Chris is just guessing and everything she says is wrong."

He put his hand on his wife's arm and held it there. "She isn't wrong, Judy. It's the way it happened. We both know it."

My heart was pounding. "I'd like you to turn yourself in. I'll drive you to the police station."

"He can't do that," Judy said, her voice losing its normal calm tone. "They'll lock him up and he won't survive."

"We can call a lawyer," I began.

"Do you know what Arthur Wien did?" Judy said. "He destroyed the life of one of the most promising musicians in this country. He had no conscience. He thought of no one but himself. After he hit the tree, he told Marsha he would go for help and she should say nothing about his being with her. He used a telephone to call the police so no one would be able to identify him. What was he doing with her anyway? He had been living with Cindy for years and they had set a date for their wedding. He was cheating on the woman he was going to marry. In the end that's what Arthur Wien was, a cheat. He pretended to be our friend so he could have access to our beautiful daughter."

"Call the lawyer, Judy," her husband said. "It's time. I have to turn myself in."

I left them making arrangements with their lawyer. When I got to my car, I decided to make one more stop before going home. I cut through Central Park to the East

Side and drove down to the Koches' building. Ellen Koch was there and she told the doorman to send me up. She didn't offer me a seat, just stood in the foyer and looked at me.

"You said you lent money once to Arthur Wien but it had nothing to do with the manuscript."

"That's right."

"About two years ago?"

"About that."

"Do you know what he used it for?"

"I don't want to talk about it."

"I gather it was a substantial sum."

"It was a lot of money, yes."

I was sure she knew. "It paid Marsha Meyer, Joe and Judy's daughter, to be quiet. He was driving the car when she had her accident."

"How did you find out?"

"I put everything together. I'm sorry."

"No sorrier than I am. It was the reason I broke off our relationship, what happened to Marsha. I couldn't believe he had done it, but he had. He told me. Have you seen her?"

"This afternoon. She didn't admit anything. But her life, her music . . ."

"Thank you for coming by."

There was a pay phone in the garage and I called Dr. Horowitz. I told him I hoped someone could post bond for Joe Meyer; he was too sick a man to stay in jail. I had some money put away myself, I said, but Dr. Horowitz said it would be taken care of. He had a patient so the conversation was necessarily short.

I got home in time to read a story to Eddie. Halfway

through, Jack pulled into the driveway, his grin telling me it hadn't been a killer of a day. I was glad his wasn't. Mine was.

I learned from one of many phone calls that night that Joe Meyer had been released until his arraignment the following morning. His lawyer guaranteed his appearance and I didn't doubt he would show up. In fact, I showed up myself, having dropped Eddie off early at Elsie's. Arraignment is at One Hundred Centre Street in downtown Manhattan. When I finally found my way to the right place, I had quite a shock. Every one of the Morris Avenue Boys had shown up, five aging men in dark suits, pale shirts, and probably sixty-dollar ties: a medical researcher who might win a Nobel Prize, a lawyer whose wife had figured in a forty-year-old story of love and deception, a gastroenterologist who was off the hook for murder, a teacher who cared about his students, a businessman who knew how it felt to be up there facing a judge, accused of a felony, instead of back here safe behind the railing and presumed to be innocent. When the question of bail came up and the judge granted it, a rather large sum, all five of them moved forward to offer to cover it. Bernie Reskin did not have the money but he had brought the deed to his house. I had seen a lot of tears in the last few days but today was my turn. I sat on the hard bench in the courtroom and cried.

The hearing was very brief. Joe pled not guilty, bail was set, and a date chosen for the next court appearance. Joe was released a few minutes later. I went to the nearest ladies room and found Judy Meyer there.

"I'm sorry," I said.

"It's not your fault. You were doing something honorable."

"At the reunion dinner, you asked Robin Horowitz to change places with you so you wouldn't have to sit next to Arthur Wien."

"She saw Arthur come in. I was sitting next to the last two empty chairs and she realized I wouldn't get through an evening rubbing shoulders with him. She got up and said she wanted to sit next to him. We traded places. Thank God," she added.

"You're the one, aren't you? You did it."

She paled. "You heard Joe yesterday."

"I heard him."

"They'll never try him."

"I know."

"And I'll take good care of him for as long as I have him."

I picked up Eddie and took him home. We had a nice conversation over lunch. He had had a good time at Elsie's.

"Maybe we'll swim this afternoon," I said.

"Wim," Eddie said with a breathy *W*.

"You have a new bathing suit and we can go to the pool after your nap."

"Pool."

"Yes. Remember we looked at the pool last week?"

"Pool."

I leaned over and kissed him.

After my own lunch I took *The Lost Boulevard* outside and sat in my chair under an old tree and read the last chapter. As I had thought, it was a wrapping up kind of chapter. The narrator took the subway to the Bronx to see his mother. It was a New York summer day, hot and very humid. By the time he got up to the street level, his shirt was sticking to his back. He walked from the Concourse to Morris Avenue and up to the apartment he had grown up in. He was in his late twenties now and had a wife and a nice little apartment in the Village. I remembered Alice's description of that first home they shared.

Inside his mother's apartment every window was open, but the air was as still as the grains of sand in the egg timer on the kitchen stove. He unbuttoned another button on his shirt, but it did no good. Even the fan in the living room seemed to have stalled.

For the first time he looked at the apartment appraisingly. It seemed very rundown. Paint was chipping in almost every room, and he wondered how long it had been since the landlord had put a fresh coat of paint on any of the walls.

The kitchen in particular looked old and grimy. The linoleum on the floor was cracked and dirt was ingrained, never to be removed. The stove looked like something from a junkyard. He remembered it from twenty years ago, the nineteen-thirties, when he was a boy. The refrigerator, one of the old gas ones, was short by modern standards and had that metal thing on top that housed the fan. If it wasn't an antique, it was surely close. The table wobbled. One of the chairs was missing.

In his shirt pocket he had a damp list of available apartments, some on the Concourse, some in Manhattan. He wondered if the Concourse buildings had become as rundown as this one or had retained the status that went back to prewar days. He showed the list to his mother. She sighed and made him a sandwich.

He told her the city was building a highway that would cut through the heart of 174th Street, that the noise of drilling through the rocks would be unbearable, that the dust and dirt that the drilling created would float into this apartment and sit on every surface, that when the highway was done there would be filthy trucks driving back and forth night and day. This was the time to leave it all behind.

She talked about the mothers of his friends. She told him how things were going with his father at work. She fanned her face with a Jewish newspaper. She couldn't think of any reason to move.

After an hour or so, he kissed her good-bye and walked back to the Concourse. It was a long trip to the Village, but the D train would take him to West Fourth Street and his apartment was an easy walk from there. He looked up and down the Concourse, accepting finally that his parents would never live there. It was too late for them as it was too late for him. His life was elsewhere, not in the Bronx.

He went down the dark stairs to the subway and waited on the almost empty platform on the downtown side, inhaling the heat. About twenty feet away, a young pretty girl in a sleeveless cotton dress and black patent shoes stood waiting for the same train. She turned and saw him. He smiled and she smiled back. He started down the platform toward her, and the train came noisily into the station, blowing hot air. She got in one car and he got in another. He sat back on the old laquered straw seat and closed his eyes. The D train would take him to a better world.

26

There's never anything clean about finishing a case. Someone is brought to what we call justice, but I am always left with a tremendous weight on my shoulders. Not only do I often feel sorry for the killer, as I did in this case, but I am left with information that puts me in a very awkward position. I do not like to lie and yet, who am I to dispense facts that are private?

I called George Fried and told him he had helped me a great deal and I would not disclose the fact that he was alive. I called Marge Beller and told her she had given me the precise piece of information that I needed to find Arthur Wien's killer. And I promised not to disclose what she had told me.

I never asked Ellen Koch whether the money she lent to Arthur Wien to pay Marsha Meyer had been paid back because I didn't think it was my business, but I did tell her her long affair with him would remain her secret.

And then there was Alice Wien, an innocent who had suffered because of her husband's behavior. Only Ellen Koch and I knew where the missing pages of the manuscript were, but I did not tell Alice. Maybe some day Ellen would give them back to Alice, with or without an explanation, and make the manuscript whole and valuable.

People rise to unexpected heights sometimes; I hoped Ellen would. She would still have the dedication that Arthur Wien had written to her in his own hand. I will never know.

A couple of weeks after the arraignment of Joe Meyer, a large, heavy box was delivered to my house. I smiled at the store name on the address label, Neiman Marcus. I could tell the contents were larger than either a lipstick or a tie, and probably more expensive.

Inside were a dozen crystal wine glasses that took my breath away and a note thanking me from Robin and Mort Horowitz. I wondered if she had guessed who had killed Arthur Wien on Father's Day. I wondered if Ellen had.

For myself, I wondered whether Joe had done it or if his wife had. Or if they had worked together. I don't think I'll ever know.

A CONVERSATION WITH LEE HARRIS

Q. *Lee, your heroine, Christine Bennett, first appeared in 1992. But you have been a published novelist since 1975. Can you fill us in on your life before Chris?*

A. Under another name I wrote mainstream novels, the last of which came out in 1989. About that time I felt I needed a change in my life. Since I was a devoted reader of mysteries, I decided to write one of my own. I used an idea I'd had for about ten years, made it the first book in a series, and the rest, as they say, is history.

Q. *We liked the author bio that appeared in your first novel—indicating that you were "at work on another book, and another book, and another book . . ." Indeed, that did happen. How many novels did you publish under your own name?*

A. Six. And I still feel I'd like to go on writing forever.

Q. *Readers, and especially fans, are always curious about an established writer's decision to adopt a pseudonym. Why, when you created Chris Bennett, did you?*

A. The mysteries were so different from my other books that my agent, the late Claire Smith, whom I loved and admired enormously, felt I should keep the two genres very separate, that the readers of my mainstream novels might be thrown for a loop by picking up a mystery. In fact, in many cases that hasn't happened, but I still keep them separate.

Q. *Who or what was the inspiration for Chris? And when you introduced her in* The Good Friday Murder, *did you envision a series? Or was* The Good Friday Murder *intended as a stand-alone novel?*

A. Chris is completely fictional, inspired by no single person. I wanted a female amateur sleuth, about thirty, a type of person who hadn't been done. Nuns have been done. Nurses have been done. Teachers have been done. An ex-nun seemed to give me a lot of opportunities for character development. I knew from the start that I was doing a series. In fact, as soon as I finished *Good Friday,* I started *The Yom Kippur Murder.*

Q. *We know that you are not a former Catholic nun, but that aside, how much of the Chris Bennett series is based on your own experience? What about background research—how vital is that for you?*
A. Only a little of my experience, like my education, the kinds of work I've done, and where I've lived, goes into my books. However, I've had to incorporate some of Chris's experiences into my own life. For *The Father's Day Murder,* besides picking the brains of my cousins who grew up in the Bronx, I drove over to where the Morris Avenue Boys came from and went through the streets taking notes. And for *The Labor Day Murder,* I spent a weekend on Fire Island. What sacrifices we writers endure!

I can't do a book without research. I have an expert on Catholicism and nuns who helps me in that area, and a retired NYPD detective who gives me hours of his expertise. They're the first two people I acknowledge in every book.

Q. *When did you settle on the title "hook"—the notion of holiday-themed mysteries?*
A. Okay, here's the truth. I was sitting at my typewriter in 1989, thinking about a murder that happened in 1950. I decided (quite by accident) that it happened on April 7. So I opened my trusty World Almanac and checked the calendar for 1950. April 7 was a Friday. It then occurred to me that Easter might have occurred around that time so I checked for movable feasts. Sure enough, Easter was on April 9 that year. And it hit me. The murder had taken place on Good Friday! The Good Friday Murder! Wow! And that, as I like to say, is how careful planning gave me a theme in my series.

Q. *The Good Friday Murder was nominated for an Edgar Award as Best Paperback Original. Did that have any impact, immediate and/or long-term, on you?*

A. The immediate impact was incredible. When I hung up from getting the news from my editor, I started to wonder if she had really called or if I had imagined it. I couldn't believe it had happened. I didn't even know that Edgars were given for that category. The longer-term effect was mixed. My next advance was no more than my last one. But suddenly, bookstores all over the country were aware of my books, were putting *Good Friday* on tables of nominated books, and my sales were up. So long-term it was all good.

Q. *Of all your novels—mystery and mainstream—which was the most fun to write? The most difficult?*

A. I can tell you this is the hardest question to answer. Maybe the answer to both parts is the same: My very first book back in the seventies. I wrote it in number 2 pencil on lined pads. I started in the middle, wrote an episode here, an episode there, then went to the beginning and started from scratch, incorporating—or tossing—the pieces I'd written before. But I loved the work; I loved seeing the characters and story grow. It took twenty-two months from day one to the end, months during which I wrote while my little child was napping, while my husband was teaching at night. And when it was sold ten days after my then-brand-new agent sent it off, it was pure bliss.

Q. *We have four words for you: "Nuns, Mothers, and Others." Please tell us about that phenomenon.*

A. Am I glad you asked! Valerie Wolzien, a well-known Fawcett author, turned out to be a neighbor of mine when *Good Friday* was published. We got to know each other through a mutual acquaintance and started promoting our books together, doing signings and even overnight trips. Then, at the Malice Domestic convention in 1994, we met Lora Roberts, another great Fawcett mystery writer, from California. Lora had a mystery writer friend, Jonnie Jacobs, whose short story is now part of a Ballantine collection, and they planned a trip that Valerie and I joined to visit bookstores throughout the Midwest in July 1995 . While trying to decide what to call ourselves for that trip, something snappy and memorable, Jonnie, in a late-night silly mood, came up with "Nuns, Mothers, and Others"—after our sleuths. And that's who we are now. We put out an irregular newsletter, we have special T-shirts we wear when we're together, and we even have a Web site (http://www.NMOMysteries.com) with all our pictures on it and lots of other good stuff. Also, we have attended mystery conventions all over the country, visited bookstores from Portsmouth, New Hampshire, to San Diego, California, and are planning more for the future. We even found we like each other more the more we see each other!

Find out more about whodunit! For sample chapters from current and upcoming Ballantine mysteries, visit us at **www.randomhouse.com/BB/mystery**